NO HIDING
IN BOISE

NO HIDING IN BOISE

KIM HOOPER

TURNER PUBLISHING COMPANY
Nashville, Tennessee
www.turnerpublishing.com

Cover design: Lauren Peters-Collaer
Book design: Karen Sheets de Gracia

9781684426232 Paperback
9781684426225 Hardcover
9781684426249 eBook

Printed in the United States of America

For Chris and Mya

ANGIE

MY RINGTONE IS THE theme song from *Sesame Street*. We just started letting Evie watch *Sesame Street* even though the American Academy of Pediatrics has strict rules about screen time for children under the age of two (Evie will be two in a few months). The American Academy of Pediatrics must not understand the daily lives of families, the need for distraction during chaotic mornings. The only way I can get ready for work is by putting Evie in her high chair and letting her watch Elmo while eating oatmeal by the fistfuls. Cale hates the oatmeal because she gets it all over herself. He suggests I buy toaster waffles, and I suggest he make breakfast; it's the same boring dance we do. Anyway, Evie loves the oatmeal, and it's healthy. The American Academy of Pediatrics would approve.

Last week, while assembling dinner—I do not cook, I assemble premade items from the refrigerated section of Trader Joe's—I'd started humming the "Letter of the Day" song that Elmo sings in every episode. Cale laughed. He was in one of his rare chipper moods, and I thought, *Maybe this will work out after all.* "This" being our marriage, our existence together as parents. When I went to the bathroom, he set the *Sesame Street* theme song as my ringtone. He probably assumed I'd change it back, but I kept it, as a reminder that he still has good days.

The phone rings in the middle of a recurring dream in which I cannot remember the combination to my high school locker.

By the time I realize the ringing is not part of the dream, by the time I reach over to the nightstand, fumbling around for the phone, the ringing has stopped. The missed call is from a number I don't recognize. It's just after midnight, a cruel time for a robocall. Must be a wrong number. I close my eyes, tell myself to go back to sleep, but then it rings again.

I answer this time so I can curse at the caller. There's something empowering about cursing at a stranger. I know I shouldn't think this, but life has been stressful and releasing a good "fuck you" takes the edge off.

"Who is this?" I whisper, not wanting to wake Cale. He's been taking something called Trazodone at night lately, for sleep. This means I'm the one who has to be ready to tend to Evie if she cries. It's a role I resent because I've had it since she was born. She's been sleeping through the night for a while now, but she still has bad nights—usually due to teething or to pee somehow escaping her diaper and soaking her pajamas.

"Is this Mrs. Matthews?"

It's a man. He sounds stern. This is not a robocall or a wrong number.

"Yes," I whisper, now more concerned than angry.

"Ma'am, this is Officer Stokes with the Boise Police Department," he says.

My first thought is Evie, though I know she's just down the hall, in her crib. I can hear the white noise machine whirring over the monitor.

"I'm sorry to disturb you at this hour, but we think your husband was involved in a shooting at Ray's Bar. He's been transferred to Saint Al's."

I'm quite confident this man has his facts wrong. Cale isn't at a bar; he's in bed next to me.

I turn in bed to wake Cale so he can tell this officer himself that there has been a misunderstanding.

But he's not there.

"Ma'am?" the man on the phone says.

I get out of bed and walk to the bathroom, sure I'll find Cale there, sitting on the toilet looking at me like I'm a mad woman. He's not there though.

"Just a minute," I tell the officer.

I walk upstairs, hoping Cale is getting a midnight snack, though I've never seen him do such a thing. Cale doesn't believe in snacking; he takes joy in fasting as long as he can and then eating an entire pizza.

"Ma'am?" the officer says again.

I can hear sirens in the background.

"I . . . I don't understand," I tell him.

"You can call the hospital for updates," he says. The sirens are louder.

"You said you *think* it's him? So you're not *sure*?"

This woman at work, a fellow copywriter, told me that the phrase "grasping at straws" is from a proverb about a drowning man reaching desperately at the surrounding grasses as he goes under. This is what I feel like right now—like I'm drowning.

"We retrieved his ID and your contact information from his wallet," he says.

The contact information. I know what he means. When I moved in with Cale and realized how often he went biking in the foothills alone, I insisted he carry certain things with him— his ID, his phone, his health insurance card, and my contact information. I'd written my name and number on a note card, under the words "In case of emergency," and folded it in half. He had rolled his eyes at me, but he complied. I'd watched him slip it into his wallet.

"I'm sorry to give you this news," the officer says.

He ends the call before I can think to ask the obvious questions:

What happened?

Was he shot?

Is he going to be okay?

I know I should be focused on that, on Cale being okay, but I can't help but fixate on another question: What was he doing at Ray's Bar in the middle of the night? I know that place. I've driven by it. It's a dive, on a quiet side street on the outskirts of downtown. From the street, there's just a brick wall, a single black door, and a sign above it that says Ray's.

If Cale wanted a beer at midnight (which would be strange), why not get one from our kitchen? We always have a few half-full six-packs in the fridge. Or, if he had to go to a bar (which would be even stranger), why not just walk five minutes up Thirteenth Street? Why get in the car and drive across town?

Plain and simple, it doesn't make sense that he was doing anything at midnight, let alone sitting at a bar. Since we've had Evie, we go to bed by eight. Both of us are exhausted. When I put her to sleep at seven, my shoulders relax away from my ears just slightly and I take pleasure in a glass of wine and whatever I've assembled for dinner. We barely make it through one episode of a show everyone says we "have to watch"— *Stranger Things* being the latest—then claim fatigue in a defeatist way and trudge to our bedroom. Cale's been having trouble with waking up in the middle of the night and not being able to fall asleep again—hence, the pills. I've known about that. I've known he's been "off." But I never would have guessed he'd be going to a bar at midnight.

I try to call him, hoping he'll defy what the police officer told me and pick up his phone. It goes straight to voice mail though, Cale's voice deep and strong, telling me to leave a message. I do, because it means I'm doing something.

"It's me. I hope you're okay. Please call me. I love you."

We haven't said those three words to each other in a while—I love you. We've said "love you" in a slapdash way when saying goodbye in the morning. We let the words run together, thoughtlessly—"loveyou." Our sex life is just as slapdash—a once-every-few-weeks item on a mental checklist. I haven't been trying hard enough, I decide.

I call my sister, Aria, because I need someone to be at the house with Evie while I drive to the hospital. And I know she'll be up because she doesn't usually go to bed before one. She's a decade younger than me, single and childless.

"A shooting? What do you mean?" she says.

"I don't know anything yet," I tell her.

"Okay, I'll be there in a few."

Aria lives a few blocks away, in one of the North End's few apartment buildings. It's purposeful, her closeness to me. I've always been like a mother to her.

I turn on the TV while I wait. There it is—breaking news on channel 7. The words across the bottom of the screen read Deadly Shooting at Ray's Bar.

Deadly.

I taste bile in my throat.

The reporter on the screen, a woman with frizzy hair and bags under her eyes, is standing in a parking lot, the sign for Ray's and police tape behind her, on the other side of the street.

"Details are still coming in, but we know there are at least three people dead," she says.

I turn off the TV, feeling like I'm going to vomit.

Then I see Aria pull into the driveway.

TESSA

I CROUCH IN THE corner of the storage closet, behind the mop bucket, covering myself as best I can with a black zip-up hoodie that was hanging from a hook on the back of the door. It's been silent for a while, but I think he's still out there, the shooter.

When the shots started, I thought they were fireworks, which didn't make sense—it's April. Even when I saw the gun, it took me a moment to realize what was happening. People started screaming, running for the exit. I just stood there, frozen, behind the bar. That song "Night Moves" was playing over the loudspeaker. Thursday is Bob Seger night.

"Tessa," a voice said. Then louder: "Tessa!"

I turned toward the man saying my name. "Cale, like the trendy lettuce stuff," he'd said when he first introduced himself. He looked frantic. "You need to find somewhere to hide. Go, now," he said.

That got me running.

I don't know what happened to him.

I WANT TO call Ryan, but my hands are shaking too much to even hold my phone. I've managed to get it out of my back pocket, but my fingers refuse to work to unlock it.

I can see I've received a dozen texts from Monica, the manager of the bar. The last one shows on the lock screen:

TELL ME U R OK

I'm assuming she got out. If she has the presence of mind to text me about my well-being, she must have gotten out. I don't know about Dan, the new guy who was behind the bar with me. I didn't see where he went. It's usually just three of us running the place, unless we have live music and a bigger crowd—then Monica makes her daughter come in to bus tables.

I don't dare move from my corner. He could be tricking me, waiting for me to emerge from the closet. I could be his final victim. I will not leave this room; someone will have to come get me.

Sometime later—a few minutes or a few hours, I have no idea—I hear the SWAT team shouting codes and commands. Even though I know they are the good guys, that they can save me, I hug my knees to my chest tighter and close my eyes. When one of them kicks in the door, I scream.

There are five of them, pointing their guns at me, telling me to put my hands up. I can't feel my arms, don't think I have control over them, but then my hands appear in the air, as if on their own accord. Everything is blurry from the tears. I am terrified.

"It's okay," someone says.

I'm ushered outside, seated on a stretcher. There are ambulances and police cars, sirens everywhere. There are others like me, on stretchers or pacing around, crying. I assume those injured, those killed, have been taken away already. It's still dark outside, so I must not have been in the closet as long as I thought.

Police officers attempt to talk to me, but I can't form sentences. One of the EMTs gives me something to calm me down. When my hands stop shaking, I call Ryan.

"Tess?" he says. It's obvious I've woken him up. His tone is that of an annoyed person trying not to sound annoyed.

"Ryan?" I manage.

It feels strange to talk. My teeth start chattering, even though it's fairly warm for April—forty-something degrees, I'd guess. I'm wearing the zip-up hoodie I found in the storage closet. I don't know who it belongs to—maybe Dan. I look around but don't see him. I hope he found somewhere to hide too.

"Is everything okay?" Ryan asks, sounding more awake now.

"No," I say.

"Tess, what's going on?"

"There was a guy. At the bar," I say.

"Did someone hurt you?"

This has always been Ryan's fear. He hates that I'm a bartender. He thinks some drunken asshole is going to wait for me to get off shift and then rape me in the parking lot. I've told him that Boise is safe; it's ranked as the seventh safest city in America (or so I heard from a guy I served at the bar a while back). Ryan grew up in a small town called Gooding. To him, Boise is a big city, dangerous. He makes me carry pepper spray on my key chain.

"No, I'm fine," I say, though I'm not sure this is exactly true.

"I'm coming down there," he says.

"No, don't."

There's no way he could get within a mile of the scene.

"You're going to have to tell me what's going on, babe," he says.

"There was a shooting."

"At the bar?"

I start crying.

"Tess, I'm coming down there."

"Okay," I say. It seems like too much effort to explain. He will see for himself.

JOYCE

HE TOLD ME HE was going to a movie, that he'd be back before midnight. It's now nearly one o'clock and he's not home. I call his phone, but there's no answer.

I know this is silly. He's a grown man, twenty-eight years old. I shouldn't be waiting up for him. Then again, he shouldn't be living with his mother. If I had it my way, he'd be married, with a child or two, by now. He would have a job that paid enough for him to have his own house—or an apartment, at the very least. As it is, he works at Home Depot, in the appliances department. For now, that is. He's never been able to hold a job longer than a few months. It's always someone else's fault. I never get the real story.

Diana says I need to cut Jed off completely. It's easy for her to say that. Her daughter is a well-to-do lawyer in Seattle, and her son is in medical school at Stanford. The biggest problem she had with either of them was a small amount of pot confiscated from a dresser drawer—a huge drama for her. She pities me, I can tell. And I'm sure she wonders what I did wrong. I wonder the same. I did my best; I don't doubt that. I just wonder if my best was good enough.

Jed's father, my husband, died of lung cancer when Jed was in elementary school. He didn't smoke. I feel the need to say that any time I tell someone how he died. I can see in their eyes that they want it to be his fault. Nobody likes to consider that some things *just happen*.

So I became a single mother with the usual sob story, working long hours to make ends meet. Maybe I didn't cook enough. Maybe I didn't help Jed with his homework enough. Maybe I should have remarried, selected a man with money so I could stay home and spend more time with Jed. It's these maybes, these doubts, that make it impossible for me to cut him off completely.

It's not like I give him money. I just give him a room to sleep in, the same room he slept in as a child. It's not like I would use the room for something else; I don't need it, is what I'm saying. I cook food for him because, after retiring from my job as a human resources manager for Albertsons, I finally have time to do that—making up for the past, I guess. I told Diana that I don't pay his car insurance anymore, and she said, "*Anymore?* Jesus, Joyce!"

Jed didn't tell me what theater he was going to. I'm assuming he went to the one downtown, though it's possible he drove further out to the IMAX. He left around eight; the movie must be over by now. The optimist in me thinks he had a date, that it went well, well enough for him to stay out this late. He never mentions dating, and I don't ask. Like I said, he's a grown man; he's allowed his privacy.

I turn on the hallway light so he can see when he comes home, and I go to bed, telling myself I am accomplishing nothing by waiting. If he comes home and sees me up, I'll get an earful about how he's not a teenager anymore, to which I'll say, "Then stop living like one." That argument will result in a sleepless night for me. So I should go to bed, end of story.

I **WAKE UP** to someone knocking on the front door. It's early—just after dawn by the looks of the light outside.

"Damn it, Jed," I mutter, swinging my legs over the side of

the bed with a groan.

How did he manage to lose his house key? Wouldn't it be on the same key chain as his car key? I wrap my robe around myself and consider that he probably lost all his keys and had to get an Uber ride home. This would be just like him. He lost his phone last month, still owes me $500 for the replacement I bought him.

"Damn it, Jed," I mutter again.

I can see the outline of him through the frosted glass window alongside the front door. I flip the lock and say, "You lost your—"

I stop.

It's not Jed.

It's a cop.

Two, actually. The other is standing by the black squad car.

My heart sinks. I know that's a common phrase, but I feel something inside me actually free-falling. My knees buckle.

The cop standing in front of me is young, Jed's age. He clears his throat.

"Ms. Ketcher?" he says.

I shake my head.

I don't want to be Ms. Ketcher.

"Are you Joyce Ketcher? Jed Ketcher's mother?"

I just keep shaking my head.

The other cop, an older man with deep-set eyes, walks over, stands alongside his partner. I stare at their shoes—so shiny.

"Was he in an accident?" I ask. My voice is strange, high-pitched.

I imagine Jed skidding off Interstate 84 in his twelve-year-old Ford Mustang, the car I bought him for his sixteenth birthday. I imagine the car flipping. I imagine him unconscious, upside down, held in place by his seat belt—god, I hope he wore his seat belt. I imagine someone driving by, spotting him, calling 911. How long was he by himself? Is he okay?

"There was a shooting," the older cop says, interrupting my thoughts.

A shooting?

I cover my mouth with my hand. I am a caricature of someone receiving shocking news.

"At a place called Ray's Bar, outskirts of downtown," he says.

Jed must have stopped in for a beer after the movie. He isn't much of a drinker, or not that I know of, but every so often a six-pack of Coors will show up in the fridge.

"Did he get shot?" My question comes out as a shriek.

The cops look at each other, as if deciding who will bear the burden of breaking the news. That's when I know that, yes, he was shot.

"Is he alright?" I ask. Another shriek.

I notice my neighbor across the street. He is getting his paper, or that's what he was doing. Now he is just staring. I am a spectacle.

"I'm afraid it appears he took his life, Ms. Ketcher," the younger cop says.

I feel faint. Am I dreaming this?

"I don't understand," I say. "The shooter shot him?"

The older cop reaches out, touches my forearm. That's when I realize my arms had been flailing about.

"Ma'am," he says.

I'm already crying.

"Ma'am," he says, again. "We have reason to believe your son was the shooter."

ANGIE

THERE ARE TWO HOSPITALS in Boise: Saint Luke's and Saint Al's. (As a kid, I thought that was the saint's name—Al. I was well into my teens when I learned that Al was short for Alphonsus.) I think of Evie any time I'm on the Connector and drive by Saint Al's. I gave birth to her there. That's my only experience with the hospital . . . until now.

I am not prepared for what I see when I get to the Intensive Care Unit. I don't even recognize Cale. At first, I'm convinced I'm in the wrong room. His head is wrapped in a turban of white gauze. His face is swollen, his eyelids purple. There are so many tubes taped to his face. A blue, snakelike one connects to what I'm fairly certain is a ventilator. It's only when I peek under the sheet covering his legs that I'm sure it's him. He has a birthmark on his knee, a brown spot that looks like an upside-down heart. This is Cale. My stomach feels like it flips over on itself, gets twisted.

One of the nurses comes in as I'm peeking under the sheet. I quickly drop it, feeling silly for needing to confirm my husband's identity. Shouldn't I know it's him on some intuitive level?

"You must be Cale's wife," she says. She's young—twenty-something, maybe early thirties. It's both strange and comforting to hear her refer to him by name, as if she is a friend caring for him.

She removes one of the IV bags, hangs a new one. There are

so many machines, multiple screens displaying information that means nothing to me.

"I am," I say.

"I'm Nicole. It's nice to meet you." She gives me a warm smile. "Dr. Harris will be in to talk with you in a minute. He's the neurosurgeon."

This mention of the neurosurgeon, along with the head bandages, confirms that Cale was shot in the head. I don't even want to ask Nurse Nicole for details; I don't want to hear it said aloud.

I stare at the braces on Cale's feet, wondering if he broke his ankles somehow. I can't help but picture him scrambling to get out of that bar, bullets from a deranged man's gun flying in all directions.

"They're to protect his heels," Nurse Nicole says, as if reading my mind.

"His heels?" I ask.

"From bedsores."

It hits me that they expect him to be lying here, immobile, long enough for sores to develop on his heels.

"Oh," I say.

"And the sleeves on his legs are what we call SCDs—sequential compression devices. They help with blood flow."

I nod, attempt a smile to show some appreciation for this information, for any information. I watch the sleeves on his calves tighten and then release. They hiss when they release. This noise and the noise of the ventilator will become the soundtrack of my life now.

"I'll be back in a little bit, but the doctor will be in shortly."

Nurse Nicole leaves, and I stare at the body of my husband. I watch his chest rise and fall. I reach for his hand, squeeze. It is warm. There is no squeeze in return. When I release it, it falls to the bed, limp.

"Mrs. Matthews?" a man says.

I turn to see a fifty-something man in blue scrubs. His cheeks are sunken; he looks gaunt.

"Yes," I say.

"I'm Dr. Harris," he says.

He shakes my hand and motions to a chair for me to sit. There are three chairs, lined up against the wall. They are chairs more appropriate for a corporate conference room. I sit in the middle one. He seats himself on a rolling stool and crosses his arms over his chest.

"Your husband sustained a very serious head injury," he begins.

I nod. "Is he going to be okay?"

"It's hard to say. Let me explain."

He rolls closer to me on his stool, almost too close. I lean back in my chair. He proceeds to give me a short lesson in brain anatomy, explaining how the brain is divided into two hemi-spheres made up of four lobes each, with each lobe serving dif-ferent functions.

"Typically, outcome is poorer for those with extensive bullet tracts, those that pass through both hemispheres or multiple lobes," he says. "A bullet that damages the right hemisphere can leave the patient with motor and sensory impairments on the left side, and vice versa. Other things like memory, speech, and vision are controlled by both sides of the brain. So what I'm saying is that the best-case scenario is when an injury is limited to one hemisphere. That means the patient may be impaired but still able to perform functions at some level, depending on what lobes are damaged."

When he says "perform functions," I imagine Cale in a wheelchair, unable to talk. I imagine drool on his chin. I think of a woman I follow on Instagram who posts about the daily care she gives her husband who was rendered paraplegic by a car accident. I think of how I told my best friend, Sahana, "I don't think I could do that." I think of how she'd said, "You could if you had to. People can do all kinds of things when they have to."

"So what's the scenario for Cale?" I ask, not sure I want to know.

"Well, unfortunately, he sustained injury to both hemispheres," he says. "The bullet entered the right side of his head, went through four lobes, and came to rest on the left side of his brain."

He pulls out a scan of what must be Cale's brain and shows me the track the bullet took.

"Is that the bullet?" I ask, pointing to a dark spot on the scan, a spot in the shape of, well, a bullet.

"Yes, we had to leave it where it was. That's not uncommon."

Not uncommon.

As if he sees this all the time, as if all kinds of people are walking around with bullets in their heads.

"There was a lot of swelling when he came in, so we performed a craniectomy."

"A what?"

He looks irritated that I'm requesting details.

"We removed part of the skull to relieve pressure."

"You removed part of his *skull*?"

I'm sure I look horrified. I can't help it.

He gives me a tight-lipped smile of pity—not pity for my situation, but pity for my stupidity, it seems. "I know it sounds bad, but this is what needs to be done to treat the swelling."

He speaks with such condescension, as if talking to a child.

I guess it's true what they say about surgeons being assholes with God complexes. I hate this man with a rage I've never felt for a stranger before.

"So now what?" I ask, keeping my tone even. He is responsible for Cale's brain; I have to be nice.

"Now, we wait," he says. "The first seventy-two hours are critical. His pupils are responsive to light, which is a sign there's no further swelling in his brain. That's a good thing. We need to keep an eye on his ICP and—"

"His what?" I interrupt. Frankly, I don't give a fuck if this jerk is irritated with me.

"ICP," he says, with that talking-to-a-child voice again. "Intracranial pressure."

"I'm sorry, this may be a stupid question," I say, playing the dumb woman because I know that's what he wants me to be, "but you're saying he's in a coma then, right?"

"Yes. We have him on sedation medications to keep him comatose. We need to give his brain time. We'll be doing CT scans to assess the damage, then see about taking him off the medications."

"And then he wakes up?"

He gives me that pitying smile again. "It's not like in the movies," he says. "Waking up is a process. And he might be a completely different person if he wakes up."

"*If?*"

He leans forward, officially invading my personal space.

"Look, in my experience, gunshot wounds like this have a ninety percent mortality rate."

I flinch at this, at his phrasing. I've worked in advertising for years, writing copy, putting a positive spin on all kinds of negatives. Why couldn't he say "a ten percent survival rate"? Why does he have to be such an asshole?

"Even if your husband survives this, he will not be the same person he was before."

I stare at his hands. He has no wedding ring. He seems like one of those married-to-the-job types. The gauntness implies he can't even be bothered to care for himself, let alone a wife.

"We will give him the very best care we can," he says.

The words sound forced, like a line he was instructed to say in a seminar about how to comfort patients' loved ones. Maybe some other wife complained about him to the hospital's HR department and he had to undergo sensitivity training. If so, it didn't do much good. Or maybe anybody in my situation is impossible to comfort. Maybe I'm just looking for someone to hate.

He stands from his stool. Clearly, he expects the information he has given me to be enough. Clearly, it is not enough.

I stand from my chair. "Wait," I say. "What am I supposed to do?"

He looks at me, seemingly baffled by the question.

"Am I supposed to stay here or go home or . . . what am I supposed to do?"

I feel the tears coming despite my attempts to keep them at bay. They are making me into the type of person he probably hates to deal with.

"It's really up to you," he says.

He starts to walk away.

"I have a baby at home. I can't . . . I don't know what to do."

He turns at the doorway, lets out an audible sigh. "You can go home to your baby. We will give him the very best care we can."

There's that line again, practiced, rehearsed.

When he leaves and it's just me with Cale again, I feel more alone and helpless than I've ever felt in my life, like I'm smack-dab in the middle of an ocean, at night, clinging to a buoy.

I turn back to Cale. I'm angry—at Dr. Asshole, but also at Cale. I know this makes me an awful person. It's just that this didn't have to happen. If he'd just been in bed next to me, he would be fine. We would wake up and watch the morning news together, shaking our heads at the reality of a shooting just minutes from our house.

I go to his bedside. I touch his hand again. It reminds me of touching Evie's hands when she is sleeping deeply, the way I can lift them to my lips and kiss them without her stirring. Her day care teacher told me I should trim her fingernails when she sleeps so she won't protest.

I make a mental note to text her day care to say she won't be there today. And my boss.

"Cale?" I whisper.

A part of me expects a response, muffled by the tubes and bandages. The only sound is the beeping of the machines, the hiss of the ventilator and compression sleeves.

"What were you doing there?" I ask.

I wipe my eyes with my sleeve.

My phone buzzes with a text from Aria.

So? What's going on?

I text her back a succinct version of reality—shot in the head, surgery, coma, waiting. Three dots appear on the screen and remain there for a while; she doesn't know what to say. Nobody is going to know what to say. Everyone is going to wonder why my husband was at a dive bar on a random Thursday night.

She texts back:

He's strong. You're strong. We'll get through this.

This is what my life will be consumed by now—platitudes,

clichés, messages of hope. I will receive "thoughts and prayers" from Facebook friends I barely know. Someone will start a meal train or a GoFundMe page. I will have to express gratitude for all this, because that's the right thing to do, but I will be exhausted and doubtful and scared. I will want to be left alone. I will resent the insistence that I trust in God and his plan. But I will have to hide that resentment. I will have to put on a "brave face," be optimistic. This will be my life now.

I text back:

Is Evie awake?

She replies:

No. Should we come there when she wakes up?

I do not want Evie to see Cale like this. Even though she's not even two years old and likely won't understand that it's her father lying in the bed, she will understand something is wrong. She will feel the tension in the room. She will be scared.

Evie adores Cale. She's oblivious to the fact that fatherhood seems to be an obligatory performance for him—*look at me, throwing my daughter up in the air*. It's no wonder he's exhausted; anything that doesn't come naturally is exhausting. But Evie doesn't know it's hard for him. She can't tell that when he sits with her and plays with blocks, every muscle in his body is tense. She doesn't know that when she goes to bed, I bear the brunt of his downcast mood, a mood he won't even acknowledge: "What's wrong?" I ask. "Nothing," he snaps. I do this for her, of course. I do this for the bliss of her ignorance.

I text:

No. I'm coming home soon.

After all, there's not much for me to do here, except continue to stare at him and whisper questions that he can't answer.

TESSA

I DON'T GET HOME, to our apartment, until evening, nearly twenty-four hours after starting what I thought would be a routine shift at the bar. I haven't slept or eaten. I have sipped water, mostly because people—Ryan, police officers—keep putting paper cups filled to the brim in front of my face.

The police wanted to know everything I saw, even though I didn't see much of anything. I couldn't describe the shooter. I couldn't even say for certain if the shooter was a man or a woman. The person was wearing all black—or maybe it was just so dark in the room that it appeared the person was wearing all black; I couldn't even be decisive about that. I couldn't say if he—assuming a male—acted alone. They wanted to know how many pops I heard. I had no idea. Ten, maybe? A hundred? They wanted to know when I went to the storage closet. I had no idea. They seemed frustrated, though they kept saying, "Teresa, you're doing great." I couldn't take them seriously; nobody calls me by my full name.

"You should really sleep," Ryan says.

We are sitting on our couch, just staring at the TV that isn't on. He has made me a cup of tea, but it just sits on the coffee table, over-steeping.

"I don't know how I could possibly sleep," I tell him.

I reach for the remote control, but Ryan stops me.

"Not sure you should be watching TV," he says.

I look at him, confused.

"It's all over the news," he explains.

This hadn't occurred to me. You see these stories all the time—shootings in movie theaters and grocery stores and schools. You don't ever expect to be the story.

"Seriously, Tess, you need to sleep."

"I don't know how to do that," I tell him, getting irritated. He wasn't the one hiding in a storage closet, listening to a horror show a wall away. He doesn't know what I need.

He stands from the couch. "Stay here," he says, holding out one "stop" hand to me, as if I'm a dog. "I'll be right back."

I curl up on the couch, hugging a throw pillow against my chest. My phone buzzes with a text message. It's my mom.

Just heard about the shooting there. Is that close to where you live??

She wouldn't even think to ask if I was okay. I've never been a bar-going type. She has no idea I work at Ray's. We haven't talked much. She's back in Oregon, in Bend. That's where I'm from. She's living with her boyfriend. To be honest, that's one of the reasons I left—the boyfriend. It used to be just me and her, against the world. Then she met Rob. Then he was eating cereal at our kitchen counter in the morning. I guess I couldn't expect my mom to stay single forever. She deserves to be happy. Like I said, I'm a brat.

She was weird about me moving to Boise. We had something of a fight about it—a spat, I guess you'd call it. I don't know what she has against Boise. I felt like she was being critical just to be critical, questioning my choices because I'd never made that many on my own before. I told her, "I can't just stay here and be your third wheel. My life is so much more than you." I regretted it the second I said it, wished I could reach out, grab the words, shove them back into my mouth. I can still see the pained expression on her face, the hurt. I haven't told her I work at a bar because I know she'd have that same expression. I told her I got a scholarship to Boise State. I didn't want her to feel bad about the fact that she doesn't have enough money to help with my tuition.

I text back:

Mom, everything in Boise is close to everything else. But I'm fine.

I don't know why I tell this blatant lie. I guess if I told her the truth, I'd have to admit it myself. Denial is easier.

She responds:

I just can't believe it—a shooting in Boise. Please stay safe, my girl xo

Ryan comes back with a bottle of Benadryl in his hand. He shakes out two pink pills and hands them to me.

"Take these," he says. "They'll help you sleep."

He thinks the mildly sedating effects of an allergy medicine will be enough to quiet my mind. I roll my eyes at him.

"If you say so," I say, humoring him.

When I first met Ryan, a little more than a year ago, I thought he was one of the smartest people I'd ever met. He scored a 172 on the LSAT; he starts law school at the University of Idaho in the fall (meaning, we will have a long-distance relationship; the university is in Moscow, a five-hour drive from Boise). He's good with textbooks, I guess. He's good with the black-and-white world of the law. When it comes to the gray area of emotion, he is somewhat of an idiot.

I close my eyes so he'll think I'm sleeping and leave me alone. Even with my eyes closed, I can feel him staring at me, worrying about me. It's a lot of pressure to have someone concerned about you in this way.

"Can you get me some ice cream at the store?" I ask him, eyes still closed.

I figure an errand will do us both good—he wants to feel helpful, and I want to be alone for a few minutes.

"Sure," he says. "Chocolate chip?"

He knows that's my favorite flavor. It was one of the topics we covered on our first date. He confessed later to going home after that first date and creating a spreadsheet of information about me, including my ice cream flavor preference. I wonder if he's kept the spreadsheet, if he updates it on a regular basis. I wonder if, after today, he will type "In crisis, she needs space."

We have never dealt with a crisis together before. We are only twenty-three years old.

"Yes," I say. "Chocolate chip."

I feel his weight leave the couch and hear his footsteps cross the room. He takes his keys off the table by the door, the door opens and shuts, and I am alone.

I wait a few minutes, until I'm sure he's taken the elevator down to the lobby and left the building. Then I turn on the TV.

Ryan was right—it is all over the news. All the major channels have reporters standing in front of the bar. I decide on channel 7 because the reporter, a youngish Asian guy, reminds me of a friend from high school, Kevin Lang.

"For anyone just joining us," the Kevin look-alike says, apparently talking to me directly, "there was a shooting at Ray's Bar last night, around eleven fifteen. Five people were killed and two injured."

He throws it back to the news desk, where the female anchor asks if there is any information about the victims. Kevin says that information has not yet been released. The woman then asks about the perpetrator. Kevin looks down at a notepad in his hands, then back at the camera.

"We have the perpetrator as twenty-eight-year-old Jed Ketcher. We're told he used a .45-caliber Glock 21 semiautomatic pistol. As we've reported, Ketcher died of a self-inflicted gunshot wound when police arrived at the scene."

Ryan was right. I shouldn't be watching TV.

I switch it off, but I keep hearing the Kevin look-alike's voice.

Five people were killed and two injured.

I think about Dan, the guy who was behind the bar with me. I barely knew him. He'd just started working at Ray's.

I reach for my phone on the side table, google "Ray's Bar shooting victims."

The victim information may not have been released to the broadcast media yet, but it's available online, like everything is these days. It's probably unverified; the internet cares more about speed than it cares about accuracy.

The online article includes names, ages, and photos of each of the five victims, photos likely taken from publicly available Facebook profiles, Instagram feeds, LinkedIn networking pages.

Robert Lang, age 62

I recognize him as a regular. He went by Bob. I never talked to him much. I'm not that chatty, which is one of the reasons Ryan says I'm in the wrong line of work. He was well liked, nice. I remember him dancing whenever we had classic rock cover bands.

Jason Maguire, age 36

He looks a little like my first boyfriend, Rich, but, besides that, he's not familiar to me. This fateful night could have been his first time visiting Ray's. If he'd only chosen another bar.

Leigh Maguire, age 37

Jason's wife, I'd guess. It doesn't say. I suppose she could be a sister. Probably wife. I wonder if it's better that they both died, that they're still together, wherever they are. I hope they didn't have kids.

Rick Reed, age 63

He's another regular, a friend of Bob's. He'd been diagnosed with Parkinson's, so whenever he held a glass of whiskey—his drink of choice—it would rattle against the wood top of the bar. He'd told me recently, "One of these days, I'm just going to ask you for a straw."

And there he is. The very last person on the page:

Dan Velasquez, age 26

They have him listed as "the bartender," as if there was only one, or as if they don't want to mention that the other one is okay; it might upset his family. I try to remember where he was when I ran to the storage closet. Did I run right past him? Could I have grabbed him, taken him with me? I just can't remember anything. I don't think I saw him. Maybe he ran to hide somewhere else. Maybe his hiding place wasn't as safe as mine. Maybe I got lucky and he didn't.

THE BENADRYL IS starting to make me a bit woozy—not tired, just woozy. I want to cry, I instruct myself to cry, but it's almost as if my body lacks the energy to do so. I wonder about Cale, the "trendy lettuce stuff" guy. Did he save my life by telling me to run? If he hadn't said anything, would I have just stood there at the bar, paralyzed? Is that what Dan did?

I'm relieved Cale isn't listed as one of the victims. If he'd died, I'd have to wonder if the seconds he spent telling me to run were what got him killed. I'll have to thank him, somehow. Maybe I will write him a letter, like little kids write to firefighters who save their homes from destruction. That's what I feel like right now—a little kid, a helpless human.

I hear Ryan's key in the lock and put my phone back on the table. Then I close my eyes and pretend to be asleep.

JOYCE

I SIT IN A dimly lit hallway of the Ada County Coroner's office, waiting for the medical examiner to summon me. They want me to identify my son—the most torturous task any parent could endure. I finger the turquoise pendant hanging around my neck, rub the stone between my thumb and index finger.

It's not him. It's not him.

That's what I keep telling myself.

I am hoping beyond all hope that the person they show me is someone else's son—a terrible thing to hope for, I know. I want to believe this is all a misunderstanding, a mix-up of wallets and IDs in the midst of the chaos at that bar. I want to believe Jed will be there when I get home, that he will say, "Mom, the craziest thing happened." I want to believe he'll be so distraught that he'll hug me, something he hasn't done since he was a small child.

The medical examiner introduces himself as Barry—not Dr. Walker, just Barry. I thought he would be wearing a white coat, like a doctor would, but he's dressed in gray slacks and a button-down blue shirt. He's younger than I expected—in his forties. Too young to be named Barry.

"Ms. Ketcher?" he says. "We're ready for you."

When they called to say they needed me to identify Jed's body, I was picturing being led into a cold, gray room where my son's body would be on a stainless steel table. One wall of this imagined room would have giant drawers, storage for dead people. I watch too much TV, apparently.

It's not like that, thank God. Instead, I'm seated in a small room and Dr. Walker (I cannot bring myself to refer to him as Barry) is telling me that I will see a photograph of my son's face—just a photograph, not his actual body.

"The gunshot wound was to his temple, so his face will appear unharmed," he says.

I stare at the photograph, facedown on the table in front of him.

"Are you ready?" he asks.

Ready? How could I be ready to see a picture of my dead son?

I nod anyway.

He slides the photograph across the table, still facedown. He sits back in his chair, his hands clasped. I wonder how often he has to do this. I wonder if he is doing this with each of the victims' families. I wonder if he ever cries.

I lift a corner of the photograph, slowly. The only thing that motivates me to reveal the whole thing is the delusional belief that maybe—just maybe—it's not him.

It is him though.

It's Jed.

His eyelids are closed, but it's clear he's not just sleeping. He's so white. The life is gone from him. I think back to when Ed—my husband, Jed's dad—died. I was holding his hand; we had hospice at home. I knew the second he left us, before the nurse even said, "He's gone."

I can't manage to verbalize "It's him," so I just look up at Dr. Walker and nod my head, my eyes begging him to let the nod be enough. He tucks his lips into his mouth and nods in return.

I assume they will let me go home, but Dr. Walker says the

detectives want to meet with me to ask questions. "Time is of the essence," he says with a sigh, expressing exhaustion on my behalf. I don't know what he means at first; then it occurs to me that the police must be wondering if Jed had other plans for doing harm, bombs set to go off in unknown locations. Or maybe they think he was working with a partner, or multiple partners. Maybe they think the Ray's Bar shooting is the first in a series. They have to presume the worst. What a terrible occupation.

Dr. Walker escorts me back to my waiting location in the hallway. I cannot let myself feel anything yet. I must just go through these motions. Perhaps if there are enough motions, I will never have to feel a thing.

A tall, formidable man in a long-sleeved black Boise Police Department shirt and black tie walks down the hallway toward me, his steps loud and deliberate. He is coming for me. When our eyes meet, he gives me a tight smile. He looks like that actor who played James Bond. What is that actor's name? Not Pierce Brosnan. Not Sean Connery. The other one. Jed and I had watched the movie together; he streamed it on his laptop, and we sat on the couch together and watched. He refused to pay for Netflix or any of those other online sites. He had a way of downloading movies for free, something I didn't want to know about because I suspected it was illegal. I had presumed those downloads and some marijuana were the extent of his dark side. People will tell me not to blame myself for all this, but how can I not?

"Ms. Ketcher?" the man says.

Daniel Craig. That's the actor's name. He looks just like him. For a split second, I wonder if we are just in a movie, if this isn't real.

"Yes," I say.

I stand to greet him because his presence seems to require such a thing. He is two heads taller than me, burly.

"I'm Detective Matt Kinsky," he says. "I apologize that we're meeting under these circumstances."

His voice is as deep as his stature demands.

"Do you mind if I ask you some questions about your son?"

I do mind, but I don't get the sense I can say that. "Okay," is all I say.

He shows me into a small room that must be used for exactly these circumstances—discussions with the loved ones of dead people. There is a round table and too many chairs—eight of them. I look around, wonder if the walls are really mirrors, if a team of people is watching me. I figure that probably isn't the case. This is the coroner's office, not the police station. I suppose Detective Kinsky wanted to spare me the ten-minute drive, a drive that would go by the mall with the Cheesecake Factory Jed and I visited for special-occasion dinners.

I sit in one of the chairs, and he sits at the table across from me.

"I'm so sorry about the loss of your son," he says. The words come out monotone; his face displays no signs of empathy.

"Thank you," I say.

He launches into all of the questions that a mother in my situation should ask herself. The questions pain me because I have no valuable answers.

Did your son talk to you about any plans to shoot others or himself?

No.

Did your son have any history of violence?

No, not that I know of.

To your knowledge, did your son own firearms?

No, not that I know of.

Did your son have any mental health issues?

He had some depression at times, but nothing major. Or not that I know of.

Are you aware of any personal incidents in your son's life recently?

Not that I know.

How long has he been living with you?

He moved back home about two years ago.

What was his reason for moving back home?

He said a business deal in Santa Cruz fell through.

What kind of business deal?

I don't know. I didn't really ask.

Did he have a significant other?

Not that I know of.

Did he leave behind any notes or writings?

Not that I know of.

Was he in communication with certain friends or associates recently?

I don't know.

THERE ARE SO many questions. My brain stops registering them. I just keep responding "Not that I know of."

By the end of it, Detective Kinsky seems slightly agitated with me. *You are his mother, how could you not know more?* That's what I hear, though all he says is, "I know this is hard. If you think of anything that could help our investigation, give me a call. Any time. Day or night."

He hands me his card.

"Also," he says, "we have a warrant for the search of your home."

I hadn't thought of that, hadn't presumed my home would contain anything they would need.

"Oh," I say. "When is that going to happen?"

He looks at his watch, and I realize it will happen *today*.

"Within the next couple hours," he says.

"Can it wait until tomorrow? I'd like to go through his room and—"

"Ms. Ketcher. I'm sorry. It's imperative we get in there."

To make sure Jed didn't have further plans.

To make sure bombs are not set to go off somewhere.

To make sure Jed wasn't part of a larger group.

To make sure this shooting isn't the beginning of a spree.

He doesn't explain these things, but I can guess.

"Okay," I say.

What else can I say? My son is dead. They can turn my house upside down if they like, take whatever they want. None of it matters.

I DON'T KNOW how I get home. It's one of those drives made by muscle memory. I am in a fog, a trance, a nightmare. I am thinking about how I want to go through Jed's room, look for a letter, clues, something. But as I turn onto my street, I see seven news vans parked in front of my house.

I consider driving past my house, but where would I go? They are going to wait there for me, however long it takes. So I push the button on the garage door opener, pretend like this is any other day, like I'm just coming home from the grocery store. There is a group of reporters congregating on the sidewalk. When they see the garage door open, when they see my car, they run toward me, not minding my flower beds, my herb garden.

I'm so harried that I pull too far into the garage, hit the front edge of the work bench that hasn't been used since Ed died.

"Joyce!"

"Ms. Ketcher!"

They are all yelling at me.

In my rearview mirror, I can see them on my driveway. I push the button to close the garage, watch it slowly angle toward the ground. A couple of them look like they might dive under the closing door, but they don't. Then they are gone, from my view at least.

I sit in the driver's seat, afraid to move.

This is my life now.

I GO INSIDE, and the phone in the kitchen is ringing. I pick it up, not thinking, and say, "Hello?"

A woman says, "Is this Joyce Ketcher?"

And I understand, again. This is my life now.

I take the phone off the hook, set it on the counter. I don't even use that phone, generally. The only reason I have a landline is because it was included in my cable package and I figured, "Eh, can't hurt." Jed made fun of me for having it, said it made me "ancient." I told him, "Well, I *am* pretty ancient. And, besides, a landline might come in handy in an emergency, if all the cell towers are down." He said, "Yeah, but you won't have anyone to call because nobody else has a landline." It was a good point.

My landline number must be listed somewhere, accessible to the public. It's probably only a matter of time before they find my cell phone number.

I hold my cell phone in my sweaty palm. Diana has texted, asking if she can do anything. I imagine her sitting on her front porch, staring at the vans in front of my house. She's probably made some popcorn for the event. I haven't returned her text.

I go to the living room, pull the curtains shut. Still, there are small slivers of space where the reporters can peer. I see them trampling my lawn. They are ruthless. I crouch behind the love seat, out of sight.

I call Gary because I can't think of who else to call. Gary and I dated. I guess that would be the term—"dated." It sounds so silly, a term that should be reserved for teenagers. But if I say we enjoyed each other's company, it sounds like I work for an escort service and he was a client. We met on an online dating site, though I told Jed we met at the downtown bookstore because I didn't want him to know his "ancient" mother was looking for men on the internet.

Gary and I broke up—another teenage phrase—because of Jed. He said I was too intertwined with Jed. He said I had to learn to let go. The final nail in our creaky coffin: "Joyce, I'm sorry, but I'm just past the point in my life when I want to date a woman with a child at home."

"Gary, it's Joyce," I whisper. The whispering is probably unnecessary, but it wouldn't surprise me if one of the reporters has affixed some kind of amplification device to the walls of my house, in hopes of hearing me inside.

"Joyce? My god. I'm watching the news. Is it true?"

The tears come again.

Is it true?

I still cannot believe he was the shooter. I want to think he was just one of the victims. *Just*. How quickly my world has changed. In this world, the best-case scenario is that my son is dead but he is innocent.

"Joyce?" Gary says.

"They say he shot those people," I say. I'm blubbering. I doubt he can even understand me.

"Are you alone right now?" he says.

"Yes."

He sighs. "You shouldn't be alone right now."

"Well, there are about a hundred people right outside my door, but you know how I feel about socializing."

He lets out a little laugh and I smile, through the sobs.

"Can I come by?" he asks.

I nod my head, vigorously. It takes me a moment to realize that he cannot see me over the phone.

"Yes," I say. "Text me when you park. I'll unlock the door at the back of the house. Just go around there. Feel free to punch a reporter or two on the way in."

"You got it," he says.

I feel better already, just knowing he's coming.

GARY ARRIVES TEN minutes later, wearing his usual uniform of khaki shorts, a collared shirt, and boat shoes. "He dresses like he lives in Florida," Jed said once. He used to refer to him as "Tommy Bahama"—"Hey, Mom, is Tommy coming over tonight?" and "Mom, Mr. Bahama said he'd be back in ten minutes."

I usher Gary in through the back door quickly, then turn the dead bolt.

He hugs me, kisses my cheek—not in a romantic way, but in the way relatives do at reunions.

"You weren't kidding about the circus out there," he says.

"The police are coming soon, with a warrant. I'm sure the reporters want to get footage of that."

"Maybe you should come stay at my place for a while," he says.

I hadn't thought of this. It's been two months since I've been to his house. It's a quaint house, charming, a craftsman built in 1919. He's constantly renovating it. We used to sit on his back porch, drinking wine. I'd be lying if I said that didn't sound nice right now—an escape from reality.

"I wouldn't want to intrude like that. I come with a lot of baggage now," I say, motioning to my surroundings.

"I have room for baggage."

"Thank you," I say, still not sure how seriously I should take his offer.

"Consider it. Really," he says, clarifying for me.

There's a knock at the front door, and I know it's the police coming to search the house and comb through all of Jed's belongings. I'm sure they'll want to take his laptop back to their lab, pore through all his files. I don't want them to find anything. If they do, that means I was blind.

Gary says he'll answer the door. I'm glad for this, content to be the damsel in distress in the background.

There are four officers, standing awkwardly close together in the tight confines of the front hallway. I tell them to come in, and they spread out in the living room. One of them presents a warrant, which I do not even bother to review. I don't care if they turn the house upside down. How could I care about that? My son did something awful; that's what they're saying, at least. They can burn my house for all I care.

"We'd like to start with your son's bedroom," one of them says. His tone is even. I can't decipher what he thinks of me, the mother of the monster.

I take them to his room. I wish I could have had some time alone here before they turn it into something that is no longer his. They do not care what I want though.

His bed is unmade, as usual. His computer is on, the screensaver a disgruntled-looking anime character—a guy with purple hair, his foot kicking outward, the computer screen made to look cracked. Jed loved anime. I never really understood it. It just seemed like disturbing cartoons to me. Was I supposed to ask him about it? It's not like he was a twelve-year-old delving into inappropriate content; he was twenty-eight!

"Why don't we go to my place?" Gary says, his hand on my shoulder.

I nod, in tacit agreement.

"Can I pack up some items in my room?" I ask an officer. It's strange, needing permission in my own house, a house I've lived in for thirty years.

"Yes, ma'am," another officer says.

I go to my room, pack an overnight bag with toiletries and some clothes. Before I go, I make my bed, for some semblance of normalcy, I suppose.

Gary and I leave out the back door. He wraps his arm around me tightly, practically carries me pressed up against his side, as we make our way to the front yard. When the reporters realize it's me, they swarm. Gary quickens his pace, our bodies like Ping-Pong balls, bouncing against other bodies, voices shouting at us:

"Ms. Ketcher, did Jed have a history of violence?"

"Were there any signs?"

"Do you have a message for the victims?"

"What do you think motivated this?"

Gary puts his hand on the back of my head, encouraging me to keep looking at the ground. Part of me wants to meet the eyes of these people, tell them that my son was not a monster. Gary must know it's best if I am silent. If they see my red eyes, if they hear my frantic responses, they will write me off as crazed. The unstable son will have the unstable mother, and their stories will be written for them. That's what they want.

Gary shoves me into the passenger's seat of his Jeep. It's only then that I look up. The reporters are at the windows, with microphones, their cameramen not far behind them. There are flashes. My photo will be online within twenty minutes. I cower in the seat, hide as best I can. Then Gary puts the key in the ignition, and we speed away.

LEIGH MAGUIRE

VICTIM #1

JASON AND I PROMISED ourselves—and our marriage—that we'd complete five therapy sessions. After all, we made those vows in front of all our loved ones seven years ago. I hate that it's been seven years. If we split up, people will chalk it up to the "seven-year itch." Maybe we should commit to making it to year eight, just so our failure can't be blamed on some notorious itch.

"So today's your last session," the therapist says.

It was my idea to do therapy. It must always be the woman's idea. I can't imagine a man saying, "We should see a therapist." Maybe there are evolved men out there who say such things, men who are in touch with their emotions, men who cry. They probably live in California. Anyway, I wouldn't be attracted to that type of man. I'm attracted to strong, stoic types—for better or worse. It's the last year or two that have revealed the "worse" part.

"Last one," Jason says.

We sit on a couch, and the therapist sits in a chair across from us. It's the exact scene you picture when you think about a therapy appointment. Jason and I are about a foot apart. I wonder if other couples touch, if they hold hands. We've never been that type of couple.

"How are you guys feeling?" Tracy asks.

She's asked us to call her Tracy, which I guess makes sense. She's not a doctor. She doesn't have a PhD or whatever the degree is that the fancy psychologists get. She's a marriage and family therapist, an MFT. These credentials make her somewhat affordable.

"Better," Jason says. "I think this has been helpful."

Jason is a good liar. He has hated every moment of therapy. He just wants to be a compliant patient in her mind.

"Leigh?" Tracy asks. "How about you?"

"I don't know," I say. The good thing about therapy is that it allows me to be honest, without having to fear being misunderstood by Jason. We have a neutral party in Tracy. She is our interpreter, our referee.

"I guess I don't feel any kind of real resolution," I say.

If I said this at home, without Tracy, Jason would throw his hands up in the air and say, "Nothing makes you happy." Here, he just has to sit. He can't fly off his usual handle. He's always cared what people think of him, which is a benefit in this situation.

"Tell me more about that," Tracy says.

Tracy says this at least five times in every session.

"I guess I was hoping to *know* at the end of this if we're meant to stay together."

I can feel Jason's eyes on me. He thinks we should stay together. He's always thought that. He doesn't understand my discontent. Tracy has tried to tell him that our strife is more about my needs not being met; his needs are mostly met, though he did express desire for more "physical contact." We are such stereotypes—me wanting more emotional connection, him wanting sex.

"And you don't know that?" Tracy asks.

"I still don't know if we're . . . compatible," I say.

Our issues started after I had Molly, our daughter. I decided to become a stay-at-home mom, mostly because my teaching job paid barely enough to put Molly in day care. It just didn't make sense. I got depressed as a stay-at-home mom. It's still something I'm ashamed to admit. I know I'm supposed to "cherish every moment" and all that, but it's difficult. I love Molly. I just miss time to myself. I miss teaching. I miss being someone besides Molly's mom. Jason says it will be better when she's older, when she starts school (she's three now). He works fifty-hour weeks at Micron; he doesn't know what it's like to be a full-time parent. He has no patience for my moods, says I'm being dramatic when I claim I'm depressed. He doesn't believe in medication. When he told me he wanted another child, I insisted on therapy. I mean, if he thinks we are in any position to have another child, he must not understand me at all.

"Can you say more about that?" Tracy prods.

"I just don't think Jason *gets* me. He doesn't really care about my happiness. He just wants our life to run smoothly."

Jason scoffs.

"That's not true at all," he says.

"Sometimes, I guess I wonder if I'd be happier being divorced."

There it is—my fantasy exposed, finally, during session number five.

I know Tracy will ask what I mean, so I get right to it.

"We'd each have our own place. We wouldn't have to deal with the daily bickering. Jason wouldn't have to hear me 'whine,' as he puts it. If I was just officially a single parent, I wouldn't resent him for all the stuff I do for Molly. I wouldn't resent all the hours he works. I wouldn't expect anything because he wouldn't *be* there, you know? We could share custody of Molly. We'd each get our days off that way. It just seems . . . nice."

Tracy nods. She does a stellar job of hiding any of her personal feelings about my admissions.

"That's ridiculous," Jason says.

I put my hand out like it's holding an invisible platter, the gesture saying, *See, this is what I'm talking about.*

"If it's the way I feel, it's inherently *not* ridiculous," I say. "That's how you should feel toward your wife. You should respect her feelings, be curious about them, ask questions. You just dismiss me. All the time."

Tracy puts her hand up like she's a crossing guard and we are approaching a busy intersection.

"Okay, let's dive deeper," she says.

This is something else she always says.

FORTY MINUTES LATER, we leave her office and walk to the car. It's awkward walking beside each other after what's just transpired.

"I can't believe this is what you really want," he says.

By the end of the session, we'd settled on considering a trial separation—not doing it, *considering* it. I have to admit, when we verbalized this possibility, I had butterflies—the good kind, the kind you get while waiting in line to ride a roller coaster at an amusement park.

"Just give me the space to think about it, okay?" I say.

I'm fairly certain it's what I want to do, but I don't want to come out and say that now. He'll write me off as impulsive, irrational. He'll take me more seriously if I claim to be "thinking about it" over the course of a week or two.

"So I get no say in the decision?"

He unlocks the car. I get in the passenger's seat; he gets behind the wheel.

"Of course you do, if you're willing to talk about it. Clearly, if I'm fantasizing about our marriage ending, I've been unhappy for a long time. Do you want to talk about that or just continue telling me I'm crazy?"

He turns the key in the ignition, and the car comes to life. He doesn't say anything as we exit the parking garage. He doesn't know what to say, I'm sure. He doesn't *really* want to understand my unhappiness, but he knows he can't admit that. He knows the right answer is to say, "Yes, talk to me."

We are starting down Main Street when he says, "Let's go get a beer. Can we do that?"

Jason always has an easier time talking after a beer or two. I can't criticize his need for it; at least he's trying.

It's just past nine o'clock. We chose to do 8:00 p.m. therapy appointments so we could put Molly to bed and the sitter just has to, well, sit. Hannah's a high school senior who lives next door. I don't trust her to do much more than sit.

"I'll text Hannah."

Two seconds later, Hannah responds, says she doesn't mind staying at all.

"Okay," I tell Jason. "Let's go get a beer."

A few minutes later, we pull into the parking lot of Ray's.

ANGIE

ARIA AND I SIT at the kitchen table, passing a bottle of wine back and forth. Evie is in her high chair, eating one pea at a time until she declares "all done" and starts playing peekaboo with us. She is endlessly entertained by this game, by her ability to make the world disappear and then suddenly reappear. It's a relief to play with her, to act as if nothing is wrong, to force a smile. I can see how it will become exhausting—pretending to be something you're not always is—but for now, it's a relief.

"Have you told Mom and Dad?" Aria asks.

I shake my head. Our parents retired to Maui five years ago, something they had always talked about doing and something Aria and I never thought they'd actually do. Our dad was a bigwig at Micron, a technology company that was founded in Boise. When he retired at sixty, he had more than enough money for them to live on for decades to come. We do Skype calls, occasionally. They've never even met Cale in person.

"I'm not up to that yet," I say.

Aria nods because she understands. Our parents raised us to be self-sufficient, for better or worse. When Evie was born, I expected they—or at least my mom—would fly in to meet her. After all, social media has made me privy to all the acquaintances I have whose moms basically move in with them for a month following the birth of their children. My mom isn't that kind of mom though. She took care of us, but she didn't weep when her nest became empty—she moved to Maui. They have

46

plans to come visit in fall; they say they never want to experience another Boise winter or summer. If the fall visit happens, it will be their first time holding their granddaughter.

"I can stay the night if you want," Aria says.

It's just after six o'clock. Aria put a frozen pizza in the oven for us, but I couldn't manage a bite.

"No, that's okay," I say. "Sahana is coming over."

Sahana, my best friend since freshman year of high school.

"You need anything before I go?" Aria asks.

I shake my head. "Thank you for being here," I say.

It's usually me coming to Aria's rescue—she is the younger sister, after all. It's always bothered Cale how I go out of my way for her. Once, after I canceled dinner plans with him to be by her side during a breakup, he said, "You will do absolutely anything for her." His tone implied this was a bad thing. I shrugged and said, "Yeah, probably. So?" He said, "I just don't think she would do the same for you." She would, though. I wish he were here so he could see for himself.

"Okay if I come back in the morning?"

She grabs her purse and keys from the kitchen island.

"That would be great," I say.

I lift Evie from her high chair and put her on the floor. She runs to Aria and wraps her chubby arms around Aria's legs.

"Bye-bye, Aya," she says.

Just as Aria leaves, Sahana pulls into the driveway, as if they have coordinated, agreeing that I should not be alone for even thirty seconds. Evie shrieks at the sight of Sahana's car. It's a red Subaru, easily identifiable for a toddler.

"Saha," Evie calls, unable to contain herself.

For a fleeting moment, I think this is just a casual visit from my best friend. We haven't seen each other in a while. Cale seems annoyed when I have Sahana over. He goes straight to the bedroom when she arrives, turns on the TV to watch whatever sporting event will lull him to sleep. The last time Sahana visited, I said, "I bet he's already passed out" at seven thirty, and she was so disbelieving that we tiptoed downstairs to see. Sure enough, he was asleep, snoring even, the TV still on. She couldn't help but laugh. His eyes flickered open and he sighed, mumbled something indecipherable, and rolled away from us. I apologized the next morning, and he said, deadpan, "I'm glad you were both entertained by my exhaustion."

"Hi, sweetie," Sahana says to Evie, with the same kind of smile I've been forcing. When her eyes lift to mine, the smile is gone and she hugs me.

"I just can't believe this is happening," she says.

Evie is oblivious—she starts babbling "Ring around the rosy" and turning in circles—but I still give Sahana a warning look.

"Let's talk after she goes to bed."

I SING EVIE the same four lullabies every night: "Hush Little Baby," "Rock-a-Bye Baby," "Twinkle Twinkle Little Star," and "You Are My Sunshine." Tonight is no different—or that's the lie I'm perpetuating for my daughter. By the end of the fourth song, her eyelids are heavy. I tell her to have sweet dreams, kiss her cheek, and then leave her to continue believing her world is safe, predictable.

Sahana is in the living room when I go upstairs, sitting cross-legged on the couch. I sit next to her, let my body fall against hers. She pets the hair on my head as if I am her lapdog.

When I left the hospital after seeing Cale, I called Sahana. In true Sahana fashion, she hadn't heard the news, knew nothing of the shooting. When I told her what had happened, the first thing she said was, "Wait, what? Cale was at some bar in the middle of the night?" Her shock was a relief; I'd been wondering if I was crazy for fixating on this fact.

"You must be exhausted," she says.

"I am," I say. "I might just fall asleep like this."

"And that will be fine with me until I have to pee. Your elbow is pressing into my bladder."

I manage a laugh and sit up.

"Have you heard from the hospital?" she asks.

I shake my head. "I'm assuming no news is good news on that front. I'll go back in the morning."

She shakes her head in disbelief of it all.

"I don't know what I'm doing," I say, feeling relieved just admitting this. "Am I supposed to stand watch over him twenty-four hours a day? Is that what most wives do?"

"In the movies, yes," she says. "But you have a toddler and a life to manage. And you need to rest and eat and things, so I don't see how you could stand watch twenty-four hours a day."

I'm grateful for this rationale. It's what I've been telling my-self, but sometimes only the words of another person will do.

We are quiet for a moment, and then Sahana acknowledges the elephant staring at us in the room.

"What was he doing there?" she wonders.

I know what she's asking—why was he at that bar, alone. Sahana has always been direct, blunt. When I've told her she needs to be "softer," she's said, in a faux accent, "I do not understand this 'softer.'" Sahana is first-generation Indian American. When we were growing up, she dealt with a fair share of teasing—jokes about turbans, call centers, 7-Elevens. Boise isn't exactly the most culturally sensitive place. She never tried to hide who she was though, never denied her heritage. One Halloween, we dressed up as a salt and pepper shaker set.

"I don't know what he was doing there," I say, staring out the window, unblinking.

"Do you think he'd been doing this for a while?" Her brows are knitted together so tightly that they appear to be one.

"Going to bars in the middle of the night?"

She nods.

"I have no idea."

She takes my hand in hers.

"Ang, I have to ask you something," she says.

I look at her. Her big brown eyes are glassy with coming tears.

"Yeah?" I say, already knowing what question is coming. It's a question I've been pondering ever since I realized Cale wasn't in bed next to me.

"Do you think Cale was . . . seeing someone?"

There it is, the biggest worm in the rusty can.

"I mean, I don't think he'd go to a bar just for the hell of it," I say.

She sighs.

Sahana knows Cale and I were having problems—not *problem* problems, but there was an undercurrent of tension, which is almost more of a threat to a marriage than a *problem* problem. I knew Cale wasn't happy, but he didn't want to talk about it, insisted he was "fine" every time I annoyed him by asking if he was okay. Sahana and I spent hours on the phone guessing at what was bothering him. We had a number of unoriginal theories:

Maybe he misses having couple time.

Maybe he misses having alone time.

Maybe he's just really, really tired.

Maybe he's overwhelmed by the responsibility of a child.

Maybe he's worried about finances.

Maybe he has postpartum depression.

That last one was Sahana's suggestion—a joke, at first. We started to wonder if it was a real thing. Sahana coined it post-*dad*um depression.

Ultimately, it didn't matter what our theories were because he wasn't going to admit to anything bothering him. Sahana—who is a psychologist—said it made sense on a psychological level. Cale is an only child, raised by a single mom who worked three jobs. His mom didn't have time for his feelings. She expected him to fend for himself, the motto of the house being "Just deal with it." Cale's always lived in a way that aims to disprove the notion that no man is an island. He prides himself on his independence and strength of will. Admitting to something bothering him would be admitting weakness; admitting weakness would be admitting the need for help on his island.

"An affair seems so cliché," I say.

Sahana shrugs. "This is how men operate. They look for escapes—women or whiskey, usually."

Sahana is steadfastly single. She claims to have zero interest in settling down, has all kinds of arguments against the institution of marriage. I think it's a front; she's just afraid of heartbreak. Despite being a successful psychologist, she's somewhat clueless about herself.

"I just can't believe he'd have the energy for an affair," I say. I keep picturing him falling asleep on the couch before eight o'clock. Was that all an act?

"Well, I bet you didn't think he'd have the energy to go to a bar in the middle of the night either."

I try to picture the woman meeting him at the bar. What would she be like? I suppose he would want someone child-less—not necessarily younger, but childless, free. She would be a reprieve from me, someone unattached to schedules and routines, someone spontaneous, the type of person to say "Let's go to the river" on a whim, then strip down and run in the current. This woman would help him forget the reality of his life—his life with me and Evie, with all its mundanity and the inevitable annoyances of clogged drains and cold viruses and property tax bills. I picture him laughing with this woman, his eyes twinkling the way they used to twinkle with me. I can't remember the last time Cale and I laughed together. It must have been when he was teasing me about humming that *Sesame Street* song. Now I wonder if he was laughing then only because he'd fallen in love with this other woman, this other life.

"Cale's going to have some 'splaining to do when he wakes up," Sahana says.

I haven't given Sahana—or anyone, for that matter—the details of Cale's prognosis. She knows he's in a coma. She knows it's serious. But she doesn't know what the doctor told me—that Cale will not be the same person ever again. Even if he does wake up, it's unlikely he'll be able to say my name, let alone tell me what he was doing at a dive bar on the outskirts of downtown. If there is another woman, he might not even remember her.

I can tell it makes Sahana feel better to be hopeful, to say things like "when he wakes up." So I don't correct her.

"Yeah," I say, "lots of explaining."

TESSA

AT FIRST, RYAN BEGGED me to sleep. Now he says I'm sleeping too much. There's no pleasing him.

The thing is, I'm not even sleeping. He just assumes that's what I'm doing because I'm in bed all day. It's been only two days since the shooting. I don't know how he expects me to be up and around.

"Did you tell your teachers you'll be missing classes?" he asks, sitting on the edge of the bed, sounding too much like someone's dad—not *my* dad, because my dad left my mom when I was six weeks old. I've never asked her much about him. Once, when I was a teenager, I told her I was curious who he was. She said she'd heard he'd OD'd—heroin. A real winner, apparently. I didn't ask anything more after that.

"Yes, I emailed them," I say.

I'm taking classes at Boise State University—a twenty-three-year-old freshman. Better late than never, I guess. They have a good nursing program. That's my goal. That's the whole reason I moved to Boise from Bend. I told myself it would be a fresh start. I broke up with my then-boyfriend, swore off men. Then I met Ryan at an off-campus house party my second week here and moved in with him a few months later. I fear I'm *that* girl, the one who can't be alone.

Ryan stands from the bed.

"Okay, well, I have to head to the firm, make up for missing yesterday," he says.

I hate how he says "the firm," as if he's already a lawyer, as if he has some big, important job. He's just an intern—unpaid. His parents pay for our apartment—or *his* apartment; he hasn't told them we live together. He says they've made it clear that they are "unwilling to fund cohabitation."

"I didn't ask you to stay home and watch over me," I snap.

"Tess, don't be like this."

He bends at the waist, kisses my forehead, diffusing my rage.

"You want to meet me somewhere for lunch?" he asks.

I haven't been eating much, despite Ryan's attempts. Still, I say, "Maybe. Text me around eleven."

He kisses my forehead again and says he loves me.

He does love me.

I'm a brat. I know that.

When I hear the front door close, I slump against the headboard and resume scrolling through Instagram on my phone.

I still haven't told anyone yet about being at Ray's during the shooting. I should have told my mom right away, but I didn't, and now it's just weird. As for friends, I don't have many in Boise. I've been texting like normal with a couple friends back in Bend, one telling me about a guy she met, the other asking me for a recipe for pot brownies that I used to make. They're going to think this is weird when they do find out what happened, but I figure I can blame post-traumatic stress. Ryan thinks I have PTSD, like, officially. Maybe I do. I'm just not ready to talk about it all with a bunch of people. I'm not ready to see their shock and horror. I just want to pretend like things are normal for a while. I want to scroll through Instagram and see that life goes on as usual. I want to entertain the delusion that I can forget Ray's and just move on.

But it's just that, a delusion.

I google "Ray's Bar shooting" at least once every ten minutes, hoping to find new information. I keep wondering about Cale. I keep replaying him shouting, "Go, now." I keep seeing his face—panicked, scared. I haven't told Ryan anything about Cale, about how he possibly saved my life. I haven't told him much of anything about that night—about hiding in the storage closet, about the black zip-up hoodie that I still have. I cling to it like a child clings to an old, worn blanket.

Five pages into search results, I find a message board with the wildly inappropriate name "Shooting the Shit." The description just says, "Thoughts and opinions on the latest mass shootings. First Amendment reigns supreme." I click. It's not a fancy website, just a black background with a white area featuring a wall of text. People hiding behind screen names say things like:

> If he really had a .45-caliber Glock 21, he must've been a terrible shot. He should've killed like 60 people with that thing.

And:

> This shooting is nothin compared to Vegas. That shit was crazy.

And:

> The shooter looks like this dude that used to work at my gym.

I refresh the page every few minutes, watching the conversation in real time. Most of the participants seem to be gossip-hungry ambulance chaser types or gun aficionados. There's a lot of talk about the shooter: Jed Ketcher. Some people think he was part of some terrorist group, but I doubt that. There are photos of him all over the message board, taken from Facebook or wherever else. He looks like an average white guy with

premature balding. He's not smiling in any of the photos—
or, rather, people have chosen not to post any photos of him
smiling. I don't know why people are so worried about ter-
rorists in this stupid country; the shooters are almost always
white guys harboring a secret grudge or a mental illness or a
gun fetish, or all three.

I create an account with the screen name TessWasHere so I
can post something:

> **Why are you guys talking so much about this Jed guy? He doesn't
> deserve attention. The victims deserve attention.**

Someone with the screen name JR2018 responds immediately:

> **Snore. Someone cue the violin.**

Someone (LvAll21) responds:

> **Shut up, JR2018. UR such a dick.**

LvAll21 responds to me too:

> **@TessWasHere, I totally agree. These shooters shouldn't get all
> this attention. Gotta remember the victims, RIP.**

I post again:

> **Does anyone know who the injured people are?**

Someone (Boyseeeee) responds immediately:

> **Ya, back a few pages. Someone posted the names yesterday.
> Someone's friend's a nurse or something at St. Al's and she leaked
> the names.**

I click back a few pages and find the names:

Cale, the guy who may have saved my life, was injured. I don't know how badly. There are no details—just his name.

Boyseeeee responds again:

Don't bother calling the hospital tho. They aren't giving out any info.

I write:

Thx.

I close out of the message board and google the hospital, Saint Al's. I've never been there. I've been to the other hospital in town—Saint Luke's. I cut my finger when slicing limes at Ray's, of all things. At the time, I would have guessed that would be the most traumatic thing to happen to me at the bar.

On the Saint Al's website, it says that visiting hours in the main hospital are 10:00 a.m. to 8:30 p.m., but visitors in the ICU are allowed only during a couple two-hour windows. I don't know if Cale is in the ICU. I hope he's not. I figure I'll just show up. It's possible they aren't even allowing visitors for the shooting victims, for privacy reasons. Maybe they will let me leave a card, though. Or one of those "Get Well Soon" balloons. The website says no latex is allowed, only Mylar. I didn't even know there were different kinds of balloons. I assume the gift shop will sell the allowable ones.

Ryan will think it's ridiculous, visiting Cale. It's just that I need him to know that I'm here, able to write him a card and buy him a balloon, because he told me to run.

JOYCE

IT'S STRANGE TO WAKE up in Gary's house—not in his bed, mind you; he has a guest room that he keeps for when his daughter visits, and that's where I stay. He says I can stay as long as I want.

I shouldn't use the term "wake up," as that implies I slept, which I did not. Every time I close my eyes, I see Jed's pale face in that photograph. It still doesn't seem real to me, the whole thing, which is probably why my brain keeps bombarding me with this image of him—a way to remind me, to say, *It really happened.*

I pull on a pair of jeans and a gray sweatshirt that I don't remember grabbing when leaving the house in such a hurry. I wonder what the police have found in Jed's room, on his computer. I wonder if they will tell me.

When I emerge from the room, I see Gary sitting on a stool at his kitchen island, the newspaper folded open in front of him. I'm sure the shooting is the front-page story.

"Good morning," I say, feeling like I'm intruding on his morning routine.

He startles, coffee sloshing about in the cup in his hand.

"Sorry," I say.

He turns the paper over, hiding the headlines from me.

"No, it's okay. I'm just not used to having someone in the house."

I wonder if he's saying this as a way of telling me that he hasn't dated since we ended things.

I run my hand over the kitchen island countertop. Toward the end of our time together, he'd been shopping around for the perfect slab of quartz. He wanted the look of marble, but didn't want marble—too expensive, not durable enough. It appears he found the elusive slab, white with gray veining.

"The counter looks nice," I say.

He looks pleased that I've noticed. "Thanks," he says. "Can I make you some toast?"

There is nothing appealing about food right now.

"Just coffee would be great," I say.

He gets up, goes to the coffeepot, pours me a cup.

I sit at the stool next to his, and he slides the cup across the island to me.

"Thank you," I say.

He resumes his seat, and I realize we must look like an old married couple on these side-by-side stools with our matching mugs of coffee.

"Did you sleep?" he asks.

I shake my head. "But the bed was extremely comfortable."

"Well, that's good."

We are silent as we sip. Then he folds the paper in half and turns to me.

"So what's on the docket for today?"

I can't help but smile at the word—*docket*. I'd forgotten about his affinity for this word. Every Friday, without fail, he used to ask, "So what's on the docket for this weekend?"

"I don't even know what day it is," I say. Because I don't. I know it's the day after I identified my son's body. That's all I know.

"It's Saturday," he says.

This means nothing to me.

"I don't have anything on the docket," I say.

"We should probably go by your house. Or I can do that, if you like."

"I can go," I say.

"You sure?"

"Cleaning up after their mess will give me something to do."

AS WE TURN the corner onto my street, my heart beats faster. I brace myself—literally, grab onto my own thighs—in preparation for the news vans, the reporters trampling my lawn. They are not there though. Once the police came and left, once I got into Gary's Jeep and sped away, they must have realized there was nothing more to see.

I'm looking down at my lap when we pull into the driveway. Gary says, "Oh, crap," and I look up, see what he sees.

Someone has spray-painted, in black, across my white garage door:

KILLER

"God dammit," Gary says, shoving the car into park and getting out, leaving his door open.

He walks to the garage, inspects the paint, shaking his head.

"I'll go to Home Depot and get some paint to cover this," he says.

Home Depot. Where Jed used to work. Gary doesn't even realize what he's said. He has no idea that I may never be able to set foot in a Home Depot again.

I sit in the passenger's seat, not ready to get out.

"Are they talking to me?" I say.

Gary leans in through his open door, his hands pressing into the driver's seat.

"Huh?" he asks.

"On the garage," I say, flicking my wrist toward the graffiti. "Is it meant for me?"

Gary looks at the garage, then back at me, then at the garage again.

"What are you talkin' about?" he says, not understanding at all.

"Are they calling me a killer?" I ask, point-blank.

Gary lets his head hang, defeated.

"Christ, Joyce, they're talking about Jed."

He speaks like I'm an idiot. Maybe I am.

"But Jed's dead. Everyone knows that. It feels like it's a message for me."

He shakes his head.

"It's just some teenager who wanted to mark the house, show all his friends on the Instagram or what have you," he says.

I can't help but smile when he says "the Instagram." Jed used to tease me about Gary being a grandpa. He's actually a few years younger than me, but he has no interest in keeping up with the times. He doesn't even use email.

"What?" he says, noticing my smile.

"Nothing."

He comes around to my side and opens my door for me. When I get out, my legs feel like Jell-O, like I walked a marathon the night before.

The lawn looks terrible, green blades smashed down, ripped out in several places. There's a Snickers bar wrapper on the front porch, a Big Gulp cup sitting on top of the mailbox.

I put my key in the door, reluctantly turn the knob.

It's not as bad as I thought—at least from what I can see. I was expecting ransacked; instead, it looks . . . investigated.

I walk through the living room, noting couch cushions slightly askew, the TV stand rolled away from the wall. Every cabinet and drawer in the kitchen is open. It seems rude. They could have just closed them on their way out.

In my bedroom, the sheets have been pulled back, dresser drawers opened, closet combed through. Shoe boxes and an assortment of hangers have been pulled out into the open, displaced from where I've stowed them at the back of the closet for years.

Gary follows me as I make my way down the hallway to Jed's room. I don't realize I'm holding my breath until I get to the threshold and exhale loudly.

His room is a mess.

The mattress is flipped over, laid to rest against the sliding glass closet door. His laptop is gone, as expected. He had a desktop computer too, which is also gone. There are drawers open, clothes strewn about—though, admittedly, some of those were there before the police came (cleanliness was never one of Jed's strong suits).

I go to the mattress, start to attempt to flip it.

Gary comes to my aid. "Let me," he says.

I do. He places the mattress back in its frame and we stand back, proud of ourselves.

"That's a start," I say.

Gary says he'll straighten out the kitchen and living room while I tend to Jed's room. He seems to understand that I want to be left alone in here, with Jed's things.

I fold his clothes, one article at a time, then place each piece back in its dresser drawer. I get choked up when folding his boxer shorts into nice, tidy squares.

Everything in his closet is in disarray. He had stacks of books. He wasn't stupid; he read heavy, philosophical texts,

Nietzsche and Dostoyevsky. He claimed to be an existentialist. There are photo albums too, dusty, memory-filled. I hope the police flipped through them, realized that my son had friends. Or he did, back then, back when people printed photos for albums.

I open one of the albums. It was filled with photos from high school. That was the time of his life I thought I had to worry about—all those hormones, teenage angst. Jed seemed to do just fine though. He wasn't popular, but he wasn't an outcast. He didn't wear a trench coat and listen to heavy metal. That's what people will want to think, isn't it?

Jed was average, that's what I thought. He was a B student; he got the occasional A, the more-occasional C. He wasn't an athlete, but I blamed that on the fact that his father died when he was young and I never tried to pretend to care about sports. He wasn't a loner, not when he was younger. They'll want to think he was, but he wasn't. His best friends were class-clown types, goof-offs. I know they all experimented with pot and drank occasionally, but they were good kids. He even had a girl-friend, or who I suspect was a girlfriend—Lindsey Benton. She was in theater, if I remember correctly. Jed always said they were just friends, but I saw the look in his eyes; if they were, in fact, just friends, he longed for something more.

He started to have trouble in college. DUI. Cocaine. He was busted for selling pot to a minor. Those are the things I know about; I'm sure there were more. I was paying his tuition at the University of California in Santa Cruz, so I got the notices about his failure to attend classes. I told him I wasn't going to continue paying his tuition. Out-of-state tuition isn't cheap. I told him he should come home, go to the local com-munity college, get back on track. He laughed at me, said he wasn't coming home, he wasn't a child. I knew he didn't have money for rent, figured he would come crawling back after a few weeks, but he didn't. I don't know if he slept on sofas or camped on the beach or what.

Over the next few years, we spoke often enough for me to know he was okay, health-wise, and not in jail. But he was distant, caught up in something he wouldn't explain. A voice whispered to me: *You've lost him.* But to others, to friends like Diana, I said he was going through a phase. I clung to this.

I hadn't seen him for four years when he showed up on my doorstep, unannounced, looking strung out and desperate as a stray cat. He didn't wait for me to invite him in; he just walked in. I should have set some kind of boundary then, I guess. I should have said, "Jed. You can't just show up like this." Would that have prevented what happened?

My phone buzzes in my pocket, jolting me from my thoughts—a blessing, probably. I don't recognize the number, so I don't answer. So many people are calling lately, mostly acquaintances who leave messages saying they are "checking in." Everyone just wants details. They are hungry for them. I understand, I do. But I am starved myself.

The voice mail notification flashes. I listen to the message, a message telling me that my son's body is ready to be released. They want to know what mortuary I want the body released to.

I need a mortuary for my son.

Gary comes into the room, asks how I'm doing. I tilt my head back and forth, indicating "so-so."

"I have a task for you," I say.

He looks at me, eager. Gary is someone who needs to feel helpful. When we dated, we argued regularly about how he couldn't just listen to me vent; he always had to offer solutions. Sometimes, I just wanted to lament the fact that my son was floundering. I just wanted hugs, assurances, nods of understanding. But he was insistent on fixing it and became frustrated when I waved off his suggestions—"You should get him to enlist in the military," "You should sign him up to run a marathon, get him committed to something," "You should sell the house and buy a place that doesn't have a room for him."

"At your service," he says.

I know he means it.

I tell him about the mortuary.

"What one did you use for Ed?" he asks.

I've always appreciated his use of Ed's name. He doesn't shy away from it, doesn't just say "your husband." He knows I loved Ed. He's never been threatened by that. It's probably because he knows about loss; his wife, Sandy, died ten years ago. Breast cancer. I have no problem mentioning her by name, either. He does, though. He doesn't like talking about her. It's too hard for him, I think.

"I don't even remember the name. It was family-run. They're not in business anymore," I say.

It was a few years ago when I drove by and saw they had turned it into a pizza place called To Die For. I was so infuriated that I posted a Yelp review—my first one—with just one word: "Tasteless."

"Do you want to bury him or . . ." Gary says.

Bury him or burn him. These are the choices, the terrible choices.

Ed wanted to be cremated. I felt strange about it at first. I had a hard time picturing his body in fire, and I struggled with accepting that there wouldn't be a gravesite that I could visit. It wasn't my choice though; he was adamant about it. He didn't like the idea of taking up unnecessary space on Earth. So I have an urn with his ashes on my nightstand. I talk to the urn some-times. I picture him chuckling when I do.

"Cremation might be best," Gary says.

I know why he thinks this. Putting Jed in the ground with a marked grave will invite people to deface that grave, spray-paint it like they did my garage door. Boise still has that small-town feel, even though it's growing, even though it keeps appearing in magazines as one of the best places to live, attracting people from other states, people nobody wants here. The small-town feel is what I've always loved about it. Now I wish we were in a sprawling metropolis with millions of people, someplace where it's easy to be anonymous, to hide. There is no hiding in Boise.

"Right," I say. It's all I can say. "I still want a service for him. He deserves a service."

"Of course," Gary says with a nod.

"Okay, then," I say.

"Okay," he echoes.

He clears his throat and scans the photo albums in front of me.

"What'cha lookin' at?" he asks.

I pat the bed, invite him to sit next to me.

"Come look," I say. "This was the Jed you didn't know."

JASON MAGUIRE

VICTIM #2

I DON'T KNOW how Leigh could think I don't love her. I work fifty hours a week to put food on the table and fund all her damn Amazon purchases. I don't say a word when those boxes arrive every freaking day. We have a nice house, health insurance, some savings for several rainy days. I've done the things we talked about in therapy—I'm making more of a point to ask her how her day is, that type of thing. And, after all that, she wants a divorce, or separation or whatever you want to call it. She *fantasizes* about it.

We sit at a high-top table along the back wall of Ray's. There are cheaply framed photos on the walls, dates scribbled in the corners: "Ray and the boys, 1992," that type of thing. This place has been here a few decades. It's a hole in the wall, but I've always liked it. I used to come here in college. It hasn't changed much since then.

"I've never been here," Leigh says.

"Really?"

She shakes her head. Leigh grew up in Boise, same as me. I thought most native Boiseans had been to Ray's at some point.

"I used to come here in college," I tell her.

"Really?"

Just like that, we have learned something new about each other. It feels, suddenly, like we're on a date. There's that rush of discovery.

"I'll get us a couple beers," I say.

I go to the bar, order from a twenty-something girl who barely looks me in the eye. She's busy, seems to be training the other bartender. She passes two pints across the bar top and thanks me.

A few sips into our first beers—I'm hoping for a few more, enough to get to the bottom of this trial separation business—I say to Leigh, "Look, I know I'm an idiot about a lot of things. But I don't want to separate. I don't want a divorce."

Her face looks softer than it did in the shrink's office. Maybe it's the dim lighting.

"You are kind of an idiot," she says, with the smile that made me fall in love with her. We met on an online dating site, back when it was taboo. We told our friends we met at the farmers market because we thought that was a better story. Most of them still don't know the truth. My sister had put my profile on the site; it definitely wasn't something I initiated on my own. She said there were several women who sent messages, but decided Leigh looked the most promising. After one date with Leigh, I told my sister she should make all my life decisions.

"You really think I've been ignoring your feelings for *years*?" I say.

I try to sound curious instead of angry, but the truth is I am angry. I don't like the implication that I've screwed up. If I'm honest, I feel like she's taking for granted all the good things I do. Like I said, I put food on the table. I fund all those Amazon purchases. Many women would be happy with a husband like that.

"I just think we don't connect, emotionally," she says. "And maybe I didn't notice that when we were dating because

I didn't need as much emotional connection then. We didn't have a child then. A child changes everything."

I nod. In one of our sessions, Tracy advised, "When in doubt, nod. Pay attention. Leigh wants to know that you're listening."

"Okay, well, I *want* to connect," I say. "You're going to have to help me with that one, though."

She lets out a little laugh. That laugh gives me hope.

NEARLY TWO HOURS later, we've each had three beers (well, Leigh had me finish half of her third one) and we both agree we need to go home. Things are better, or maybe they aren't. I suppose I'll find out the reality tomorrow, when the alcohol has left our systems. Leigh says she'll give it a few weeks, though. She says we can try "connecting" and see how it goes. We agree we'll be completely honest with each other. We say this now, of course. The beers help us make grand promises.

"Text Hannah that we'll be home in ten," I say.

We both stand. I go to the bar to pay my tab. The bartender girl is talking to a guy sitting on a stool across from her. She is telling him to calm down—about what, I don't know. I feel for her. She must have to counsel men on a nightly basis, and she doesn't get paid the same as Therapist Tracy does.

I turn to head for the exit, where Leigh is waiting. That's when a man barges in through the front door, knocking Leigh backward. She looks up at me from the floor, shock on her face.

"Hey!" I scream, charging at the guy, ready to throw a punch.

That's love, isn't it—being ready to fight anyone who disrespects your wife? Shouldn't that matter more than *connecting emotionally*?

This is what I'm thinking when I realize he has a gun. Leigh sees it at the same time I do.

"No!" she shrieks.

There is a bang. All goes black.

ANGIE

SAHANA LIES NEXT to me in bed, in Cale's spot. She wears earplugs and a silk eye mask, which is a very Sahana thing to do. She would be horrified to know that she snores. It didn't wake me; I was up anyway, my mind unable to quiet.

I keep playing back scenes of Cale and me. We were happy in the early days—at least that's what my memories tell me. Memories, I suppose, can deceive.

We met at a speed dating event at the historic Owyhee building downtown. I'd been dragged there by Sahana; he was dragged there by his coworker, a guy named Jeff. It was a simple premise: The women were each seated at individual tables, a full wine glass in front of them, an empty chair across from them. The men rotated from table to table, spending five minutes with each woman. There was a loud buzzer when the five minutes were up, like we were on a game show. The women and the men were each given a note card to rank their top three "dates," and if two people picked each other, it was a match.

There were about twenty people there, and I had my eye on one guy in particular—the quintessential tall, dark, handsome. He had a cleft chin, something I've always liked that Sahana does not understand ("It's like there's a butt on his face," she argued). That guy was the first one to sit across from me, and my hopes were up. Then he started talking. I asked him about his hobbies, and he spent the entire five minutes telling me about the love he had for his sports car (it should say something that I can't remember this guy's name, but I know the sports car was a Nissan GT-R). When the buzzer went off, he hadn't asked me a single thing about myself. I took a long sip of wine and prepared myself for an exhausting evening of disappointment.

Then Cale sat down.

I could see right away that he was older than me (by ten years, I'd learn). When he smiled, lines fanned out around his eyes. He had a good smile—kind and genuine. I was surprised when he said he worked in sales. Usually those guys are as fake as they come. He said his job was boring (he sells mutual funds to financial advisors) and then turned the conversation to me. He didn't ask me the routine questions I'd had in mind: What do you do for work? What are your hobbies? Instead, he asked me my ideal Friday night and ideal Saturday morning. For Friday night, I said, "Takeout, wine, early bedtime." When I was younger, I would have lied, said something about dressing up and checking out the newest restaurant downtown—to sound cool or something. My thirties, I'd decided, were all about honesty. He nodded, poker-faced, and then I told him Saturday morning would involve a hike and breakfast at a café. He nodded again. He was about to say something when the buzzer went off. He stood, shook my hand, smiled without showing teeth, then turned his attention to the woman at the table next to me. I had no idea what he thought of me, but I was smitten.

When it came time to write my top three men on my note card, I just wrote one—Cale. I had absolutely no interest in the other men I met. From recollection, there was an incredibly nervous guy with hairy arms who looked down at his lap the whole time, a guy with braces ("Braces!" Sahana would shriek on the car ride home), and a guy who admitted to having an on-again-off-again girlfriend who he wanted to make jealous.

Jeff, Cale's coworker, was nice enough, but he'd quite obviously had his eye on a brunette in her twenties. At the end of the dates, while the organizer of the event analyzed our cards, looking for matches, Sahana and I got our second glasses of wine and swapped stories.

"That guy," she said, her eyes flicking in the direction of the nerdy forty-something guy who'd told me he worked for the parks and recreation department. "He opened with, 'Do you know where the name Owyhee comes from?' Then he went on and on about how some Hawaiian fur trappers were part of an expedition and went exploring and never came back, so some British guys named the region after them, just spelling it phonetically because they didn't know what Hawaii was."

She lets her head fall back and pretends to fall asleep.

"Well, that's kind of interesting. All he told me is that the zoo renovation project is almost done."

"I told him this was a dating event, not trivia night. He didn't even smile. Zero sense of humor."

She took a long sip of wine.

"This was a total bust," she concluded.

"I don't know, I liked one of them," I confessed.

She looked horrified.

"God, which one?"

"Cale," I said.

I nodded in his direction. He was standing by one of the tables, looking at something on his phone.

"Huh," she said, looking back and forth between us, assessing.

"Yeah, you two could make sense."

"You didn't like him?"

"I tuned out after he mentioned hiking," she said, mock vomiting.

The organizer gathered us all together and said there were six matches—a new record. Sahana and I eyed each other, disbelieving this statement. Our cards were given back to us. I was privately embarrassed at how my heart was pounding in anticipation. When I flipped over the card, the word "MATCH" was stamped next to Cale's name. I looked up at him immediately, and he was already looking at me. We both looked down, shyly, then up again. He gave me a nod, and we walked toward each other.

"So," I said, "I'm one of your matches?"

I figured he'd matched with all three of the women on his card; after all, he was the least offensive man in the room. I figured if there were six matches, three were with him.

"You're my only match," he said.

This became our line, the line we would say to each other in lieu of the overused "I love you." Cale's wedding vows ended with that line.

"Well, then" was all I managed to say.

"What about you? I'm guessing you have the awkward duty of greeting your other matches," he said.

"You're my only one too," I said.

I felt my cheeks flushing, had to look away for a second.

"That makes things much easier."

"Much," I agreed.

He leaned in, whispered in a conspiring tone that made me feel like we were already friends (or more than friends), "Who do you think the other matches are?"

"I have no idea."

We looked around the room and, sure enough, there were five other insta-couples, chatting. Someone had paired with the Nissan GT-R guy—a shock. Sahana was stuck talking to the guy with braces who, like her, hadn't matched with anyone.

"I'm glad my coworker and I took separate cars," he said, nodding toward Jeff, who was canoodling—an obnoxious word, but perfectly descriptive of the scene—with the twenty-something brunette.

"Smart of you," I said.

"I had a feeling he was here for a hookup."

I finger-combed a strand of hair behind my ear. "And what are you here for?"

"I just came for the comedy," he said. "Meeting you is an unexpected plus."

"'An unexpected plus,'" I echoed. "Might be the strangest compliment I've ever received on a first date."

"I wouldn't count this as a first date," he said. "I have to at least buy you a drink or something."

Sahana appeared beside us.

"Did you just mention buying her a drink?" she said to Cale.

He laughed good-naturedly. "I did."

"Can you do that *now*? And can I be a third wheel?"

Cale looked at me, and I just shrugged.

From there, Cale, Sahana, and I walked ten minutes to a Mexican restaurant because Sahana wanted margaritas. We shared a pitcher, though I think Sahana drank most of it. Cale was quiet, but not in a strange way. He just struck me as more of an observer. Sahana is always more than happy to do the majority of the talking in any social situation, and he seemed amused by her, and by the way I was amused by her. We covered basics: he hadn't been married before, didn't have kids, voted Democrat, liked dogs but didn't have any pets. When we parted ways—with each other's numbers entered into our phones—Sahana admitted that she didn't see any red flags. And Sahana always sees red flags.

"Maybe this one is a good one," she said.

"Or maybe you're drunk," I told her.

"Maybe."

A COUPLE MONTHS into our relationship—which consisted largely of hiking in the foothills, drinking wine, and trying out new recipes—Cale and I were driving back from a day hike at Bogus Basin when he told me, "I don't know if we should see each other anymore."

The statement was prefaced by nothing. We'd had a nice time on the hike, even took a selfie at a particularly pretty lookout.

"What do you mean?" I asked him.

I was already mentally texting Sahana in my head, telling her that we'd been wrong about Cale being one of the good ones.

"It's just gotten serious pretty fast and . . . I guess I'm just not sure, and it doesn't feel fair to you if I'm not sure."

"Not sure of what, exactly?" I asked him.

"Not sure about marriage and all that."

I feigned shock. Of course, I'd thought about marrying him—every woman in her thirties is thinking about marriage when she dates someone longer than a few weeks.

"Who said anything about marriage?" I said, hoping my tone made him feel stupid for classifying me as a ring chaser.

Looking back, maybe this was a mistake. Maybe I shouldn't have been trying to convince him to stay with me. Maybe I should have let him go, if that's what he'd wanted.

"I guess I just assumed," he said.

"You should stop that," I said, sassy.

I suppose I gave him the impression I was a confident, cool girl who would never expect too much. This impression was false. I maintained it until Evie was born, and then I became a woman who expected a lot.

"I've never met anyone quite like you," he said, taking his eyes off the road and smiling at me for a quick second.

It's then I knew that we wouldn't break up, and I wouldn't mention this to Sahana. She would want to analyze it to death. She would label him an "avoidant personality," the type of personality I always seem attracted to, though I just refer to it as "mysterious" or "complicated." I don't know what it is about that type; I like the challenge, I suppose. I like the feeling of winning when they bite at my bait, even if I've exhausted myself with my line in the water for days on end.

WE DATED A year before Cale invited me to move in with him. Even at the age of thirty-three, I'd never lived with a man before. I prided myself on having my own place—a town house right next to the Greenbelt that I'd bought just six months before meeting Cale. I was nervous because, even though Cale hadn't mentioned breaking up again, I still felt like he wasn't completely mine. He was reserved with his emotion. He'd waited eight months to say, "You're my only match," and he doled out "I love yous" sparingly, as if he had a lifetime limited supply.

When I talked to him about my nervousness, I framed it as my being tentative about giving up my independence—again, an attempt to be that cool girl. I *was* independent, but it wasn't because I was someone who didn't need a mate; it was out of necessity. I wanted nothing more than closeness with another human. I wanted all the mush and gooeyness of romantic comedies. I wanted someone who would stay up with me for hours talking, someone truly interested in my every thought and feeling. I wanted a soul mate.

"I mean, what if you want to break up and then I've sold my town house and I'm homeless?" I said, daring to give him a partial glimpse into my true concerns.

He sighed the sigh that men give women when they are being irrational. "Ang, I wouldn't ask you to move in with me if I thought I'd ever ask you to move out."

It was one of the sweetest things he'd ever said to me, and I could tell by his tone that he didn't say it to be sweet; he said it because that's what he felt in a very practical way.

"Okay then," I said.

I moved in two weeks later.

A few months after that, I got pregnant.

THE SHEETS RUSTLE, and I turn to see Sahana stirring in bed. She pulls off her eye mask and squints, noticeably offended by the morning sun.

"How long you been up?" she asks, her voice groggy. Sahana is not a morning person. She sees to it that her first client of the day is no earlier than ten o'clock.

"I didn't really sleep," I say.

She leans up, resting on her elbows. "I was hoping you'd get at least a couple hours."

"No such luck."

"You going to see him?" she says.

I nod. "Aria is coming over, but can you stay here with Evie until she gets here?"

"Of course," Sahana says. "Just know that her breakfast is going to consist of one of those squeeze pouch thingies and graham crackers."

"I call that the Cale Special."

She laughs, then stops. "I'm allowed to laugh at that, right?"

"If you aren't, then all is truly lost."

"Okay, good," she says.

I get out of bed, go to the closet, pull out a pair of yoga pants and an oversize sweater—comfortable clothes since I figure I'll be spending the day curled up in a chair at my husband's bedside, waiting for him to wake up, or not wake up, or . . . something.

"Call me, for any reason at all," I say.

"Same," she says.

I go upstairs. Our house (which began as Cale's house, became our house, and may end up my house) has the entry-way, living room, and kitchen on the upper floor, the bedrooms downstairs. I busy myself cleaning the dishes in the sink. I fold and refold dish towels, stack them in their drawer with a precise orderliness that Cale would appreciate. He's a fan of order, which is probably why having a baby has caused him so much angst. Babies are destroyers of order, the epitome of chaos.

After wiping down the shelves of the refrigerator, I decide I've procrastinated enough. It is time to get in my car, drive to the hospital, and see my husband.

TESSA

I SEVERELY UNDERESTIMATED HOW difficult it would be for me to leave the house. Maybe Ryan is right to worry.

Getting out of bed and walking through our apartment wasn't a big deal, but the moment I stepped into the elevator, I felt like I couldn't catch my breath. Then I started panicking about not being able to catch my breath. I imagined Ryan finding me dead in the elevator, literally scared to death. I managed to push the button to take me to the ground floor, and when the doors opened, I told my legs to walk, but they wouldn't. So I crouched there in the elevator, hoping nobody would come by and ask if I was okay.

After a few minutes, I felt more composed, so I got out of the elevator and went to the parking garage. That's when I started to panic again. Even though it was light outside, the garage was still dark, and in my mind, I went right back there, to Ray's, to that night. My heart pounded so hard I could feel the pulsing in my ears. My palms got sweaty. I had to crouch again. At that point, I almost gave up and decided to go back upstairs, forget my little mission to visit Cale Matthews at the hospital. But then I spotted my car, and I thought, *I just have to get there. I am safe there*. I crawled. I'm sure the garage has security cameras and I probably look like an insane person crawling on the ground, but I don't care. It was the only way I could do it.

I did feel better in my car—safe, contained. I locked my doors, looked in the back seat to make sure nobody was hiding. I felt like a little kid, checking the closet for the bogeyman before bed. I put the hospital address into my phone, and the robotic voice started giving me directions. There was something comforting about that voice—so even, steady, unemotional.

The drive to the hospital was fine, but I got panicky again when I realized I'd have to park in another dark parking garage. I knew I'd panic in there, feel like I was trapped, with just one way out. I decided to park on a side street instead, a few blocks from the hospital, figuring the walk would be good for my nerves.

So now I'm at the hospital. It's busy, people coming and going. Someone bumps my elbow as I pass through the sliding doors, and I jump about three feet in the air. I'm on edge, on guard. I wonder if I'll always be this way, if the shooting will make me into a person who can't go on airplanes, a person traumatized by fireworks on the Fourth of July, a person who refuses to sit with her back to the door, like someone in the mafia.

I make my way to the information desk in the lobby area and stand in line behind a couple other people, my head on a swivel, checking my surroundings. A voice comes over the loudspeaker, calling someone's name, and it's so loud I flinch.

When I get to the desk, I tell the woman I'm here to see a patient. She gives me a tight smile.

"Name?" she says.

"Cale Matthews," I say, clearing my throat.

I notice someone passing by out of the corner of my eye. I notice this person coming closer. I turn, heart racing.

It's a woman.

She is looking at me funny.

"Did you say Cale Matthews?" she asks.

I wonder if she's a reporter, lurking at the hospital, looking for friends and family members of those injured at Ray's. She looks too disheveled to be a reporter though. Her hair is in a messy bun, she isn't wearing any makeup, and there are plump bags under her eyes.

I'm just standing there, dumb, when she says again, "Cale Matthews?"

"Um, yeah," I say.

She's still looking at me funny, scanning me up and down.

"Who are you?" she asks.

The person in line behind me sighs loudly so I step away, mumbling a half-hearted "thank you" to the woman behind the desk.

"I'm Tessa," I say to the mystery woman once I'm a good couple feet away from the information desk.

The woman looks impatient, annoyed.

"How do you know my husband?" she says.

So she's Cale Matthews's wife.

I realize quickly how this must look to her—a young woman coming to the hospital, asking to visit her husband.

"I don't really know him," I say.

She doesn't look convinced.

"I was . . . I was at the bar the night of the shooting," I say.

"With him?"

Her eyes are big, wild.

"No, no," I say. I reach out to touch her arm, a reflexive gesture, an attempt at assurance. She steps back, as if my touch is a bite.

"I was the bartender there," I clarify.

Her face relaxes, just slightly.

"I was working that night. I feel like he maybe, like, saved my life," I tell her.

"Oh," she says.

"Yeah, I know, it's weird of me to visit. I just . . . I wanted to thank him, I guess."

"Well, he's in a coma," she says.

I'm not sure what upsets me more—this news of his condition or the anger in her tone, as if I'm at fault.

"I'm sorry," I say, the tears coming embarrassingly fast, too fast to be stopped.

She exhales loud enough for me to hear and says, "No, I'm sorry. I shouldn't have snapped like that. I'm just . . . It's been stressful."

I wipe my eyes with the back of my hand. "I understand," I say.

"Do you want to sit down somewhere?" she asks.

She looks irritated, like, *God, now I made this girl cry and I have to console her*.

"No, no, I'm fine," I say. "I shouldn't have imposed. This is your family's private situation and—"

"Let's just sit."

She walks with a brisk pace to the far end of the waiting area, where there is an empty love seat and chair. She sits on the love seat, placing her purse on the cushion next to her, as if to make it clear that I am not to sit there. I sit in the chair across from her which, thankfully, faces the center of the room so I can see everything going on. I fear I am now a person who must always know everything going on.

"I'm sorry," she says, suddenly calmer.

"It's okay."

There is a terribly awkward silence, me still sniveling a bit, despite ordering myself to get it together.

Finally, she says, "So you saw Cale?"

I nod. "He was sitting at the bar. I think he got a beer."

I *know* he got a beer, but I don't want her to think I've kept track of this detail about her husband. He got the White Dog

Hazy IPA.

"Did you talk to him at all?"

"A little," I say. "We were busy that night, so I didn't talk to him as much as usual."

She looks confused. "As usual?"

I sense I've made a mistake.

"He was a regular or something?" she presses.

The truth: I'd seen him at Ray's a handful of times over the past few months. I don't know if I should share this though. It's clear he didn't tell her about coming to Ray's; it's clear I'm in on a marital secret.

"I wouldn't say that," I say. "I'd seen him a couple times."

"Was he with someone?" she asks.

I shake my head. "Not that I saw."

The first time Cale came in, he sat right in front of me at the bar, started making small talk. I could tell he hadn't been out in a while, that he was rusty. He wore a wedding ring, but I'd seen all kinds of guys wearing wedding rings and meeting women who weren't their wives. I'd told Ryan once that it was enough to make me swear off men forever.

That night, I asked him, point-blank, "So you meeting someone?"

I let curiosity get the best of me, which isn't a great trait for a bartender who is supposed to look the other way, not notice, not care.

"Meeting someone?" he'd asked, repeating the question, as if to make sure he'd heard it correctly.

"Yeah," I'd said. "Are you meeting someone?"

And he'd said, with a smirk, "Something like that."

But, thing is, I never saw someone show.

I figured he'd been stood up, thought he deserved that for stepping out on his wife. Normally, I'd have written him off as just another asshole having a midlife crisis that involved online dating, but he seemed nice enough. A bit strange, but nice.

His wife crosses and uncrosses her legs, like she can't get comfortable.

"You think he saved your life?" she says.

Her tone says she disbelieves this.

I shrug. "I think he did. I was just standing there, behind the bar, like, frozen, when the shots started. I couldn't move. He snapped me out of it and told me to find somewhere to hide. That's when I ran to the storage closet."

Even just recounting these details brings goose bumps to my arms and legs.

Tears begin to fill her eyes. She shakes her head, trying to shake them away.

"God, it must have been terrifying," she says, dabbing at her eyes with the end of her sweater sleeve.

"It was."

We sit there in silence again.

"Is he going to be okay?" I dare to ask.

She looks at me, her eyes watery. "I don't know," she says.

I want to pry, but know I can't.

"Do you mind if I, like, get your number?" I ask her. "Just so I can check in. I mean, if that's weird, just—"

She interrupts me again. "Of course," she says. She paws through her purse, retrieves her phone. "Here, I'll text you so you have it. What's your number?"

I give it to her, and a moment later a text appears. It just says, "Hi."

"Thanks," I say.

She stands to leave.

"Thank you for telling me what you know," she says.

"No problem."

"If you think of anything else, you have my number."

She is starting to walk away when I say, "Wait, I don't have your name."

She playfully hits herself in the forehead with her palm.

"You can call me Moron," she says. "Or Angie."

JOYCE

I NEED TO DELETE my Facebook account. I only have it to communicate with members of my book club and keep in touch with a select few old friends. Facebook was thrilling at first—finding all those faces from the past. Now it's just a way for people to find Joyce Ketcher, mother of the Ray's Bar shooter.

It's Monday morning, and I've made the mistake of checking my messages on the app. There are a slew of them from acquaintances and used-to-be-friends, feigning concern for my well-being. That's how it seems to me—fake. They say things like, "You are in my thoughts, and I want you to know I'm here if you need to talk" and "These things are never as simple as they seem. If you need a shoulder, I'm here." They just want to be "Joyce Ketcher's friend." They want inside information they can share at their next dinner parties and Sunday brunches.

There are a few nice messages from strangers, very religious people, telling me they will pray for Jed's soul. But there are also messages filled with rage, chastising me for my parenting skills (or lack thereof), telling me I could have prevented all this. My first reaction is a rage that trumps theirs. I want to yell at these people that my son was a grown man. He was twenty-eight years old. He had his own life. I suppose this argument would be easier to make if he hadn't been living under my roof.

"Just delete it," I tell Gary, slamming my phone onto his brand-new kitchen island countertop and going to the bathroom.

"Delete what?" he asks, dumbfounded.

"Facebook," I yell from my seat on the toilet.

Of course, he has no idea how to delete Facebook. He doesn't use Facebook. He has a flip phone.

I come back and take the phone from his idiotic hands. "Never mind," I say.

"Haven't I always said there's nothing good that comes from all that stuff," he says, motioning toward my phone.

"Not now," I tell him.

I go to the app, delete it. A prompt asks me if I'm sure, and I say, "Yes, damn it."

Then it's gone.

One thing accomplished.

"I'm going to put the second coat of paint on your garage today," Gary says, trying to calm me with evidence of his helpfulness.

"Okay, fine, great," I tell him. I'm well aware I'm taking my anger out on him. He is a good, cooperative punching bag. He just sways about, awaiting my next outburst.

"Is there anything else I can do?" he asks.

"The mortuary. The service. Have you done that yet?" I ask him.

I can't control the bitchiness in my voice; I just can't.

"I'm working on it," he says.

He goes to the sink, rinses our cereal bowls.

"What do you mean *working on it*?"

It should be a simple task, after all.

"Just trust me. I'm working on it," he says.

He's being strange, evasive.

"What is it?"

He lingers at the sink, now drying the dishes he's just washed, instead of just leaving them to drip-dry on the rack like he usually does.

"Joyce, I don't want to add to your plate, okay?" he says.

He is looking at me now, his eyes pleading. He seems tired. I've brought this mess of my life to him and exhausted him.

"What? Is it the cost? You don't have to protect me from that. I know funerals are expensive. I *have* money, Gary. You don't have to treat me like—"

He interrupts my defensive tirade: "It's not the fucking cost."

That shuts me up. I don't think I've ever heard him say "fucking." He is the type to say things like "Dang it" and "God Almighty."

"Sorry," I say.

I see the frustration leave his face as his skin turns from red back to white.

"It's okay," he says. "I'm sorry too."

"I'm not myself."

"How could I expect you to be?"

I take a final sip of my now-cold coffee.

I bring my mug to the sink, where he's still standing. I squeeze his forearm, which is the most we've touched since he first came to my house and wrapped his arms around me. He removes my hand from his arm, which I take as rejection until I realize he wants to hold my hand in his. Our fingers interlace. He lifts our hands to his face, kisses my knuckle gently, then lets go. My nose tingles, a precursor to tears, in response to this unexpected show of affection.

"I'm having trouble finding a place," he says. "That's the thing."

I'm still thinking about holding his hand. I'm not sure what he's talking about.

"A funeral home," he clarifies. "I'm having trouble finding one."

"Oh," I say. "Really? There's the one over on Fairview, and I think there's one by the mall, and—"

"It's not that," he says.

I still don't understand.

"When I tell them who the service is for . . ."

He waits for me to get it.

Finally, I say, "Oh."

Nobody wants to host a service for my son. That is the crux of the matter.

"The one on Fairview, the one by the mall, they're working with victims' families and there's a conflict of interest there. It's not that they think Jed is . . ."

"Evil?" I say, knowing that is exactly what they think. It might be what Gary thinks.

"Joyce, I don't think it's that. They're just trying to be good businesspeople for their other clients."

"Right," I say.

"Like I said, I'm working on it," he says. "I have a few other places to contact. We will find one. Don't worry about it. Please."

I nod.

"Should only take me an hour or so to paint the garage. You going to be okay here?" he asks.

I nod again.

Then he is gone, busying himself with the tasks of this new life of mine.

I suppose I need to consider how long I'll be staying with Gary. I'm sure he expected just a couple days. I don't want the embarrassment of being asked to leave. But I can't imagine going home at this point, being alone there, noticing the absence of Jed.

I called the lead detective yesterday, Detective Kinsky, asking for any information about what they found in Jed's room. He said they are still poring through everything, but that he could confirm that Jed had a private journal online that "shed light on his mindset." I don't know what that means, exactly. I'm not sure I want to know.

When Jed was a toddler—two or three—he would have such horrible tantrums. He would scream and pull out tufts of his own hair. There was no calming him. It scared me, but Ed said it was just the age. I read all kinds of books on toddler behavior, deciding that we just had what one book called a "spirited" toddler. There were three categories of temperaments according to this book—easy, shy, and spirited. I chose to put a positive spin on Jed's tantrums. He was passionate, I told myself.

Maybe I was delusional.

When Jed was six, Ed and I took him to see a child psychologist because his kindergarten teacher said he was having problems with "impulse control." We saw this at home too. If something didn't go his way, he would get so angry, often resorting to hitting whoever (or whatever) was closest to him. We did time-outs on a bench in our front entryway, and he complied, flaring his nostrils and staring daggers the whole time. The time-outs didn't seem to curb the behavior though. This was the age of gentle parenting, and we were probably too easy on him, thinking it was our job to walk alongside him as he discovered his "passionate" self. The psychologist seemed concerned when we mentioned that Jed often banged his head against the wall or on the hard tile floor in the kitchen. He said something about "early signs of self-injury." I remember Ed laughed at this. I remember Ed saying, "Self-injury? He's *six*!"

Maybe Ed was delusional.

I thought he grew out of all these things. It's not like he was still banging his head on walls and pulling out tufts of hair when he was a teenager. But maybe those behaviors turned into something else, something hidden, something I didn't see.

Detective Kinsky said he would release the online journal to me "soon." I don't know if I can read it though. There is comfort in delusion.

Last night, I found a message board online about the shooting—a disgusting thing called "Shooting the Shit." There are pages and pages of people talking about Jed, about the gun he used, about the victims. It's quickly become a train wreck I cannot turn away from. I was up until dawn reading, feeling nauseated.

They say he got the gun legally a year ago. Whoever he bought it from must have come forward with a receipt or something. Had he been planning this for a year? Did he keep the gun in my house?

I log on to the message board again, surprised to see there has been more conversation since I logged off a few hours ago. I know the frequent posters now—JR2018 seems to be the ringleader, obsessed with mass shootings. I should probably mention him to Detective Kinsky, before he shoots up a bar himself and his poor mother is shocked, unaware of this message board, of her son's fascination with violence.

TessWasHere has just posted a question. I've seen her post only a couple things—asking about the victims, mostly.

> **Does anyone know about the funeral services for the victims? Are any of them open to the public?**

Another frequent poster, Boyseeeee, responds:

> **No info on funerals yet. Prob too soon. Candlelight vigil at the capitol building tonight tho. I'm gonna go. U going?**

TessWasHere doesn't respond. That's the last of the conversation for now.

I would like to go to the vigil. It's public, seemingly open to everyone, even the mother of the killer. It's not like I'm going to be welcomed at any of the funeral services. This may be my only chance to pay my respects.

Of course, I have to assume loved ones of the victims will recognize me, thanks to social media. My Facebook profile picture was on that damn message board, after all. I have to assume they will want to direct their anger at me, because Jed came from me. I created him.

Maybe I can go, wear a ball cap to disguise myself, watch from a distance, then leave flowers when everyone has gone. It will make me feel better, I think. I can almost hear Jed scolding me: *Mom, this isn't about you.* And I know he's right. It's not about me. But I can't just sit here, in Gary's kitchen, too full-up with guilt to even eat my damn breakfast. I have to do something. I have to buy the prettiest lilies I can find and pay my respects. I can hear Jed scoff.

"Jed," I whisper, "stop."

ANGIE

SAHANA THINKS IT'S STRANGE that I want to go to work on Monday morning. She keeps texting, asking if I'm sure. It's not like there is paid leave for employees with spouses in comas. I have some vacation time built up, about a week. I figure I should save that for when I really need it—like when Cale comes home . . . or when he doesn't.

I can't just stop working. There are bills to pay—the regular ones, as well as the medical ones that I expect to start arriving soon. I figure I can visit Cale on lunch breaks; Madison & Brightly, the ad agency where I work, is about a ten-minute drive from the hospital. If I'm honest, I *want* to go to work. I want to pretend like it's any other Monday. I don't know how to accept that it's not.

Evie usually wakes around six in the morning, but today she sleeps until seven, giving me time to shower and dress and make my own breakfast and hers. It's as if she understands I am alone. There is only one pair of hands to tend to her, to feed her and get her ready for day care and play with her on the kitchen floor. Then again, it's usually my hands doing this work most mornings. Cale makes himself present—usually standing at the kitchen island, doing something on his computer. He acts as if this presence is enough. He is there, but not *there*. He is with his family, physically, but only physically. Whenever I'd ask what he was doing on his computer, he'd claim he was getting a head start on his work day. But usually, when I dared to glance, he was just looking at sports scores. It angered me, but I didn't say anything. His silence, his detachment, was hostile enough; I didn't know if I could handle an actual fight.

Sahana texts me again as I sit Evie in her high chair and turn on an episode of *Sesame Street*. She will sit there, watching, content and quiet, for a half hour. I can count on this. I used to say things to Cale like "We are so lucky to have an easy kid" and "Kids like this are the reason people have ten kids." It was my way of trying to get him to be happier as a father. But now I think comments like this drove him away, made him feel unallowed to be unhappy.

Does Cale's boss know?

I hadn't even thought of that.

Shit. I'll call him.

I know Cale's boss's name, but I don't know his number. I look up the company online—Gingham Funds—and scan for Cale's boss's name. Nathan McClintock. I clear my throat and dial the number. He answers, sounding rushed and formal.

"Hi, Nathan, this is Angie Matthews, Cale's wife," I say.

It's quiet for a moment, and then he says, "Oh, yes, Angie. Right."

I've met him several times, never liked him. There's something slimy about him. His hair is always shellacked into place. I told Cale he looked like a Ken doll—plastic, phony.

"I wanted to let you know that Cale's in the hospital," I say.

"The hospital? What happened?"

I realize I'll have to get used to telling this story. The names of the deceased are in the news, but the names of the injured are not. Nobody has any idea Cale was shot.

"Well, did you hear about the bar shooting?" I ask.

He's quiet again. I don't think someone like Nathan pays attention to anything but the stock market.

"My wife said something about that," he says.

"Cale was shot," I tell him.

"You're serious?" he asks.

"It would be strange of me to make this up," I say, getting irritated.

"Man, wow, I'm so sorry. He gonna be okay?"

"He's in a coma," I say, purposefully blunt, the way I was with that girl, that bartender, Tessa. It's like I want to hurt people with this news, shock them into pitying me. Then I remember how I hate pity and regret my tone.

"Wow," he says. "I'm sorry. Wow."

That's all he says. I wait for more but get impatient.

"So he won't be at work," I say. "Obviously."

"Of course, right, of course," he says. "I'll have Nancy give you a call. She's our HR person. Short-term disability benefits, all that."

Disability benefits—something else I hadn't thought of. I am strangely grateful to Nathan in this moment, appreciative of his lack of emotion, his ability to focus on logistics.

"Thank you," I say.

Evie clings to me like a koala to a eucalyptus tree when we get to day care. She's been going to day care since she was a few months old, when my maternity leave ended. She likes it, generally, which alleviates my maternal guilt. It's only recently that she's developed separation anxiety, clinging to me at drop-off time, crying when I pry her off me and sit her on the floor of the playroom.

"Mama will miss you too," I say as she begins her dramatic display of despair.

I give her a hug.

"I'll pick you up after work," I tell her.

"Evie, did you hear that? Mama is picking you up today," the teacher, Ms. Janie, says to her, exaggerated excitement all over her face.

Usually, Cale picks up Evie, my attempt at equity—I drop off, he picks up. So much of the caretaking has been lopsided, me doing most of everything, though Cale frequently denied this. "I'd say we're fifty-fifty parents," he said a few months ago, a statement that floored me. I couldn't understand how he would believe this, given the objective list of tasks with my name next to them. Then it occurred to me that his small parenting role *felt* huge to him, huge enough for him to see our efforts as equal.

"Is Dad out of town?" Ms. Janie asks me. She is not prying; she is just making conversation.

"Um, kind of," I say.

Ms. Janie gives me a curious look, but then she turns her attention to one of the kids throwing a wood train against the wall. Evie, also distracted by this show of disobedience, abruptly leaves my side, with just a flick of the wrist to say "bye."

I slip out of the room and then out of the school, thinking about how I'll need to tell Ms. Janie about Cale. She will have to know. I can keep this to myself for only so long.

WHEN I GET to work, my first stop is the company kitchen to get a cup of coffee. Two of the art directors are at the machine and just happen to be talking about the shooting.

"I've *been* to that bar," one of them, Scott, says. "It was one of our stops at my buddy's bachelor party a few years back."

Scott and I have both worked at Madison & Brightly for nearly ten years, but all I know about him on a personal level is that he plays in an adult soccer league that requires him to leave work early on Thursdays.

"Me too, man," the other one says. I can't remember his name; he just started a few weeks ago.

I decide to try out my truth.

"My husband was there," I say.

They don't seem to realize I am talking to them, contributing to their conversation.

"My husband was there," I say again, a bit louder.

They both turn to look now.

"At the bar?" Scott says.

"Yes. He was shot," I say.

Their jaws literally drop.

"Holy shit," the not-Scott guy says. "Is he okay?"

"He's in the hospital," I say.

They wait for me to say more, but I don't want to get into the details of the coma, the unlikelihood of Cale being okay.

I go about getting my coffee, feeling their eyes boring into me.

"I hope he gets better soon," Scott says.

"Thanks," I mutter.

I can still feel their eyes on me, even as I turn around and walk away.

Because ad agencies are like high school campuses, everyone will know about Cale within the next hour. I close the door to my office and await the knocks.

My boss, Raquel—an all-business woman who is constantly on the brink of divorce with her husband because she refuses to work fewer than eighty hours a week—is the first to knock. She doesn't really knock, though; she taps the door a couple times, like as a warning, then barges in.

"Ang, are you kidding me? I just heard. What the hell are

you doing here?"

Raquel is what I call a hard blinker; she has this nervous tic that involves blinking so hard and fast that her nose scrunches. She has lines across the bridge of her nose from all the scrunching—bunny lines, they call them, something I know from years of working on the Dermatica Skincare account.

"I wanted to come in," I say. "Keep up some kind of normalcy."

"And I thought I was a workaholic," she says.

You are, I want to say.

"I just don't want to spend all day sitting at the hospital or at home, feeling helpless. That seems like torture," I tell her.

She blinks.

"I guess I understand," she says. "Well, just know I want you to take it easy. Only participate in projects as you see fit. You got it?"

"Understood," I tell her. "Thank you."

She turns to leave, then turns back, abruptly, as if her central processing unit has set off an alarm.

"And I hope he's okay," she says, stiff and unnatural. This is her attempt to "be human." One of my coworkers, Dave, has a theory that Raquel is a robot programmed by aliens wanting to learn about human behavior. It's a valid theory.

"Thanks, Raquel," I say. "I hope so too."

"It's just terrible, what happened."

The furrow of her brows that accompanies her words translates to the most emotion I've ever seen from this woman.

She closes the door behind her, but that doesn't stop the parade of well-wishers. They are mostly women; men, I've learned, are not that interested in people's personal lives.

When I tell the story, about how Cale was at the bar that night, nearly everyone says, "You weren't with him?" And when

I say no, they say some version of "Thank god," but I can see the questioning in their eyes. I know they will convene in someone's office and gossip. They will consider how I've come to work, just days after this tragedy, and conclude that my marriage was in trouble. They will ask the same thing Sahana did—was he having an affair? All of this makes me the center of attention I don't want. I've never liked having all eyes on me, which is why Cale and I didn't have an aisle for me to walk down when we got married; we just stood together, holding hands, promising for better or worse, having no idea what "worse" could entail.

I try to ignore the buzz of the office and just sit at my desk, with my door closed, reading through emails. I'm a director of copy, meaning I write brochures and websites and whatever else for our various clients and I supervise a team of writers beneath me. Most of my energy is spent on the Dermatica account. They are about to launch a new product for hyperpigmentation (a fancy name for sunspots). I figure writing headlines like "It's Glow Time!" is a good way to get my mind off everything else. It's simple enough, or it should be. But as I sit, staring at my computer screen, I can't even bring myself to review a single job brief.

By lunchtime, I haven't done any actual work, but I figure that's fine. Raquel said to take it easy. I take my brown-bag lunch from the kitchen fridge, keeping my head down to avoid any eye contact, then head to my car to drive to the hospital. This is my routine now. I have no idea how long this will be my routine. I have no idea what my routine will be when this one is obsolete.

WHEN I GET to Cale's room, Nurse Nicole is there.

"Hi," she says with her warm, sympathetic smile. I wonder if she also thinks Dr. Harris is an asshole.

"How's he doing?" I ask.

He looks the same—his head bandaged, his face swollen, tubes everywhere.

"He's stable. His ICP spiked a bit overnight, but it's back down around ten now," she says.

I don't know what this means, exactly, but I can tell it's good. Or, at least, not bad.

"I was just going to remove his gauze to adjust his brain wave monitors," she says.

"Oh," I say, "okay."

I watch as she removes the gauze carefully. There are so many layers of it. When she is done, Cale's head is revealed. It's cartoonishly large, swollen, and partially shaved in a haphazard pattern. I wonder why they didn't just shave the whole thing. Then I remember that aesthetics is not their concern.

My eyes well up looking at him there, with his head exposed. I don't know what it is; he just looks so vulnerable, so bare.

Nurse Nicole puts her hand on my shoulder.

"I don't know what's wrong with me," I tell her.

"You don't? Your husband is in a coma," she says. I appreciate her attempt at a light joke. It means she thinks I'm capable of hearing such a thing.

"It's just weird seeing his head," I say.

"I know. Lots of loved ones say that."

She seems too young to have encountered "lots of loved ones" in situations similar to mine.

As she starts adjusting the monitors, Dr. Asshole walks in with his arrogant swagger.

"Oh, hello," he says when he sees me.

I keep my eyes on Nurse Nicole as she adjusts the wires.

"Well, as you can see, his brain is active," he says, nodding toward the wires.

I don't want to admit that, actually, I can't see that. I have no idea what anything means.

"He's showing brain activity," Nurse Nicole translates. "That's a good thing."

She gives me a wink.

"If his ICP continues to lower, we'll see about turning off the sedation medications in a few days."

"And then he'll wake up?"

He looks at me like *Haven't we been over this?*

"We will have to see," he says.

He looks down at the pager affixed to the waistband of his pants. Then he mutters something under his breath and leaves.

"He's not exactly warm and fuzzy," I say to Nurse Nicole.

She laughs. "He's not. But he's an amazing doctor."

"That's good to know."

"Between you and me," I say, "what should I expect? With Cale?"

She takes a roll of gauze and starts rewrapping Cale's head.

"It's so hard to say. I know you want answers . . ."

I go to Cale, touch his hand. I don't know why, but it's something I need to do whenever I see him, to confirm its warmth, to confirm his life.

"I know you can't give me answers," I tell her. "I'll settle for information."

She exhales, as if preparing for a long speech.

"Well, the hope is that the pressure in his brain lowers and we can take him off the sedation medications, like Dr. Harris said," Nurse Nicole says. "Then we wait and see. Brain injuries are like that. Sometimes it's impossible to know the real damage until the patient wakes up. It's all kind of a mystery, even to us."

This is not what anyone visiting a loved one in a hospital wants to hear.

"Okay," I say. "Thank you for that."

She smiles. "I have to make some rounds, but I'll be back in a bit if you have more questions."

I just nod, not wanting to tell her I have to get back to work, not wanting to feel her judgment.

As she's walking out, she turns.

"Oh!" she says, one finger in the air. "I keep forgetting. We have some of his things here if you want them."

She walks to a small table near his bed and retrieves a clear plastic bag, gives it to me. It contains Cale's keys, his phone, his wallet. It's strange to see them there—these familiar possessions of my husband's.

"Oh, right, of course," I say, feeling stupid for not asking about them sooner. Most wives probably ask. "Thank you."

She leaves, and I open the bag and take out his wallet. There are his credit cards, a couple twenty-dollar bills, a few one-dollar bills. This wallet has changed so many hands and nobody has touched his money; there may be hope for humanity yet.

There is nothing else of note in his wallet—his driver's license, a health insurance card, the "In case of emergency" card they used to contact me. I take out his phone. I press the "home" button to turn it on, but nothing happens. I figure it's dead, out of battery. I fish around in my purse for the spare charging cord I take with me everywhere, affix it to the phone, and plug the other end into the wall. The phone comes to life and, within a few minutes, it has enough power to turn on.

The photo on the screen is from a backpacking trip in the Sawtooth Mountains, a trip we took before Evie, before we even moved in together. I remember Cale taking the picture, kneeling down to get the crystal-blue water of the lake with the snowcapped mountains behind it.

I touch the home screen to open the phone. I'm holding my breath. I know the truth of Cale could be on this phone. Everything about everyone is on their phones. I prepare myself to see texts with the woman he was seeing, or a dating app recently used, or a Google search history revealing someone completely different from the man I married.

The phone doesn't open though. It's locked. Of course.

I'm prompted to enter a six-digit passcode.

I don't know Cale's passcode. He's never shared it with me. We've never had reason to share passcodes with each other. But if I know Cale—and I have to wonder at this point if I do—I know his passcode would be simple, easy to remember.

I try his birthday.

031574.

And it opens right up.

TESSA

I'VE CHANGED OUTFITS THREE times, finally settling on a maxi dress I bought when Ryan and I went to San Diego last summer. It's black with embroidered pink flowers. Ryan catches me analyzing myself in the mirror.

"You look nice," he says.

As if we're going on a date.

"I don't know what to wear to a vigil," I tell him.

Not that it really matters, of course. I am obsessing about my outfit in lieu of obsessing about being in public with hundreds of unpredictable human beings.

"You sure you don't want me to go?" he asks.

"I'm sure," I tell him.

If I get there and freak out, I don't want him to see it. He's already worried about me, I can tell. I didn't tell him about visiting the hospital the other day, about how jittery I was, about talking with Angie. I met him for lunch after, got there early so I could choose a booth in a back that felt safe, and I had every intention of telling him. But I just . . . didn't.

I wonder if Angie will be at the vigil. I was tempted to text her, but I didn't. We are not friends. I have to remember this. We are people whose association is based upon this horrible, strange tragedy.

"Where is it?" he asks.

"In front of the capitol building," I tell him.

He wraps his arms around my middle. "I love you," he says.

I turn around, look in his eyes. "Thank you for that."

"We'll get through this," he says. "You're strong."

I don't feel strong though. I feel anything but.

I GET THERE around seven forty-five. I anticipated needing time to find a place to park, but I didn't anticipate the crowd to be as big as it is. My heart races as I drive through the downtown streets. I find a spot on Sixth Street and sit in my car a moment, eyes closed, taking deep breaths.

When I start my walk, I feel like I'm at a rally or a music festival; the energy is more electric than somber. Some people are carrying signs that read Disarm Hate and Protect People, Not Guns. A few posters-on-sticks have photos of victims, faces I've come to know.

It's loud. I feel a little dizzy. I wonder if I should go back to my car.

"Tess?" a man's voice shouts.

I flinch, stop, look around.

"Tess!" he shouts again.

That's when I spot him—Ray, *the* Ray. Of Ray's Bar. He's sixty-something but has the life story of someone who's lived a few hundred years. Monica, the woman he hired to manage the bar (he retired from official management a few years ago, though he still comes in frequently), calls him the Most Interesting Man in the World. He played professional baseball (minor leagues, but still), served in Vietnam, lost a thumb and two fingers, got involved with the Guadalajara drug cartel in the '80s (supposedly), was friends with James Hetfield (lead singer of Metallica), and supposedly had a brief relationship with a Playboy bunny in the '90s (though "relationship" may be an embellishment). These days, it's hard to believe any of that is true. He's a grandfather, and looks like one. The only remnant of his past is a straggly gray ponytail at the nape of his neck.

"Ray," I say.

Ray wasn't at the bar the night of the shooting. Monica was managing that night, though she'd been out front, having a smoke, when the shooting began. Because she'd sent me all those texts while I was in the storage closet, she was the first person I texted when my fingers stopped shaking.

Ray is with a group of people, but he tells them to go on ahead.

"I was just asking Monica about you," he says.

Monica has been texting every day, just to check in. I don't think I even responded to her last "How are you?" text. It's not like Monica and I were close before the shooting. I realize we now share this *thing* between us, and we always will, but the fact remains that I haven't even talked to my mom about what happened yet.

"Yeah, it's been a strange few days," I say.

"To say the least."

He tilts his head, attempting to make eye contact, but I keep staring at my feet, at the polish chipping on my toenails. I close my eyes to try to stop the dizziness, but that just makes it worse.

"I'm guessing you heard about Dan," he says.

I nod.

"I spoke with his mother. They're planning a service for next weekend," he says. "I'll tell Monica to send you the details . . . if you want to come."

"Thanks," I say, though I know I won't be able to go. I won't be able to stand being "the bartender who survived," on display for all the mourners.

"I'm sorry you were there," he says. "I haven't slept since, just thinking about you guys in there."

I look up at him, meet his eyes. Most of the crowd is past us now, so it's just us on the sidewalk. My heart rate slows, the dizziness calms.

"You don't owe any apology," I say. "It's not your fault."

He lets out a deep, loud sigh. "Jan keeps sayin' that same thing."

Jan is "his gal." I don't think they are officially married, but they've been together for decades. They wear matching turquoise rings and have each other's names tattooed on the inside of their wrists.

"Well, she's right," I tell him.

"I just think if I was there, I would've been able to do something about it," he says.

To most people, the response would be *There's nothing you could have done*. But Ray is the Most Interesting Man in the World. It's hard to believe there isn't something he could have done.

I change the subject. "What's going to happen to the bar?"

He sighs again. "Don't know. Monica asked the same thing. Feels wrong to open it again. But I don't want you guys out of a job."

I laugh for what feels like the first time in years. It's rusty, sounds more like a cough.

"You can't reopen the bar just to give us jobs," I tell him. What I don't say is that it's insane of him to think I'll ever be able to set foot inside a bar again.

"Yeah, yeah," he says. "Jan said that too."

"Have the police told you anything about why?"

He looks at me curiously. "Why what?"

"Why *your* bar? Did you know him or something?"

I've been wondering this—if Jed Ketcher chose Ray's for a

reason. In a way, I want there to be a reason. There's something terrifying about accepting the complete randomness of it all. It's the randomness that makes it so hard for me to leave the house.

"Him? You mean Jed Ketcher?"

I nod.

He shakes his head. "Never heard of the kid before this."

He wasn't really a kid—he was twenty-eight—but I don't correct him.

Another large group of people nears. A girl yelps and I crouch down, instinctively. The yelp turns into laughter. Her boyfriend just tickled her or something, and here I am ducking for cover.

"You okay?" Ray asks, looking down at me, his hand outstretched to help me up.

"Yeah, yeah, I'm fine," I tell him, standing, not accepting his hand. "Hey, I forgot something in my car. I'll see you over there?"

Before he can say goodbye, I am walking back toward my car, against the force of the large group with the yelping girl. My vision is blurry, my heart pounding.

I can't do this.

I thought I could, but I can't.

When I get to my car, I feel as if I've been walking for miles, though it's just a couple blocks. I fall against the driver's side door, rest my head on the roof of the car. I try my deep breaths again, but I can't get enough air in my lungs. Before I know it, I'm legitimately hyperventilating.

I can hear the event beginning, someone on a microphone thanking everyone for coming.

"Excuse me?" a voice says, behind me.

I jump, turn around.

"Sorry, I didn't mean to scare you," the woman says. "I just saw you and . . . are you okay?"

I recognize this woman. I can see her face underneath the bill of her baseball cap, and I recognize her.

I know who she is.

I summon enough breath to say, "I think so."

This is a lie. I don't think I'm okay at all. And she can tell.

"How about you sit?" she says.

She takes me by the arm, and we sit on the curb. She tells me to put my head between my knees.

It works.

After a few moments, I feel better.

I look up at her.

I know this woman.

She is Joyce Ketcher. Jed's mother. The shooter's mother.

I expect the panic to return as I come to this realization, but it doesn't. It's as if I'm paralyzed, just like I was when the shooting started. I read online that there are not just two ways to respond to a crisis—fight or flight; there's a third—freeze. I am experiencing the third. I freeze.

"It's okay, it's okay," she says.

She is stroking my back. I am letting the mother of the shooter stroke my back.

"I don't like crowds either," she says.

Strangely, I'm not scared of her. I've studied photos of Jed Ketcher, and I can see the resemblance. They have similar eyes. But this doesn't frighten me. She seems kind, gentle, nothing like what I'd expect of the mother of a killer.

"I have bottles of water in the trunk of my car," she says. "You should have some water."

I let her help me stand and we walk on Sixth Street, away from the vigil. We stop at a gray Honda Accord. She goes to the trunk and I look inside the car, see several bouquets of lilies in a bucket on the passenger's seat. She must be planning to leave them after the vigil. Tomorrow, the area in front of the Capitol will be adorned with so many flowers, balloons, and candles.

"Did you know someone in the shooting?" I ask her, giving her this opportunity to tell me, to confess.

She closes the trunk and comes back with two bottles of water, giving both to me.

"I did," she says.

I wait for more and when she says nothing, I say, "I was there that night."

Her eyes widen. She puts her hand to her chest.

"My god, I'm so sorry," she says.

The apology, if I didn't know who she was, would sound strange, overly heartfelt, too dramatic.

There are so many questions I want to ask her—about her son, about what happened, about why. It's possible she doesn't have all the answers, but she must have some. She is his mother, after all.

"I'm just glad I made it out," I tell her.

She sighs. "Do you want to go to the vigil? I'll walk with you."

I bite my bottom lip. "I think it might be too much for me," I say.

"I understand."

We start walking, stop when we get to my car.

"Well, it was nice meeting you," I say to her, switching both water bottles to one hand so I can shake her hand. "Thank you for helping me."

She nods as she takes my hand, holds it in hers for a couple seconds beyond what would be considered normal.

I open my car door, sit in the driver's seat. I watch her walk until I can't see her anymore. Then I reach into my center console for the Post-its and pen I keep there. On one of the neon-orange sticky notes, I write:

Thank you, again, for helping me. If you ever want to talk, call me. —Tessa

I add my phone number, then walk back to her car and tuck the note under her windshield wiper. It's a long shot, I know. But maybe she really does need someone to talk to. Ryan will think this is insane, my reaching out to the shooter's mother this way. He just doesn't understand how desperately I need to know more—about Jed, about why. I don't like keeping secrets from Ryan. But, like I said, it's unlikely she'll actually call, so the only secret will be that I left a neon-orange Post-it under some woman's windshield wiper.

JOYCE

WHEN I GET BACK to Gary's condo after the vigil, I open the front door as quietly as I can, not wanting to wake him. It's after eleven o'clock. The vigil ended around ten, then I walked back to my car for the lilies. That's when I saw the note stuck under my windshield. I thought it was going to be a sorry-I-hit-your-car kind of note, so I grumbled to myself, asking the universe, "What now?" It wasn't that though. It was a note from that poor girl who was at the bar the night of the shooting. That's how I keep referring to it—the night of the shooting. At some point, I'm going to have to accept that it was the night my son shot people.

For whatever reason, the girl, Tessa, left me her phone number. And for whatever reason, I want to use it—if only to make sure she's okay, to assuage my own guilt about that night. I hear Jed's voice again: *Mom, this isn't about you.* I want to shout at him: *You did this and I'm your mother, so you've made this about me.*

The TV is still on in the living room. Gary must have forgotten to turn it off. I go in search of the remote and find him on the couch, sitting up, his head hanging forward awkwardly, like someone trying to sleep on an airplane. He was waiting up for me—or trying to. Gary is usually unyielding about his nine o'clock bedtime.

I tap him gently on the shoulder. I would leave him be except that I know he'll have a neck ache in the morning if he stays sleeping as he is. He stirs.

"You're home," he says, suddenly alert.

Home.

As if we live here together.

"How was it?" he asks. He leans forward, palms on his knees.

"It was fine," I say, though it wasn't "fine." It was awful—awful to see loved ones of the people my son killed, awful to hear their sobs, awful to realize the impact of what he did. I don't regret going though. I deserve the awfulness. My son is not here to suffer the consequences of his actions, so I will do that for him. It will be my last sacrifice for him, as his mother.

"You didn't have to wait up," I say.

"Sure I did," he says.

"Well, thank you. I'm going to head to bed then."

I turn to go to the bedroom that's become "my bedroom," but Gary says, "Hold on a sec."

I think this is when he will tell me that we need to talk about when I'll be going back home—to my real home. That's why he waited up, to have this conversation.

"I found a funeral home," he says. "It's in Caldwell. Family-run. Really nice people."

Caldwell is a half-hour drive, on a good day.

"Oh," I say. "Thank you."

"I put down the deposit and—"

"You didn't have to do that," I say.

He waves me off. "They need to know when you want to do the service. I wasn't sure what to tell 'em. Didn't know if you needed time to invite people and whatnot."

Invite people? I can't imagine who on earth would want to come to my son's funeral. I've had some very-extended family members reach out to me, before I deleted my Facebook account. But they didn't *know* Jed. They didn't love him. I don't know any of Jed's friends. There are coworkers at Home Depot, but I don't want to have a funeral service with just me and some Home Depot employees.

"The service is really just for me," I admit.

Gary doesn't seem surprised. "Well, I hope I can go too," he says.

I can't help but smile, even though we're talking about the worst possible thing.

"Okay, then," I say. "You and me."

He nods. It's settled.

"When?" he asks.

I shrug. "Wednesday? Thursday?"

He nods again. "I'll take care of it."

"Thank you," I tell him.

I give him a little wave and retreat to my bedroom.

I change into what's become my pajama shirt—an old T-shirt with an Albertsons logo on the front of it, something I got at a company picnic years ago. They had only extra-extra larges, so it has no use apart from sleeping. As I fold my jeans and put them back in the one drawer I've allowed myself to use (I keep reminding myself this situation is temporary), I take out the Post-it note in the pocket and read it again.

Then I do something impulsive and probably stupid.

I text Tessa.

This is Joyce, from the vigil. Got your note. I know it's late.
Just wanted to make sure you were feeling okay.

I get into bed, not expecting a response at this hour. I turn off the bedside light and close my eyes. Then I hear my phone buzz. I reach for it.

Hi, Joyce. Good to hear from you. This might sound weird, but do
you want to meet up for coffee sometime?

It does sound weird. But I suppose she doesn't know who I am. If she did, she wouldn't want to have coffee with me.

I text back:

Sure. I'd like that.

She suggests tomorrow at a coffee shop called Bean There, Done That. And, just like that, I have a date with one of the people who escaped my son's wrath. I hear him again: *Mom, this isn't about you.*

I whisper back to him, "Yes, it is."

ROBERT LANG

VICTIM #3

I GUESS I SHOULD have known. If Marilyn were still alive, that's what she would say. I can hear her now: "You've been bleeding out of your ass for a few months and you didn't think you were dying?" Marilyn isn't here though. Cancer took her a couple years ago. It's my turn now. According to the doctors, I'll get to see her soon—six months to a year, they told me today.

I don't much feel like going to Ray's, but I haven't missed a Thursday at Ray's in as long as I can remember. The guys and I, it's our thing. It's been our thing since Rick, Cliff, Randy, and I were in our forties, dealing with all the things forty-year-old men deal with: ball-and-chain jobs, nagging wives, narcissistic teenagers. We're retired now. Our kids are all grown, and the wives nag less (probably because the kids are all grown). Rick, Cliff, and Randy still have their wives, something I envy. They're careful not to complain about them, even though I'm sure it's warranted at times. They know I wish I had the luxury of complaining about Marilyn.

When I show up, they're there, at our usual table in the back. They've each downed a quarter of their beers already; my full pint is sitting in front of an empty stool, waiting for me.

"Well, look what the cat dragged in," Rick says, standing and giving me a clap on the back.

Rick always acts like it's been years since we've seen each other, though we do this every week.

"You losin' weight, Bob?" Cliff says, scanning me up and down.

I am, in fact. According to the doctor's scale, I'm about twenty pounds less than I used to be. I'd noticed it happening over the last month or so but blamed it on not having Marilyn around to cook for me. I'm completely useless on my own, something I'm not too proud to admit. The doctor said weight loss is one of the symptoms. And weakness and fatigue, which I've also had. I blamed that on Marilyn too. My body was tired without her, finding little in life deserving of energy.

"I am down a few pounds," I say, tugging at the belt buckle of my jeans, demonstrating the small gap between it and my still-round belly.

On my drive here, I debated whether or not I should tell the guys. Rick told all of us when he found out he has Parkinson's. He made an event of it, announced it before we even got our beers: "Guys, I have some bad news to share with you." We all clapped him on the back, the male sign of affection, said we would be there for him however he needed. It was the first health crisis for our immediate group. Marilyn's passing was the first death.

I just don't want to tell them though. Not now, at least. Not before I tell Greta. Greta is our daughter—mine and Marilyn's—our only child. When we first got married, Marilyn wanted a litter of kids, but that wasn't in the cards for us. It took us years to get pregnant with Greta. By the time she came, we were so grateful to have her that we didn't want to press our luck. Greta looks so much like Marilyn these days—same auburn tinge to her brown hair, same lines around her eyes when she smiles. She turns thirty next month. Her husband's throwing her a big party. I can't tell her about the cancer before then. She's just now getting her footing after her mother's passing. I can't hit her with this.

"You want another?" Randy asks me, rising from his stool and heading toward the bar.

I'm the only one of us who hasn't finished his first beer.

"Nah, I'm okay," I say. "In a bit, maybe."

"Guess you're a lightweight now," Cliff teases.

WE SPEND AN hour talking about the things men our age talk about—local news, sports, our adult children, the things we do to fill our time because we don't work anymore. Men become strange creatures when they don't have official jobs. They tinker. Rick has started a little piano repair business. Cliff makes homemade ice cream, brings it to us in cardboard pints because he says Gina (his wife) is fed up with the lack of freezer space. Randy golfs when the weather allows, goes bowling when it doesn't. I don't really have a *thing*. Marilyn and I used to go for our morning walks, do crosswords together, garden (never very successfully). My thing seems to be missing her, which is pitiful, I know.

I notice a guy come into the bar, a guy I've seen before. I keep tabs. In what feels like a past life, I was an officer with the Boise Police Department. I'm used to noticing signs of trouble. The guy seems frazzled. He sits at the bar. I watch the bartender, a twenty-something named Tessa who the guys and I are hesitant to like because it feels disloyal to the old bartender, Heather. We all loved Heather, had innocent crushes on her. She was in her late forties, so closer in age to us than Tessa. Tessa reminds us too much of our daughters.

Tessa hands the guy a beer. He appears to calm down.

Then another guy comes into the bar. This guy seems angry,

his footsteps forceful and fast. On instinct, I rise from my stool. I see Rick watch me.

"Bob?" Rick says.

He knows I see something.

He has a gun, the guy.

I go toward him. Rick is behind me, on my heels. He must see the gun too.

The guy with the gun shoves a woman out of his way. She falls to the ground. A man, the woman's husband or boyfriend probably, approaches the guy. The guy shoots. The woman screams, scrambles to her feet. He shoots her too.

"Hey!" I shout, now running toward the guy with the gun.

The bar erupts in a frenzy of people screaming, running. I see Tessa at the bar, just standing there.

The guy with the gun is looking around, as if he has someone specific in mind.

"Hey!" I shout again.

He doesn't acknowledge me.

I run at him, decide I need to tackle him.

He must see me out of the corner of his eye because he turns.

He looks scared.

He looks like a scared little boy.

"Give me the gun," I say.

He fumbles with it in his hand. I know what's going to happen before it does.

It occurs to me that I might not die of cancer after all.

ANGIE

I CAN'T STOP THINKING about what I've found on Cale's phone. I almost get in two car accidents on my way to pick up Evie from day care. I text Sahana, telling her I need her to come over after I put Evie to bed. I can't sit with this information alone.

I try to look like I'm paying attention while Ms. Janie recaps Evie's day for me.

"She ate all her broccoli today. She didn't nap great, but that's nothing new," she says.

Evie has never been much of a napper. When she was an infant, we would put her in the swing. It was the only way to get her to sleep. We got the portable kind, carried it from room to room. We used it so often that the batteries ran out every week. When she grew out of the swing, I resorted to putting her in the jogging stroller and taking her for long walks at nap times. The movement put her to sleep. I begrudged Cale on those walks, begrudged that he got time to himself in the house to relax while I worked up a literal sweat. I waited for him to offer to do the Nap Walk, but he didn't. Sahana said I should just ask him to do it, and I said what every disgruntled wife-mother says: "I don't want to ask him. I want him to *want* to do it on his own."

Evie tugs on my skirt.

"Do you want to show mommy the sandbox?" Ms. Janie asks. "She was *so* into the sandbox today."

Evie nods, her eyes full of light and glee.

"Go and play. I'll be there in a minute," I tell her.

She holds up one finger, parrots back, "A minute." It's her newest thing.

When Evie is out of earshot, scooping and dumping sand repeatedly and laughing like a maniac, I say to Ms. Janie, "I need to tell you something."

She raises her eyebrows almost to her hairline.

"Cale is in the hospital," I say.

Ms. Janie is so young—early twenties. She is all sunshine and rainbows. I feel like in telling her about Cale, I am contributing to the inevitable disillusionment all of us experience as we get older and realize how cruel the world can be.

"Oh no," she says, her blue eyes big and wide.

"Yeah, so I'll be doing drop-off and pick-up for a while," I say. "And I haven't really explained anything to Evie. She hasn't asked where he is yet."

Evie is accustomed to Cale being away for two- or three-day business trips. Even on those trips, she doesn't ask about him, which both relieves and saddens me. I feel like she would ask about him more if she saw him as an essential part of her daily life. But maybe I'm making more of it than it is. Maybe toddlers are kind of like dogs—living only in the present, abiding by the "out of sight, out of mind" principle.

Ms. Janie nods her head and says, "She seemed as happy as can be today, but I will let you know if she asks about her daddy."

Those words—*her daddy*—make my heart clench. No matter what problems existed between Cale and me, he will always be her daddy. Evie will always be blissfully unaware of his shortcomings and my resentments. Or that's the hope.

"Thank you," I say.

Ms. Janie twists her mouth to one side, as if contemplating something. Then she says, "I hope it's nothing serious."

This is her way of asking what's happened, why Cale is in the hospital.

"It is pretty serious, I'm afraid," I say.

I can't bring myself to tell her about the shooting. I feel as compelled to protect her innocence as I do to protect Evie's.

"Evie," I call, using my daughter to get me out of this conversation with Ms. Janie, "we have to get home for dinner, okay?"

Evie looks up, mid-sand-scoop, and gives me a pouty face. I go to her, kneel next to the sandbox, take the blue plastic shovel when she hands it to me.

"This is fun, isn't it?" I tell her.

She dumps a shovelful of sand on my hand and laughs.

I do the same back to her.

Sometimes I wonder if this—the often mindless and repetitive toddler play—is one of the reasons for Cale's funk. If he would talk to me, I would assure him that nobody loves taking a doll's shoes on and off one hundred times or pretending to drink tea from tiny plastic cups for an hour. The trick is to imitate Evie's joy. Somehow, in doing that, I feel some of my own.

We dump sand on each other's hands a few times before I tell her that we have to go home for dinner. When she whines, I tell her I have crackers in the car. Evie loves crackers—Goldfish, graham, Ritz, saltine. They are approximately 80 percent of her diet.

We wave to Ms. Janie on our way out. She gives me a sorrowful look that is supposed to convey pity, I guess. It annoys me.

EVIE AND I go through our evening routine. I try to be engaged, though I can't stop thinking about what's on Cale's phone. Evie eats her pasta—she will eat only penne noodles, no other shape—and a handful of Ritz crackers. I consider that good enough. We play on the floor of the kitchen with her dolls. I wait for her to poop so I can change her diaper and put on her pajamas. When she is changed, I heat up her bottle of milk. I'm sure I was supposed to stop giving her a bottle months ago, but it calms her before bed. She loves it, and it gives her nutrition that I figure she needs; she's not big on drinking milk at any other point in the day. I used to walk her around while she drank her bottle, but she's gotten so heavy. We sit now, her on my lap, and I watch her suckle. It feels like years ago that she was on my breast. Just recently, we've started taking baths together. She always looks at my nipples curiously, as if she's perplexed by them, as if she has no recollection of them being her former food source. Sometimes she pinches them and laughs when I say, "Ouch."

"All done?" I say to her when the bottle is empty.

"All done," she says.

"Ready for night-night?"

She nods.

She doesn't fight bedtime, probably because she is so tired from refusing to nap.

When I lay her in her crib, I sing my usual lullabies and then say, "Sweet dreams. Mommy and Daddy love you." She usually just stares at me when I whisper, but tonight she whispers back:

"Daddy?" It's a question more than a statement.

"Yes, Daddy loves you," I say.

"Daddy?" she says again.

It's as if she's just realized she hasn't seen him in a few days.

"We love you, sweetheart," I say.

She furrows her little brows.

I go through another round of the lullabies and she starts to doze off, whatever concerns she had forgotten in the name of needed rest.

I LEAVE THE front door open for Sahana and go to the kitchen to wash dishes. I'm at the sink when I hear her come in, talking on her cell phone. She lowers her voice, knowing I will kill her if she wakes Evie.

She paces the kitchen while finishing her call, then sets her phone on the counter and says, "What a day."

I raise my eyebrows. "I bet my day beats yours."

"No doubt," she says. "But can I vent anyway?"

I appreciate this about Sahana—her honesty, her refusal to pity me.

"This guy wants to sue me because he says I'm responsible for his wife filing for divorce. His wife is my client," she says.

I roll my eyes. "There can't be any merit to a lawsuit like that."

"I wouldn't think so, but I still had to call my lawyer. Just that phone call alone is probably going to cost me three hundred bucks."

I wince.

"Anyway," she says. She does a little shimmy with her whole body, as if shaking off the day, and then sits at the kitchen table. "Give me wine and tell me everything."

I retrieve a bottle of red from the wine fridge that Cale bought with his last bonus. I pour two glasses, then sit across from her at the table.

"So, work was actually fine," I tell her, because I know she was worried about me going back so soon. "It was good to kind of go through the motions, ya know?"

"Classic distraction mechanism," she says. "Not that I'm judging. Sometimes survival is dependent upon distraction."

"Okay, Dr. Ravani," I say.

Sahana takes a long sip of wine, and I do the same.

"I visited Cale at lunch," I say.

"Any news?"

I shake my head. "He's stable, they say. For now. They're monitoring the pressure in his brain. They may start to take him off the sedation medications in a few days."

"What does that mean?"

"I ask that question a lot. I guess they'll see if he comes out of the coma on his own. Nobody seems to know anything for sure."

"How helpful," she says.

"I keep torturing myself with all the what-ifs. What if he doesn't wake up? What if he does, but he's not really Cale? What if—"

She puts her hand up, like a crossing guard. "Stop right there. You'll drive yourself crazy."

"Oh, I'm way past crazy at this point."

"Well, you started off a little crazy, so that complicates things."

I roll my eyes.

"There's something else," I say. "The nurse gave me his belongings—wallet, phone, keys."

She looks at me expectantly.

"I didn't know if I'd be able to get into his phone, but I guessed his passcode."

"Of course you did," she says without hesitation. "Men are idiots."

I take another sip.

"And?" she asks.

She is leaning so far forward that her chin almost touches the table.

"Texts with the other woman?" she guesses, impatiently.

There were no texts of interest, actually. Nearly all of the texts were work-related. Cale doesn't even have a personal phone, didn't see the point of paying for a separate phone when he could just use his company-paid work phone.

"No texts," I say. "But he had something weird in his Notes app."

I wouldn't have guessed Cale even used the Notes app. I use it all the time—for my running grocery list, a list of funny things Evie says or does that I want to remember to tell her one day, a list of Netflix shows everyone says I need to watch. Cale had just a few notes: one related to fantasy football, which I couldn't make sense of, one titled "Stocks" with a list of— not surprisingly—stocks, and the last one, which is the one I haven't been able to stop thinking about.

"What?" Sahana asks. "You are telling this story way too slowly."

"Sorry," I say. I don't know why I'm hesitating. I guess I'm afraid of the face Sahana will make. It will be a face that confirms that my husband is not who we thought he was, a face that confirms that my marriage was deeply troubled.

"Remember Tessa?" I say.

I'd called Sahana after meeting Tessa at the hospital. She was immediately suspicious of the whole thing. Her first question: "Was she pretty?"

"Yes," Sahana says, the "I told you so" already in her tone.

"Cale had a note in his phone titled 'Tessa,'" I say.

There it is—the face I feared.

"What was in the note?" she asks, though I feel like her conclusion has already been drawn: my husband is an asshole.

"That's what's weird," I say. "It was like a list of things about her. Like he was stalking her or something."

Sahana looks disturbed. "Let me see."

I knew she would ask. I go to my purse, take out Cale's phone, enter the passcode. I set the phone on the table, in front of Sahana, and let her read what I've already read a hundred times.

Tessa

23 years old

Works Tu, Th, F, Sa, Su; 6pm-2am

Has boyfriend (Ryan)

Boise State U—wants to be nurse

Likes classic rock

Honda Civic (black)

Moved from Bend last year

Tattoo—birds flying—starts at wrist, up underside of arm

"You could have done better but I don't mind"

IPAs = favorite beer

Sahana pushes the phone away from her, as if it's diseased, and looks up at me.

"Ang, this is weird."

"I know," I say.

"It's like he's obsessed with her."

"My thoughts exactly."

"I guess it makes sense why he 'saved her life,' as she put it," Sahana says, using air quotes.

"Do you think she knew about this? Like they had a *thing* and she lied to me?"

Sahana shrugs. "I never trusted her from the moment you

mentioned her name. I mean, she came to visit him in the hospital? That's strange."

"It is, right?" I say.

She nods. "It is."

"What does 'You could have done better but I don't mind' mean?"

She shrugs again. "Sounds like words exchanged between disgruntled lovers, if you ask me."

"What am I supposed to do now?" I ask.

"Well, you can't exactly confront Cale about it."

"Nope."

"You have her number, right?"

"Tessa?"

"Tessa."

"Yes, we traded numbers."

"Which is also extremely strange," Sahana says.

I don't know how to explain that it didn't seem strange at the time. Maybe it's just that everything seems strange lately. I've lost touch with normalcy.

"What do I say to her?"

Sahana thinks about this. "Text her. Ask if she can meet in person. It'll be easier to tell in person if she's lying or not."

"I don't know," I say.

Sahana stands from the table and goes to my purse.

"What are you doing?"

"Getting your phone," she says, holding it up for me to see. "I bet I can guess your passcode."

I cross my arms over my chest and let her try.

"Damn it," she says. "I could have sworn it would be Evie's birthday."

I take the phone from her. "It's my and Cale's anniversary, actually."

I feel embarrassed admitting this, like a teenager confessing to a completely unattainable crush.

"Aw, Ang," Sahana says. She attempts a hug, but I push her away. I can't handle sentiment right now.

I open my phone and go to the text I sent Tessa, just "Hi."

I type something new:

Tessa? Hi, it's Angie. Cale's wife. I was wondering if we could meet in person sometime soon.

Sahana tells me to keep it short and simple, not elaborate on why. I set my phone on the table and pour myself a second glass of wine. Before I can take a sip, my phone buzzes again. Sahana grabs it before I can. She looks at the screen, then up at me.

"Looks like you two have a date."

TESSA

ON TUESDAY MORNING, I'm getting dressed and ready for the day when Ryan's alarm goes off. I'm standing at the vanity in our bathroom. In the mirror, I can see him sit up in bed. I can see the surprise on his face when he sees me.

"You're up early," he says groggily as I pat my face with powder.

"Couldn't sleep," I say.

This has been true since the shooting. It's just that usually I stay in bed, staring at the ceiling, watching the fan blades go 'round and 'round. Today, though, I have a 9:00 a.m. coffee date with Jed Ketcher's mother, who does not know that I know who she is. Tomorrow, I have a coffee date with Cale's wife, Angie.

"You have class today?" he asks.

Normally, on Tuesday mornings, I do have class. I can't even think about school though. Even if I was able to sit in the lecture hall without having a panic attack, I wouldn't retain any information. I emailed my teachers last night, telling them what happened:

I was at the scene of the Ray's Bar shooting and will need some time to get my bearings.

They said to take as much time as I need.

I still haven't told my mom, a fact that is getting weirder by the day.

"Yeah, I have class today," I say.

I tell myself this isn't really a lie; I do have class, I'm just not going. I want to be completely honest with him, but I know the truth will scare him. He wants to think I'm getting back to normal, whatever that means. He won't consider meeting Joyce Ketcher or Angie Matthews "normal," that's for sure. In a week or two, I bet I'll be back to my classes, feeling better. For now, though, I need to talk to Jed's mother, and I need to find out why Angie wants to talk to me.

"Come here," Ryan says, motioning for me to join him in bed.

I comply, sitting on the edge of the bed. He wraps his arms around me, pulls me down against his body. He wants to have sex. Morning is our usual time; we both like the thrill of rushing, trying not to be late.

I squirm in his grasp, giggle to disguise my discomfort. I have no interest in sex right now. I haven't had interest since the shooting. I want to be annoyed at him for thinking I'm able to close my eyes, press my body against his, and have an orgasm with ease, as if I didn't just go through a traumatic event. But I know I can't be annoyed; I am at fault for perpetuating the idea that I'm fine.

"Babe, I have to get ready," I say. Normally, saying such a thing is part of our foreplay.

He reaches his hand under the waistband of my skirt.

"Babe, I mean it," I say.

I press myself off him, careful not to look at his face because I don't want to see what's on it—irritation, impatience, frustration.

He lets out a sigh and falls back on his pillow. Everything in me wants to say, "I'm sorry," but I don't want to make this a *thing*.

"I'll see you later?" I say, still not looking at him.

"Yeah," he says. And, because he's sweet to me even when he's annoyed, he adds, "Have a good day at school."

THE COFFEE SHOP is downtown, on Main Street. It used to be called something else, a woman's name I can't remember. Antoine's? Annabelle's? Something like that. Ever since I saw the new name—Bean There, Done That—I've been meaning to come in. It's a cute place. They have a small, fenced patio out front with a few tables. Inside, there are a handful of tables, a couple couches, a few chairs that look like they belong in front of a fireplace in an old mansion. A chalkboard listing all their drinks hangs from the ceiling. I order a tea and peruse the selection of baked goods in a case by the register before deciding on a carrot cake muffin.

I'm ten minutes early, on purpose. I want time to find a table in a corner, a seat against a wall. Just as I'm starting to scan my options, tea and muffin in hand, I hear, "Tessa?"

I look in the direction of the voice to see that Joyce has also come early. I should have guessed.

I didn't even see her when I walked in. She's sitting at a small, round table next to the floor-to-ceiling windows that look out onto Main Street. This table does not feel safe to me.

"Oh, hi," I say, giving an awkward wave.

"Is this table okay?" she asks, as if sensing my unease.

I see a more suitable table in the back. "Actually, do you mind if we sit over there?"

"Of course not," she says, standing hurriedly, apologizing when her purse brushes my arm as she maneuvers her way between the tables.

I take the seat against the wall, take a deep breath. *You're okay, you're okay*, I tell myself—my new mantra.

"I was thinking about getting that muffin," she says. Her hands are wrapped around a cup of tea, the string from the bag hanging over the side, steam escaping through the tiny hole in the lid.

I look at the muffin like I don't know where it came from. It was stupid to order it; I have no appetite.

"And you're a tea person too," she says.

I'm not actually. Before the shooting, I drank coffee every day. The morning after, I made a cup out of habit and was jittery and panicky the entire day. Maybe it had nothing to do with the coffee, but I've still abstained since.

"I'm a recent tea person," I say.

She nods. I wonder how many minutes we are going to spend talking about tea.

"I like coffee too, but only first thing in the morning," she says.

I give her a small smile, a smile that says I'm slightly bored. She seems to get the hint because she sits back in her chair and says, "So, how are you doing?"

Sometimes, people ask this question as a formality only, expecting a hurried, "Good, fine" in response. But, occasionally, people ask it with weighted meaning, with true inquiry. This is one of those times.

"Okay," I say. "It's still hard to go out in public."

It feels good to admit this simple truth, even if it's to someone who is a virtual stranger. This must be what therapy is like.

"I can only imagine," she says.

She takes a sip from her tea, winces a bit, like it's still too hot.

"It must have been terrifying," she says, her eyes begging me to tell her about it, to explain the terror.

"It was," I say.

"Do you mind if I ask what happened?" she says.

I came to this coffee shop with the hope of finding out more about Jed Ketcher; now I realize that she came with the same objective.

I tell her the bits and pieces I remember, the bits and pieces that come to me in nightmares whenever I dare to fall asleep. I tell her about being behind the bar, about the shots, about how I thought they were fireworks. I tell her about everything being dark, about the confusion, about people screaming. I tell her about Cale. I tell her about the storage closet, about the zip-up black hoodie, about the SWAT team. My rescue is the happy ending, I suppose. But a part of me still feels trapped in that storage closet.

I only realize I've been telling my story to the tabletop when I finally look up and see tears in Joyce's eyes.

"I am so sorry this happened to you," she says.

"It's not your fault."

I mean this, even though I know who her son is—or was. I'm sure she feels at fault. I'm sure that's why there are tears.

She uses a brown paper napkin to dab at her eyes.

"Did you lose someone in the shooting?" I say carefully, tentatively.

She crumples the napkin and puts it in her purse, then looks at me.

"I did," she says. Then: "My son."

I don't want to ask his name, don't want to force her to reveal who he was, so I just say, "I'm so sorry."

Her tears come again. She reaches into her purse, uncrumples the napkin, and uses it again to dab her eyes. I get the feeling nobody has said these words to her—"I'm so sorry." Nobody has acknowledged the loss of her son as a valid loss. Nobody has considered her sadness.

"It still doesn't feel real," she says.

"I know."

She must feel as I do—as if the shooting was part of some strange dream. I feel as if I'm still waiting to wake up, to turn to

Ryan and say, "You won't believe the nightmare I had."

"The service is on Thursday, so I suppose it will feel more real then."

According to the message boards, the funerals for the victims start on Friday. I hadn't even thought about the funeral for Jed. Nobody on the message boards has mentioned his funeral. To most people, he was a monster, undeserving of ceremony.

"I hope you have supportive family, friends," I say.

She shrugs. "I have Gary."

She says it as if I know who Gary is. She stares off behind me.

"I haven't even told my mom," I say, in an attempt to jolt her out of this moment of grief. It works. Her eyes shift back to me.

"Why not?" she asks.

"I don't know," I say. "Normally, I tell her everything. We had a little bit of a falling out—nothing major though. I guess maybe I think telling her will make it real. Which is stupid. I know it's real. I just . . . I don't know."

"I understand," she says. "I haven't reached out to many people either."

"My mom will freak out," I say. "She's going to cry, and it's going to make me cry. I feel like I'm keeping it together pretty well . . . or I'm faking it or something. But if she knows what happened and jumps in her car to see me, I'll lose it."

She nods. "Where does she live?"

"In Oregon. Bend. That's where I'm from."

It's just a five-hour drive. I could call my mom right now and she'd be here before dinner.

"She must miss you."

"I don't know. She has this boyfriend now. Rob. It's . . . different."

"It was always just the two of you?" she asks.

I nod. "My father took off when I was a baby."

"My son's father died when he was young. After that it was just the two of us too," she says.

Jed Ketcher was without a father. Maybe this explains something; maybe it doesn't at all.

"I'm sure she misses you."

It takes me a second to realize she's referring to my mom.

"Yeah, I know," I say. "I'll tell her soon."

"Tell her when you're ready. She'll want to know. She'll want to support you."

These words make her cry again. The brown napkin is nearly shredded to bits, useless.

"Have you been in touch with anyone else who was there that night?" I ask.

She shakes her head. "Just you."

"I'm glad we met," I say. "I'm glad I hyperventilated and you were there."

She manages a little laugh.

"It is nice to talk to someone who understands."

I muster up the courage to ask the question that's been sitting on my tongue since she mentioned the funeral on Thursday.

"Would it be okay if I came?" I say.

She looks at me, quizzically.

"To the funeral, I mean."

Her eyes go wide. I may have gone too far.

"It's going to be small, private—"

"I'm sorry," I interrupt. "I shouldn't have—"

"You can come," she says. "If you'd like."

"You don't have to say that. I've overstepped my bounds. It's the chatty bartender in me," I say, though I was never that chatty of a bartender.

"No," she says. "You can come."

She must know that if I come, I will find out his name. I will find out who he was. I want this to happen, of course. She needs to know I know who he was before I can ask her questions about him—how he thought, what he felt, why he did what he did.

"You're sure?"

She doesn't seem sure, but she says, "I am."

"Okay," I say.

"I can text you the details. I don't even know them yet. Gary is organizing it."

Again with Gary. Whoever he is, at least she has him.

She takes another sip of her tea and doesn't wince this time. This always happens with coffee dates—the coffee or tea is finally an appropriate temperature for drinking by the time the conversation has come to its natural conclusion.

Joyce pushes her chair from the table and stands. I do the same.

"Thank you," she says, "for meeting me."

"I'm the one who should be thanking you," I say. "It was my crazy idea."

"It was a good one."

We walk out together. To any bystanders, we would appear to be friends, or mother and daughter. If they only knew.

We turn to face each other when we're outside. For a second, I think Joyce Ketcher is going to hug me. She doesn't though. She just sticks out her hand, as if we are concluding a business meeting. I take it, squeeze it instead of shake it.

"Until next time," she says.

JOYCE

"IT'S SADISTIC," GARY says when I tell him about meeting Tessa.

"Sadistic?"

"Yes. You're just bringing more pain on yourself," he says.

"You mean 'masochistic'?"

He looks thoroughly annoyed with me. "Whatever. It's wrong is what it is."

"It's wrong to want to talk to people hurt by my son? It's wrong to want to make some amends?"

"They aren't your amends to make. They're Jed's."

"Well, Jed isn't here."

We are in the garage. Gary was tinkering with something at his workbench when I came home. He stopped tinkering when I told him about meeting Tessa.

"Look, you can do what you want," he says. He stands from his stool, noticeably flustered. "It's your life."

The words sting. I suppose a part of me had thought— stupidly—that he'd begun to see this as "our life."

"I don't understand why you're so upset," I say.

He marches inside the house. I follow. He paces from one end of the kitchen to the other, hands on his hips.

"I'm upset because I care about you, okay? And what you're doing—talking to this woman—it's just going to make things worse."

"I felt better after talking to her."

He just shakes his head. "You know you're going to have to tell her who he is at some point."

I haven't told him yet that I've invited her to the service. Or, rather, she invited herself and I didn't object.

"I know I have to tell her. I will."

He raises his eyebrows. "And you think she's going to still be your friend, or whatever she is, when she finds out who he is?"

This confirms my suspicion—Gary thinks my son is someone I should be ashamed of, someone I will have to apologize for and condemn for the rest of my life.

"You're an asshole," I say.

With that, I retreat to my bedroom. I can feel him follow me, can sense him standing in the doorway of the bedroom as I sort through a pile of clothes for no reason except to have something to do with my hands.

"I don't want to overstay my welcome," I tell him. "I'll go back home today."

"You don't have to do that," he says.

I turn, face him. "I think I do."

"It doesn't make any sense," he says. I feel a rush of relief that he wants me to stay. Then he adds, "Stay until after the funeral, at least."

So he wants me to stay until Thursday. He feels it's his duty, clearly, to make sure I don't lose it after burying my son. I am Gary's obligation.

"I'll leave today," I say.

He rolls his eyes. "Whatever you want, Joyce."

I hate when he uses my name like this, as if we are not two people who know each other well enough to bypass our given names, as if our association with each other has a formality to it.

I resume sorting through my clothes, deciding that I'm folding for the sake of packing. Yes, I am packing. I am going home.

IT'S ONLY WHEN I've finished packing my things that I realize my exit from Gary's house cannot be as dramatic as I desire. I need him to give me a ride. My car is still at my house. He's back in the garage, tinkering. I approach him, trying to look proud instead of sheepish.

"I'm ready," I say, my chin held high, like the Queen of England making a proclamation.

He looks at me over the top of his glasses.

"Ready for what?"

"To go," I say. "Home."

He doesn't seem to remember yet that he is my ride.

"Okay then," he says, turning back to his workbench.

I'm going to have to just admit that I need him. "My car is at my house."

He understands now. He sets down whatever he's working on—from my perspective, he always seems to be fiddling with the same piece of wood and an assortment of screws—and hops off his stool.

"I'll get my keys."

THE DRIVE BACK to my house is silent. I'm too busy trying to appear undaunted by the tension that I don't prepare myself for what it will be like to be in my driveway again. Once we are there, I can't catch my breath. I feel what Tessa must feel all the time.

The car is in park, but I stay seated, feeling as if a boulder is on my lap, pinning me down.

"Okay then," Gary says, as if he's just dropping me off after one of our weekend dates.

Gary's always been kind of dense about reading me, understanding my feelings—a stereotypical man, I guess. It's only when I started dating again—a few years after Ed died—that I understood the grievances of my girlfriends lamenting their clueless husbands. Ed was incredibly sensitive and attentive to me, but also strong, breadwinning, and committed to the traditional male role—a unicorn of a man. I was lucky to have him as long as I did, but he made it impossible for me to ever be truly satisfied with someone else.

I open the car door but remain seated.

"Thanks for the ride," I say.

I can feel him looking at me. "You sure you're okay?"

The sensitivity of the question surprises me.

I look at him. "Nope, but I have to go home sometime."

He sighs. "You don't have to—"

"I do," I say.

For once, I'm the one whose ego is getting in the way.

"I'll give you a call later," he says.

It's that ego that enables me to get out of his car. I don't look back at him when I get to the front door, but I hear him drive away.

THE HOUSE IS eerily quiet. The first thing I do is turn on all the lights and the TV. The sound, the chatter of a rerun of *The Office*, tricks me into thinking I'm not alone. Jed used to love *The Office*. He wasn't much for comedies, in general, but he laughed at that show. He said it was the only show on TV that "exposed the absurdity of the American dream." Or something. I didn't really understand what he was getting at—still don't, frankly; I was just happy something made him laugh.

I wonder if they have burned his body yet. They probably have. I will myself not to think about it. They will give me the urn at the service, and I will place it on the nightstand, next to Ed's. How strange—to have these remains of the human beings I've loved most.

I decide I need a task, something to keep me busy. The service is in two days, and I want it to be special, even if it's just me there. I assume Gary will still come; he isn't the grudge-holding type, and he always does the "right" thing. Most funerals have photos—enlarged, mounted on easels. I want that for Jed. I go to the linen closet in the hallway, where I've always kept our photo albums (I've never seen the need for *that* many linens). I stand atop a kitchen chair to retrieve the albums on the top shelf. These are the old ones, the ones from my wedding, the ones from Jed's baby and toddler years. On the middle shelf are albums with the rest of Jed's childhood. I stopped keeping albums of photos when he was a teenager. That's when he took over, creating albums of his own, the ones in his closet.

I carry five albums in my arms, precariously, to Jed's room. I let them topple over onto his bed. I take his high school albums from his closet, add them to my pile. This will be my task—going through photos of my son, choosing a handful of favorites. That's what people do when they say goodbye—they attempt to distill a lifetime down to a handful of favorites.

I open the first album, the one that begins with a photo of me in a hospital bed with Jed, the one that has his hospital band tucked into a slot meant for a picture. My throat constricts, feels suddenly like it's the size of a drinking straw. I close the album and chastise myself for thinking I could do this. I'm suddenly exhausted—by the task, by everything. I push the albums to the side of the bed and lie next to them, spooning them as if they are him. I used to sleep with him like this, after Ed died, when we both needed a warm body at night.

I stroke one of the albums, as if it is his back, making clockwise circles. I did this when he was a baby, when I was putting him to sleep at night. All the books said I should leave his room before he fell asleep, so he would learn how to "self-soothe." He would scream and scream though, so I'd come back. Maybe I shouldn't have. Maybe he never learned to manage his emotions because of me.

I'd do those circles on his back for however long it took. Even when I was sure he was asleep, when I saw his little clenched fists release and his eyelids flutter, I would wait until I made a hundred circles with my hand on his back before leaving his room.

I start counting now.

One. Two. Three.

Sometime before one hundred, I fall asleep.

ANGIE

I NEVER WOULD HAVE guessed Cale would be pursuing another woman, let alone a woman in her twenties. He's not the type to be *obsessed* with someone; I don't think he was ever obsessed with me. We got along well. We had fun, but I wouldn't say there were fireworks. I assumed mature romance was less about fireworks, more about friendship. Maybe I was wrong. Maybe he wanted fireworks.

The list in his phone—it's just weird. Why was he so into this woman? I met her. She was pretty, sweet. But obsession-worthy? I don't get it. Maybe he was just desperate for distraction from his life, our life. Maybe he craved freedom. A twenty-something bartender is the epitome of freedom.

BEFORE I GOT pregnant, we'd talked vaguely about having kids. I'd said I wasn't sure about them. This wasn't an attempt to be the cool girl, the girl who promises her guy a future in which he is her sole focus; at the time, I really wasn't sure. I was old enough to have several friends who had kids, and I'd seen how their lives had diverted drastically from what they had been before. I liked what Cale and I had. I liked that we could hike Hulls Gulch on a whim, visit breweries whenever we wanted, take the canoe to the river on weekends. I still felt like I had selfishness and hedonism to indulge. And I was aware that meant I wasn't ready to be a mother.

Condoms work about 90 percent of the time. When you hear that, you assume the 10 percent is reserved for idiots who use them incorrectly or say they used them and didn't. You don't think you could be in the 10 percent until your period is a week late, your boobs feel strangely tender, and there's a weird metallic taste in your mouth, like you've been sucking on pennies. That was what I googled—*metallic taste in mouth*. One of the common causes: pregnancy. Something to do with hormones. My first thought was, *No, it couldn't be*. But when I considered the lateness of my period and my tender breasts, I knew it could be. I went to Walgreens on my lunch break, bought three different pregnancy tests, and took each of them to the Walgreens bathroom. My fingers trembled as I set the alarm on my phone for three minutes. I closed my eyes for those three minutes. When the alarm beeped, I looked. Two of the tests were the kind with lines—one showed two lines side by side, the other showed two lines crossing each other. The third test said "Pregnant" in a little window. There was no denying it.

Sahana was the first person I told. I had to tell her first because I needed her guidance on how to tell Cale. He would be shocked, as I was. A small part of me was excited by the unknown, by how this unexpected thing would change our lives. We hadn't talked much about the future, though moving in together suggested we had one. Now there was something growing inside me that would start making decisions for us.

Sahana was shocked too. I'm not the type to have unexpected things happen to me. I'm a planner, by nature.

"I know this sounds lame," she said, "but I feel like any sperm that got past a latex barrier deserves to become a kid."

I laughed. I was giddy. "I kind of agree," I say. "I'm oddly proud of my child's resolve."

"Well, it's the sperm's resolve. Your egg was just hanging out. Women are always waiting on men, remember?"

I laughed again.

"I don't know how to tell Cale."

"Whatever you do, don't post it on Instagram."

"Oh god no," I say.

I knew, right then, that even if I did take a video of the moment, Cale's reaction would not be Instagram-worthy. I knew he wouldn't be the guy breaking into the biggest smile of his life, the guy hugging his wife gleefully, the guy jumping up and down. I didn't expect him to be excited.

That night, after scooping pasta into bowls for us, I said, "I have something to tell you." I couldn't help but smile as I said it. He smiled in response. I think he was expecting me to say I got a promotion.

"I know this is crazy, but I'm pregnant," I said.

He was stunned. That much I'd predicted. But there was something else too—fear, I think. It was on his face for just a split second before he smiled. At the time, I thought it was genuine. In retrospect, I think he smiled because he knew that was what he was supposed to do.

"I hope it's mine," he joked.

AT EIGHT WEEKS, I had my first doctor's appointment. I went by myself, told Cale not to worry about it (he had a busy day with work, I remember). In this instance, I *was* trying to be the cool girl, not one of those annoying pregnant women demanding her husband's presence at every ultrasound. Once I was there, though, I wished he was too. I got tears in my eyes hearing the heartbeat. I was *that* woman. Maybe it was better I was alone; if he'd been there, I would have been a little embarrassed by my reaction.

He proposed shortly after that first appointment. He got down on one knee at our house, on a not-otherwise-special Friday night. I told him he didn't have to do this just because we were having a baby. He said, "You're ruining the moment." I laughed, let him put the ring on my finger. It was beautiful—two carats, round cut, classic. I didn't think I was someone who cared about diamonds until one was presented to me.

"We're really doing this?" I asked him. Tears were threatening. There I was, being *that* woman again.

He shrugged. He was still down on his knee. "I don't know. You haven't said yes yet."

I knelt on the floor so I could look in his eyes and said, "Yes. Duh."

THIS IS WHAT I'm thinking about as I sit in this annoyingly charming coffee shop, waiting for my husband's apparent love interest to walk through the door. It's 11:00 a.m. I told work I had an appointment. Nobody asked questions. Before the sentence even got out of my mouth ("I have to leave for an appoint—"), they were saying, "Yes, of course. Go ahead." They seem uncomfortable with me there, going about life. I'm sure they're all thinking, *If that happened to me, I wouldn't be able to function*. My functioning is perplexing to them. They don't know the whole story. I'm not just a grieving, worried wife; I am a betrayed, confused wife. "Of course you're angry," Sahana said yesterday. She is the only one who knows, who understands. I haven't told Aria the whole truth yet, the truth that my husband wasn't just at a bar randomly. He was at a bar in pursuit of a twenty-something-year-old girl.

And that twenty-something-year-old girl has just walked in.

I stand from my chair, as if I'm an audience member at a wedding and she is the bride. When she spots me, she quickens her pace and sits in the seat immediately next to mine, instead of the one across from me, which would be more socially appropriate.

"Sorry," she says. "Since the shooting, I can't have my back to doors."

She seems embarrassed of this, though it makes total sense. In this moment, I feel sorry for her; the hatred I'd developed for her since discovering the note in Cale's phone suddenly dissipates.

I shift to the seat across from the one she has chosen, settle into this more comfortable position.

"Thanks for coming," I say to her, straightening in my chair, giving myself the posture of a powerful woman. I need her to know that I am in control of this situation, whatever it is. I need her to know I won't tolerate bullshit—Cale's or hers.

She finger-combs a strand of sandy-blonde hair behind her ear. She has beautiful hair, Pantene commercial hair. I can see the appeal of her, to a man, to Cale. She seems innocent, simple; but then there's that tattoo on her arm, black silhouettes of birds flying, the one Cale mentioned in his note about her. Something about her seems complex, deep. An old soul, as they say.

"Is this about Cale?" she says.

I look at her, stunned. Is she going to just come out with it?

"What do you mean?" I ask.

She furrows her brows. "I assumed you wanted to give me an update. Is he okay or . . ."

"Oh," I say. "They say he's stable. I'm going to the hospital after I meet with you."

She nods solemnly.

"You seem awfully curious about his condition," I say, trying to lead the conversation where I want it to go.

She cocks her head to one side, like a dog questioning a sound off in the distance.

"I just mean . . . he's basically a stranger to you, right?"

"Not a stranger," she says.

I wait for more.

She looks down.

"Like I said, I feel like he may have saved my life."

Not this again.

I sigh.

"So that's all there is to it?"

"To what?" she asks.

"To your interest in him?"

She looks confused again.

"Look," I say, "I have reason to believe that Cale had a . . . thing for you."

Her already-large blue eyes become bigger.

"A thing for me?" she asks.

I try to find deceit on her face, but her surprise seems genuine.

"A crush or something," I say, because "crush" seems like something that someone her age would understand. And "obsession" might scare her.

"Really?" she says. She shakes her head in apparent disbelief.

"You didn't know?"

She keeps shaking her head. "I didn't see it," she says.

"So this is news to you."

She holds up one hand, like a Girl Scout taking an oath.

"I swear," she says.

She seems so young. I half expect her to stick out a pinky, ask to link it with mine.

I believe her.

I believe she didn't know.

In a way, I'd prefer they had a thing together. I'd prefer a mutual crush. As it is, Cale just seems like a creep, a forty-five-year-old man inappropriately invested in a younger woman.

I touch the home button of my phone, look at the time. I suppose I've gotten what I came for, though it's only raised more questions.

"I should get going," I tell her.

She looks surprised, maybe a little disappointed, like she thought we were going to *hang out* or something.

"To the hospital," she says. "Right, of course, yeah."

We both stand.

"Can I just ask," she says, "what makes you think he had a . . . thing . . . for me?"

Her voice is timid, unsure. She stands with one foot crossed over the other, teetering slightly to one side.

I wonder if I should tell her. Considering her fragile emotional state, her paranoia, her inability to sit with her back to doors, I decide she doesn't need to know about the note in his phone. She doesn't need to also worry about older men stalking her.

"Just wife's intuition, I guess."

She looks doubtful but doesn't press further.

We walk out together, turn to face each other when we get to the sidewalk.

"Thank you, again, for meeting me," I tell her. "Sorry I have to run."

She nods once. "Of course."

I take my keys out of my purse, signaling that I'm on my way.

"Well, have a good day," I say, bringing this awkward meeting to an appropriately awkward conclusion.

"You too."

I give her a wave and make my way to my car a block away. When I turn around, she's still just standing there outside the coffee shop, looking in my direction.

TESSA

THE FIRST NIGHT HE came in was a Friday. It was busy. We had a Rolling Stones cover band playing, which always drew a large crowd. They called themselves Wild Horses. I've always loved that song—"Wild Horses Couldn't Drag Me Away." My mom was always playing the Rolling Stones when I was little. And Bob Dylan, Creedence Clearwater Revival, Van Morrison. Our favorite song was "Wild Night." We'd dance around the kitchen to that, using wooden spoons as microphones. By the end of the song, we were sweaty, hair sticking to the backs of our necks. It always took us a minute to catch our breath. Just thinking of it now makes me want to cry with missing her.

I need to call her, tell her. Soon.

He was wearing a button-down flannel shirt. It wasn't buttoned correctly—one button in the wrong hole and the whole thing went awry. His hair was wet, like he'd just gone to the bathroom, wet his hands, and ran them through his hair. It was close to one o'clock, an hour from closing. The band had finished at midnight, but there were still about fifty people or so lingering, laughing, drinking. It was loud. Drunkenness at 1:00 a.m. is always loud.

He sat at a stool right in front of me as I was pouring vodka into four glasses for some regulars—one of them was Bob, who was killed in the shooting.

I squeezed a lime in each glass, and he said, "I think you got me."

He meant with the lime.

I looked up. "Oh, sorry," I said.

To be honest, I was irritated with him for calling my attention to this. I didn't have time to apologize to some guy for a squirt of lime juice. I was dealing with a pack of rowdy drunkards and I was the only one tending bar; Heather had quit, and we hadn't hired Dan yet. Monica was outside smoking, per usual.

"Can I bother you for a beer?" he asked. He had to shout at me, because of the noise.

"Sure, yeah," I said. "One minute."

I held up a finger, telling him to wait, then gathered up the glasses of vodka and delivered them to Bob and his trio of buddies. One of them made a comment about my shirt being sized for a toddler; it was a crop top, baring my belly. I snapped, "Maybe you should tip more so I can buy new clothes."

The regulars liked when I gave them a hard time. One of Bob's buddies, Randy, used to call me Testy Tessa.

"So, what can I get you?" I asked when I came back to take his order.

"What do you recommend?"

Most men do not ask me this. They have a drink of choice. They take pride in it.

"For beer?" I asked.

He nodded. He had this dopey smile on his face.

"IPAs are my favorite. Hoppy, if you like that."

"Sure," he said with a shrug.

I turned around, pulled the tap for the White Dog Hazy IPA we had that night.

When I set the pint glass down next to him, some foam sloshed out.

"How long have you been doing this?" he asked.

I took it as criticism.

"Long enough," I said, defensively. If he didn't want to deal with a little beer foam and squirt of lime, what was he doing in a shitty bar like Ray's?

"I didn't mean it like that," he said. "Sorry."

He shook his head at himself and took a sip.

"It's good."

I grabbed a towel from under the bar, ran it across the bar top.

"I've been doing this for a year," I told him. "And it's just to pay the bills. I'm going to school."

He raised his eyebrows. "That's great," he said. "What school?"

I thought it was weird that he was asking, that he was interested. Any woman who has lived in the world for any length of time has a radar for creepy men. That's when I looked at his ring finger, saw he was married.

"Boise State," I said. He probably thought I was going to the local community college. I relished the opportunity to shock him.

He didn't look shocked though. He just said, "What are you studying?"

I stared at the ring finger long enough for him to see me staring. I wanted him to know that I knew he was married.

"Just general stuff now. I want to be a nurse," I told him.

"That's great," he said.

He took a long sip.

That's when I asked, "So you meeting someone?"

And he said, "Something like that."

It seemed strange—coming to a bar an hour before closing to meet someone. But I didn't know much about clandestine affairs.

Just before two o'clock, Monica turned the lights on in the bar and said, "Alright, bedtime, folks."

There were the usual groans. At that point, only a handful of people were left—all men.

He stood up from his stool and downed the rest of his beer—his second pint of the Hazy IPA. Whoever he was supposed to meet hadn't shown up, but he didn't seem to care.

That's when he said, "It was nice chatting. Thanks for the beer."

He pulled two twenties out of his pocket, set them on the bar top. I thought he'd made a mistake—pulled an extra bill. I handed one back to him.

"Oh no, that's for you. To buy new clothes or whatever," he said with a wink. I usually associate winks with creepy men, but his seemed friendly. I couldn't help but smile.

"Uh, thanks," I said.

His two beers were $12 total, so he'd tipped me $28, which made no sense.

"My name's Cale, by the way," he said.

"Cale?"

I wasn't sure I'd heard him correctly. My hearing's always kind of shot by the end of the night when we have live music.

"Yeah, like the trendy lettuce stuff."

Again, I couldn't help but smile.

Now, in retrospect, I guess I have to wonder if he was flirting with me.

"Well, I'm Tessa," I told him. Then I said what I always say when someone I serve at the bar is leaving: "See you around."

Monica said she was going to lock up, so I grabbed my purse from where I'd stashed it under the sink, then made my way to the parking lot. I had an eerie feeling, like I wasn't alone. I thought of Ryan's ongoing fear of me being attacked on the way to my car after work. I was less scared of the attack than I was of having to admit to him that he was right.

I picked up my pace until I was jogging. When I got inside my car, I exhaled. I turned the key in the ignition, and all the locks engaged. I was fine. Then I looked up and saw the reason I'd felt like I wasn't alone.

He was sitting in his car and looking at me.

Cale.

When he saw me catch him, he looked away quickly.

It was weird, but I didn't think much of it at the time. After all, he'd stayed until closing. So what if he lingered in his car for a few minutes? He was probably checking his phone, trying to get ahold of whoever had stood him up. He'd seemed harmless. So harmless that when he showed up again a few nights later, I'd already forgotten about the eerie feeling I'd had in the parking lot. I just got him an IPA, and we chatted again.

Honestly, I didn't think anything of it.

Ryan always says I'm too naïve.

JOYCE

TODAY IS THE DAY I say goodbye to my son.

They say no parent should have to do this, that it's the worst thing a human being could possibly endure, and I am about to do it.

Jed is gone. Jed is gone. I say these words with the hope that they will lose their impact, but they do not.

We named him Jed in an awkward attempt to combine our names—Joyce and Ed. We took the "J" from my name and the "ed" from his. It was silly, I suppose. At the time, it seemed appropriate; we had created the ultimate something together, and we were so awed by that. Jed thought it was cool until he was a teenager. Then he thought it was lame.

I wish Ed were here. That's selfish, I know. I wouldn't want him to suffer this. Misery loves company though, and Ed is the only person who would share my misery. Gary didn't know Jed like I did; Gary didn't even like Jed.

I suppose there is comfort in Ed *not* being here. There is comfort in knowing he is with Jed, on the other side. I've never believed in a conventional heaven, but I do believe in an "other side." I'm relieved Jed didn't arrive there alone. I can picture Ed greeting him, his arms stretched out wide. I can picture Jed falling into those arms—father and son reunited. They have each other now.

I am alone.

THERE IS A knock at the front door. Gary. He called early this morning, said he was going to pick me up at ten o'clock. He didn't *ask* if I wanted him to drive me, which was smart on his part; I would have said no, out of stubbornness. He just said, "I'll be there," and I didn't have it in me to say anything besides, "Okay."

I've never seen Gary in a suit. He is not a suit-wearing type. Before he retired, he worked in construction his whole life. He's accustomed to jeans and T-shirts on a daily basis. The Tommy Bahama shirts and khakis are his version of "dressing up." But today he is wearing a suit, even though he knows I will be the only one to see it; there are not multitudes of guests to dress for. The suit jacket and pants are black. He is wearing a button-down light gray shirt, a black tie.

"You look nice," I say.

It's probably not the right thing to say to someone going to a funeral, but it is the truth.

"Thank you," he says.

He tugs on the collar of the shirt. I'm sure he is uncomfortable.

"You look nice too."

I'm wearing a black dress that I found at the back of my closet, something I don't think I've worn in at least fifteen years. I'd bought it for a company holiday dinner at Capitol Cellars, one of Boise's nicer restaurants. I wore it just the one time. Now that I have it on, I remember why—the bottom of the dress, around my calves, is too tight, forcing me to shorten my stride. I wonder what bereaved mothers are supposed to wear to their child's funeral service. Should I have bought something new? How could I be expected to go dress shopping at a time like this?

There don't seem to be any rules for mothers who have lost children. Nobody wants to make rules for such a thing because that would be acknowledging that it happens. Most of us would rather ignore the possibility. We have a term for someone who loses a spouse—a widow or widower. We have a term for a child who loses parents—an orphan. But there is no term for a mother who has lost a child. I guess everyone is in denial of the need for this term.

CALDWELL ISN'T A great town. It's kind of a "wrong side of the tracks" town, in my opinion. I saw a report on the news a few months back about how it has one of the top crime rates in our state. Overall, Idaho has low crime rates, so I'm sure it's not *that* bad. But, still, it's worse than Boise.

I don't like that this is where I have to come to say goodbye to Jed. It still bothers me that the funeral homes in Boise wanted nothing to do with my son. I feel the same rage I felt when he'd come home in elementary school and tell me about the kids making fun of him for wearing overalls. He had this tan pair that he just loved. I told him kids can be cruel. I never anticipated his retaliating against the world in such a dramatic way. I never anticipated him being the cruel one.

As we approach the funeral home, I see a small crowd of people outside the gate. At first, I assume they are there for another service. But then it occurs to me that they don't look to be there for a service; they are wearing jeans, regular clothes, not funereal attire. Then I see the camera propped up on a man's shoulder and realize the press has found out about Jed's service.

"You've got to be kidding me," Gary says, coming to the same realization as me.

As we drive through the gate, they peer at us. I'm sure they recognize me. If they are invested enough in what my son did to come here, they have seen my photo online. I watch as one of them, a girl, points at me and then says something to the guy next to her. All at once, the crowd of them, maybe twelve people, follows the car.

"What are they doing here?" I ask.

Gary's nostrils are flaring. His face is red. I've never seen him quite this angry.

He parks the car in the lot outside the chapel. By the time we open the doors, the crowd of people is waiting for us.

"Joyce Ketcher?" a girl says. Her tone is harsh.

Gary tugs on my arm, says, "Come on."

I keep my head down as we try to walk toward the funeral home. I just stare at my feet, trusting that Gary is leading me.

"Your son killed my brother," the girl says.

She is clearly the leader of this group.

"Jason Maguire," she says. "And his wife, Leigh."

Without thinking of it, I put my hands over my ears.

"Oh, you don't want to hear it?" she says. "You don't want to hear that he killed people who had a child at home? Well, we have to *live* it. His family has to live it."

They had a child.

Jed created an orphan.

I glance up, in an attempt to make eye contact with this person. But I don't see her. The camera is in my face. I look down again.

Gary pulls me inside what must be the administrative office, the place visitors go to discuss the cost of cremation and whatnot. He locks the door behind him, shutting out the angry mob. I hear a woman's heels clicking down the hallway and look to see a woman wearing a black pantsuit, which must be the uniform in a business like this. Her hair is pulled up in a tight bun.

"What the hell is going on?" Gary shouts at her.

"I'm sorry, Mister . . . ?"

"McKee. Gary McKee. I don't know how many times I told you the importance of this service being private."

"I'm sorry, Mr. McKee. I can assure you—"

"You already assured me. You assured me it would be private, that your employees were—what did you say?—'respectful professionals.' Clearly, someone spilled the damn beans."

The woman is looking out the window, at the people waiting at the door. She's flustered now.

"I don't know—"

"Right. You don't know," Gary snaps. "Can you please get someone in security to escort these people off the premises?"

She looks behind her, to the left and right, as if in search of security personnel who I am sure do not exist.

I tap Gary on the elbow, gently. "Gary, it's okay. Let's just go. We'll have our ceremony in the chapel. They'll leave us alone."

He looks at me as if I am one of the intruders, his eyes so wide that I can see the whites all the way around the pupils.

"You think they'll leave us alone? Isn't it clear they have no intention of doing that?"

He waves his hand toward the door, toward the group of people still standing there.

"Let's just go," I say.

I give the woman a conciliatory smile, and she gives me one in return.

"Our director, Marcus, is presiding over your service today, Mr. McKee," the woman says. "He's ready in the chapel."

It is time to say goodbye to my son.

WHEN WE OPEN the door to go back outside, I keep my head up.

"Do you have anything to say for your son?" a man says. He has a microphone. He is a reporter.

Gary's hand is on my back, urging me forward, but I resist. I stop. I think of Jed in those tan overalls, think of how they were just a bit too short for him. I look at the man with the microphone. I stare into the camera wielded by his colleague.

"I am sorry for what he did. I am ashamed of what he did. But please, let me say goodbye to my child."

I take a step forward, and the man with the camera backs up. This is a victory.

I reach back for Gary's hand, grabbing at the air until he gets the hint. He presses his palm against mine as I march toward the chapel. I don't hear footsteps behind us. They are not following. That's all they wanted from me—an apology, an admission that my son did something horrific, a confirmation that I am human . . . not a monster like him.

I don't realize I'm holding my breath until we enter the chapel and I crouch, gasping for air. Gary is still holding my hand.

"Joyce?" I hear a voice say.

I look up to see Tessa. I'm surprised she's here, even though she said she would be. I am embarrassed of the angry mob. She must know now who Jed was.

When I stand, I see they have the photos I selected of Jed displayed—three enlarged and on easels, ten others in a framed collage. The urn is at the front of the room, looking small and almost silly. The bouquet of lilies towers over the urn. Still, Gary has done a good job. When I look at him—his face now a normal color, the rage gone—I love him a little.

"Thank you for coming," I say to Tessa. "Tessa, this is Gary. Gary, Tessa."

They shake hands.

I know Gary thinks it's strange, my budding relationship with a woman who was almost killed by Jed. I don't think it's strange though. I think it's right. In a way, Tessa and I have something in common—we both survived Jed.

"I was just looking at the photos," Tessa says.

This is her way of telling me she knows. This and the redness of her eyes, the puffiness, the evidence of her crying.

I nod.

"His eyes . . . he looks like he felt everything," she says. "I don't know if that makes sense."

"It does," I tell her.

The funeral director walks from the front of the room to greet us. He introduces himself as Marcus, says he's ready to get started whenever we are. I'm not ready to get started, but I walk to the front of the room anyway. The first pew has a placard that says Reserved for Family on it, as if they expected a room full of people, like any other funeral. Tessa sits in the second row, in accordance with the placard, pretending along with the funeral home staff that social norms still apply, even though what Jed did violated every norm.

Marcus doesn't read passages from the Bible. Gary must have told him I'm not religious (and Jed certainly wasn't). He reads from a sheet of paper, something he must keep in a file titled "Agnostic Ceremonies." It's all generic stuff; he didn't know Jed, after all, and I'm sure whatever Gary told him didn't elicit much compassion. If I close my eyes, I can imagine Jed next to me, slouched against the pew, his legs stretched out in front of him, arms crossed over his chest. He wouldn't enjoy this service. I imagine him rolling his eyes, sighing as the funeral director speaks.

Mom, was this really necessary?

Yes, Jed. This is about me too, remember?

Marcus starts to read from that famous poem—"Do Not Stand at My Grave and Weep." I can hear Jed groan.

"Do not stand at my grave and weep," Marcus begins. "I am not there, I do not sleep."

Jed chuckles. *Oh, no, I am there. And I do sleep.*

I shush him. I don't realize I do it out loud until Gary turns and whispers, "You okay?"

I open my eyes, see Jed is not next to me. I nod at Gary.

I DON'T LISTEN to much of what Marcus says after the poem. It's a short service, a half hour or so. At the end, organ music starts playing—not from an actual organ, but from a recording over speakers. Gary must not have requested a live performance. I'm glad he didn't. I wouldn't want yet another person who didn't know Jed in this room.

Marcus places the urn in my hands. It's heavier than I expect. I remember this about Ed's too. Gary helps me stand and we file out of the chapel, Tessa in our wake, a three-person procession. As we approach the double doors leading outside, I look up and see a woman standing there. She is familiar, but I can't place her. She is wearing a flowy black dress, hoop earrings.

As I come closer, I realize who it is.

"Lindsey?" I say.

Lindsey Benton. Jed's friend—or girlfriend, it was never really clear—from high school.

Gary and Tessa stop when I do. I can tell they are unsure if they should proceed outside or if they should wait, eavesdrop on my conversation with this woman they don't know.

"Hi, Ms. Ketcher," she says.

I always loved Lindsey, secretly hoped she and Jed would get married. They were just kids, of course. I think I was more brokenhearted when they went their separate ways than Jed was.

"I'm sorry to just show up like this," she says.

"Oh, you don't have to apologize. Thank you for coming."

Just as I'm wondering how she found out about the service, she says, "I saw the funeral information online."

The message board, most likely. I should have known.

Gary leans in to me, says, "We'll be outside."

He and Tessa walk out into the sunlight. Just the sliver of it through the doors is blinding. It seems like it should be dark. It seems like it should always be dark now.

"We're just going to lunch, if you'd like to join," I say.

"Oh, that's okay. I don't want to impose. I just . . . I wanted to be here. And I wanted to talk with you."

"Talk with me?"

Her eyes are on the urn. When she looks up, I see they are glassy, wet.

"About Jed," she says.

I was not under the impression that Lindsey and Jed were in touch after high school. He hadn't mentioned her in years. I know she meant a lot to him. I'm sure he thought of her as "the one that got away." But he never said as much.

"I talked to Jed the night he died," she says, the words coming out fast and furious, like they've been restrained too long, like bulls charging against a closed gate.

"Oh," I say.

"I've been wanting to talk to you. To tell you," she says.

The urgency in her tone scares me.

"Okay," I say. "Now?"

She shakes her head. "No. I'm sorry. I shouldn't be bombarding you with this. I just . . . Sorry."

I put my hand on her arm. "It's okay," I tell her.

Of course, I want to know what she has to tell me. I want to know now. I feel self-conscious of my eagerness, afraid I might be foaming at the mouth, salivating like a hungry dog staring down a bone.

"Can I come over tomorrow?" she asks me in a small voice.

It's like she is fifteen years old again: *Can I come by tomorrow, Ms. Ketcher?*

"Sure," I say. "Tomorrow."

I know I will not be able to sleep tonight. Not that I've been sleeping much anyway. But now I won't even try. I will just pace the room, talking to my urns.

"Are you sure you don't want to join us for lunch?" I ask.

She nods. "Yes," she says. "I have to get home. I just had a baby a few weeks ago."

She glances down at her chest, gives a shrug. She's breastfeeding, that's what she's telling me. Lindsey Benton has a child. She probably has the life I always wanted for Jed—something boring and domestic.

"Congratulations," I tell her, though I hate her now, just a little, for having what Jed never will.

She thanks me. We exchange phone numbers. She says she will call me in the morning. Then she is gone, and I do what I must do—I walk toward the doors, push them open, wince at the light.

RICK REED

VICTIM #4

I'M GOING TO MISS the guys when we move. I need to tell them soon—tonight, maybe. Sherry and I met with our Realtor today. We're ready to pull the trigger, put the house on the market. We've owned it outright for twenty years, and the housing market in Boise has gone bananas, so we should make a few hundred grand on the sale. That will be enough for a shack in California. I suppose that's all we need.

Sherry's had this dream of retiring in California for as long as I've known her. I thought it would vanish, like so many dreams do over the years, but it hasn't. I don't really want to move. I've always lived in Boise. But I owe it to her. She's been good to me all these years. When we got my Parkinson's diagnosis, she didn't flinch. She just said, "Okay, what do we need to do?" She knows all about the latest clinical studies, the latest medications. I don't know what I'd do without her.

It makes sense to move now. The kids are both out of state. It still baffles me that they are functioning adults with jobs and spouses. We raised them right, all the while feeling like we had no idea what we were doing. What a relief it would have been to have a Magic 8 Ball during all those years when we lost sleep wondering what mistakes we were making.

Now I lose sleep about different things. The Parkinson's, how much time I have left. Nobody knows for sure. It depends on how fast the disease progresses. Sherry says California will be good for me—winters won't be as cold, summers won't be as hot. She wants to make it a goal to put our feet in the ocean every day. She has visions of eating healthier food, laughing more. We're going to rent a condo in San Clemente. We already have a complex picked out, about a mile from the beach. Then we'll see about buying that shack.

I'M THE FIRST one at Ray's tonight. As I take a seat at what's become Our Table, I get a little choked up thinking about not coming here every Thursday. The guys always give me grief for being the softy. It's nice to be old, to not give a shit what people think. I'm no longer a man who's ashamed of his occasional tears.

Cliff and Randy show up at the same time. They are talking about how Cliff's son just got a big finance job in Manhattan. All of us are dumbfounded by the successes of our children. We've all been spared major problems. The teenage years were challenging—that's when we started these guys' nights—but nothing abnormal. Somehow, everyone has turned out okay. We are in the clear now. We can breathe sighs of relief, drink beers, enjoy the golden years. I'd dare to say this is the happiest time of my life—even with the Parkinson's. I'd say the same for Cliff and Randy. Bob's having a hard time since he lost Marilyn. Sherry and I were set to list the house right before Marilyn died, actually. When that happened, I told her we needed to give it time. Bob would never admit that my moving would be hard for him, but I knew it would, and he'd had enough "hard" for a while. He still doesn't seem quite like himself, but he's better. Maybe he'll never be quite like himself again. Maybe that's just what happens. In a way, I'm comforted by the fact that I'll die before Sherry. If she went first, I'd be lost.

Cliff goes to the bar to buy our first round. We take big first sips—gulps, really. We don't gulp because of hard days anymore; we gulp because we can, because we don't have jobs to go to in the morning.

I see Bob walk in. He's been looking thinner lately, but none of us have mentioned anything yet. We are stereotypical men in this way; we don't talk about things like weight loss because we are uncomfortable delving into the likely emotional reasons for that weight loss. As Sherry said once, "Men are emotionally inept."

Just seeing him makes me nervous to tell the guys about the move. Maybe I'll wait until next week. Even if the house sells in a few days—a realistic proposition in this real estate market—we won't actually move for a month or two, at the earliest.

Bob gives us his usual smile when he sees us. I stand, give him a good clap on the back.

"Well, look what the cat dragged in," I say.

ANGIE

"CALE?" I WHISPER.

I do this every time I visit—attempt to talk to him. I feel like if he hears my voice, his brain will register, "Oh, Angie's here," and he will wake up. I know that's not how it works. I know he's on medications that keep him comatose. And, even if he wasn't, even if his eyes did open right now, it's possible he wouldn't even know who I am. But, still, I whisper his name.

I listen to the rhythmic sound of the ventilator, bringing predictability and order to the chaos of all this.

"Cale, tell me about Tessa," I say.

I try to sound kind, understanding. I don't want him to sense my anger. I don't want him to stay where he is, in this limbo, because of my anger.

I stare at his eyes. They're less swollen, more normal-looking. In the movie version of this, they would flutter open and he would explain everything. There would be an extraordinary explanation—he is a secret CIA agent and Tessa is a Russian spy he was investigating.

But, of course, that's ridiculous. And this isn't a movie.

BEFORE THE SHOOTING, when Sahana and I talked about the problems Cale and I were having, I told her how Cale seemed like a different person. Sahana said, "When did he change?" and I said, "The day Evie was born." Sahana had laughed, but I was being serious. It was exactly that day when something shifted.

I had a long labor. My contractions started at seven o'clock on a Tuesday evening. I wasn't even sure they were contractions. My water didn't break. I just started to feel tightening, cramping every so often. I retrieved a notepad from the junk drawer in the kitchen and wrote down the times the cramps occurred and how long they lasted. When an obvious pattern developed, Aria was the first person I called: "I think I'm in labor."

It was eight days before Evie's due date.

"I can't believe we get to meet her today," I told Cale.

I drank a protein shake and ate toast with peanut butter, then lay in bed. I'd made Cale take prenatal classes with me, and in the classes they said not to go to the hospital until you have to grab onto furniture when a contraction comes. For several hours, I just felt like I had bad menstrual cramps. I couldn't sleep, even though I knew I should. I was too excited. Cale slept, deeply enough that he snored.

The next morning, I was in more pain. The contractions were a few minutes apart, each one about a minute long. In our classes, we learned all kinds of techniques for Cale to use to help alleviate my pain. Several involved me on all fours, him standing over me, holding a blanket around my belly, pulling up. We didn't use any of the techniques though. Cale just stared at me, dumbstruck. At nine o'clock, I told him we should just go to the hospital.

When we got to Saint Al's, I was only one centimeter dilated. The nurse was a bitch. She didn't believe I'd been having contractions for fourteen hours. She said I should go home, take a bath, that the baby probably wasn't going to come for a week or so. A week! I told the nurse there was no way in hell I was going back home.

I walked through the hospital parking lot, a spectacle, I'm sure. Cale seemed more concerned about people staring than he was about my pain. This only bothered me in retrospect; in the moment, I wasn't thinking about him at all. I was thinking only of what was happening to my body.

A few hours later, I was five centimeters dilated and they admitted me. I'd loosely committed to a "natural birth" (no epidural, no pain medications), but any woman who says she "loosely commits" to such a thing will surely ask for drugs. Cale stood in the corner of the room, as if he were afraid to touch me, as if I were a wild animal. I guess I was, in a way.

By the time I was eight centimeters dilated, I was begging for an epidural. My contractions were coupling—coming in twos, no break or rest in between. When the anesthesiologist came and stuck the needle in my back, I didn't feel a thing. Whatever pain was caused by that sharp instrument in my spine was nothing compared to the contractions.

Once I was sufficiently numbed, I opened my eyes for the first time since I'd been admitted. I didn't even realize they'd been squeezed shut until the nurse said, "I can actually see you now. What pretty eyes." I laughed. That's the joy of an epidural—while your body endures a horrendous pain, you feel nothing, you *laugh*. I wondered why I'd waited for it, why I'd attempted this "natural birth" to begin with.

"Cale, I'm starving," I said to him.

They don't let you eat while you're in labor. They don't want you to have anything in your system in case they have to rush you in for an emergency C-section.

"When I have this baby, I'm going to need you to get me a breakfast burrito from Goldy's," I told him.

The nurse said, "That's the easiest push present I've ever heard of."

I'd told Cale about push presents—gifts husbands get their wives for going through labor. I'd made fun of them, made a show of rolling my eyes when telling him about the friends I had who had requested them. But, secretly, I hoped he would get me something—a necklace, flowers, something to show he was proud of me, grateful for my effort in bringing our child into the world.

Evie was born just after ten o'clock—twenty-seven hours after my first contraction. I cried when they put her in my arms. Cale stood next to the bed. I don't remember him kissing my cheek or gazing at the baby. He was just standing there, looking lost, as if he'd wandered into some other woman's delivery room. After Evie was cleaned and warmed and swaddled, they placed her in Cale's arms and his shoulders went straight to his ears. He looked so uncomfortable, so hesitant. I remembered something the teacher in our prenatal classes had said—"Most men have never held a baby until they have their own."

I told Cale to go home, get some rest. I applauded myself for being such a nice wife, still attentive to his needs, unlike all those other wives who forgot their husbands existed the moment they had a child. The next morning, they brought me breakfast from the cafeteria: dry eggs, rubbery pancakes, syrupy fruit from a can, a juice box. I left my tray untouched, waiting for Cale, for my burrito.

He came just after nine, bags under his eyes, like he hadn't slept at all, even though I'd sent him home so he could do just that. It was like I'd given him a gift and he'd thrown it out the window. Again, it was only in retrospect that I was annoyed. At the time, I was too enamored with our daughter, all six-and-a-half pounds of her.

It took me a moment to notice that he had nothing with him. His car keys and wallet were in his pockets, as usual. There was no takeout bag, no burrito. It's a small thing. Maybe the birth of his daughter had been so momentous that he'd forgotten about the stupid burrito. Maybe it was silly of me to remember such a thing. But, I don't know, there was something foreshadowing about that burrito. The burrito was the beginning of him distancing himself, pushing away from our life as a family. The burrito was the beginning of something that culminated with him going to a bar in the middle of the night in pursuit of a girl.

TESSA

RYAN AND I SIT on the couch, watching one of those survival shows where the contestants are naked and left in some remote location without food or water. He is deeply involved in the episode, and I pretend to be as long as I can, then reach for my phone on the coffee table.

There are several new posts since I last checked the message board. I scroll back to the beginning of the new-to-me posts.

Boyseeeee:

Latest intel says Ketcher's funeral is gonna be in Caldwell tomorrow. Parsons Funeral Home.

That was posted on Wednesday night. So this is how people found out about the service. I wish I'd checked the message board before the funeral. Maybe I could have arrived early, tried to talk sense into the angry people, spared Joyce the pain of seeing them there.

JJ1356:

At least they were smart enough not to do it in Boise. Anyone going?

Mags4Ever:

I'll be there. Five people had to die terrible deaths at the hands of this man. Doesn't feel right for him to have a peaceful send-off.

JJ1356:

Srsly. Why even do a service? Just asking for trouble.

I can't help but type a response.

TessWasHere:

**He's still someone's kid. I mean, what he did was awful.
But his mother should be able to say goodbye.**

Mags4Ever:

Why tho? None of us who lost loved ones got to say goodbye.

JJ1356:

@TessWasHere, u actually defending this asshole?

TessWasHere:

**Not defending. Just saying his mother knew him for 28 years.
I doubt he was all bad for all those years.**

Mags4Ever:

**Wow. U crazy. I bet u would feel different if he'd killed someone
u loved.**

JJ1356:

**Ya. I didn't even know the victims and I think u crazy, @
TessWasHere. His mother raised a killer. She's basically a killer
in my mind.**

LvAll21:

Anyone read that book by Dylan Klebold's mom?

JJ1356:

The Columbine kid?

LvAll21:

Ya, his mom wrote a book.

JJ1356:

Is it titled "I Raised a Killer"?

Mags4Ever:

Lol. Should be.

"Whatcha doing?" Ryan asks.

He's fast-forwarding through the commercials—the benefits of DVR recordings.

"Nothing," I say. "Instagram."

"You are always on that phone," he says.

He resumes the show. The female contestant has banana leaves over her boobs. I make a comment about the woman's fashion sense. Ryan laughs. I've done it again—convinced him I'm fine, we're fine, everything is going back to normal.

I can't stop thinking about Jed though. Those photos, the ones Joyce had at the service, I can't stop seeing them. It's hard for me to imagine that the man firing shots while I hid in that storage closet was once a boy with his two front teeth missing, blowing out candles on a birthday cake. That was my favorite photo—the one of him with the cake. He looked so happy. He looked like a person who would never *not* be happy.

After the service, Joyce invited me to lunch with her and Gary. I declined, didn't feel like it was my place. But I didn't want her to think I declined because I'd figured out who Jed was, so I sent her a text message later:

I can see how much you loved your son. I will be thinking of you.

She hasn't responded yet. Maybe she is embarrassed that I know. I want her to know it doesn't change anything. I want her to be comfortable enough with me to tell me what he was like. I still feel this intense need to understand—why he shot those people, why I survived.

"Tess? You hear me?" Ryan says.

I hear him now, but it's clear I've completely missed another question.

"What? Yeah?" I say.

"You want to try that new Thai place this weekend?"

"Oh, sure," I say.

It's the end of the episode, when they reveal how much weight each contestant lost. We always like to guess; winner gets a back massage.

Ryan pauses it before they reveal and says, "Eighteen pounds for the woman, thirty-three for the man. So, total of fifty-one."

"Good guess," I say, playing along. "I'll say fifteen for the woman, twenty-eight for the man."

"So, total of forty-three."

He hits play, and the announcer says that the woman lost seventeen pounds and the man lost twenty-five—a total of forty-two.

"I win," I say, trying to look happy, though I couldn't care less. Ryan makes a show of his disappointment.

"I guess massaging you isn't the worst thing," he says with a smirk.

He is going to want to have sex later. I am going to have to deny him, again.

"You want any ice cream?" he asks as he gets up and heads toward the kitchen.

I shake my head. "No, thanks."

He stops. "You okay, Tess?"

I give him a smile that doesn't show teeth. "Uh huh."

He doesn't seem to believe me, but he goes to the kitchen anyway. While he's gone, my phone buzzes with a text message.

Thank you for the message, Tessa. And thank you for coming today. It means so much to me.

My heart bangs in my chest, as if I'm a teenager who's just received a text from her longtime crush.

I am so glad I was there. Let me know if you want to meet for coffee again soon.

I start biting at my thumbnail nervously, awaiting her reply.

How about this weekend?

I can't help but write back, too quickly, too eagerly.

Yes! Tell me when and where.

Ryan returns with a bowl of chocolate chip. I resent that I have to look up at him, interact with him, when I really want to text Joyce. It occurs to me, in this moment, that maybe Ryan and I can't survive this. Maybe we can't be together. Maybe he will go to law school five hours upstate and I will stay here, and we will pretend that works for a while until we both get tired. *It's not you, it's me.* That's what I would say, because it's the truth, but those words have been so overused that they would do nothing but aggravate him.

"You sure you're okay?" Ryan says, sitting next to me.

He offers me a spoonful of ice cream, and I eat it.

I nod.

"You sure *we're* okay?" he asks.

"Yeah," I say.

As I say it, I know it's a lie. And the knowledge of that lie makes my throat tighten and my eyes well up.

"Hey," he says, setting his bowl on the coffee table.

He pulls me into him. He's a good guy. It really isn't him; it really is me. It's not his fault that I was alone in that storage closet, that he wasn't there. It's not his fault that he can't possibly understand.

My phone buzzes again, and I pull away from Ryan.

It's Joyce, suggesting we meet at the same coffee shop on Saturday at 10:00 a.m.

Ryan eyes me as I text back to say I'll be there.

"Who you texting?" he asks.

He seems suspicious. Maybe he thinks it's another guy. That would be an easier story to tell his friends—*Oh, she was cheating on me*. The reality will be harder to explain.

"A friend of mine," I say.

He nods, doesn't ask which friend. And as he sits back into the couch, slumping against the back cushion, there is a look of defeat on his face that says he knows what I know—we are at the beginning of our end.

JOYCE

I WAKE UP TO the two urns on my nightstand, seemingly staring at me. Jed's is a graphite gray color; Ed's is navy blue. Jed's is slightly smaller than Ed's, which seems fitting—father and son. I think of the stick figure family decals people put on the back windows of their cars—the father figure the tallest, then the mother, then the children. When Ed and I got married, we thought we would have two children. I always pictured a son and daughter, a little bit of the American dream, a real-life Norman Rockwell painting. Jed wasn't an easy baby though. I thought, *We can try for another one when he's a little older*. But then he wasn't an easy toddler either. When he was five, we decided the time was right (or as right as it would ever be). A few months passed with no luck. Then Ed was diagnosed with cancer.

"You awake?"

This voice startles me. I turn over, face him.

"You forgot I was here, didn't you?" he says.

I did, in fact. I'd expected to be up all night, wondering what Lindsey Benton has to tell me, but I slept hard—because of the wine at our post-funeral lunch, or the vodka after lunch, or the emotional exhaustion of saying goodbye to Jed.

Gary sits up against the headboard. He is naked, except for his boxer shorts. I stare at the curls of gray chest hair. There are patches of it in locations other than his chest—the back of his upper arms, the middle of his lower back. It's as if the hairs were originally planted on his chest, but some seedlings migrated to other locations and grew unexpectedly.

I certainly didn't plan on him being here—in my house, in my bed. I pull the sheets up to my chin, embarrassed, which is silly. He's already seen my body—last night and so many nights before.

He gets out of bed, walks to the bathroom. I stare at the back of him, the way his boxer shorts gather between his legs, the thickness of his tree-trunk thighs. He turns on the shower. He doesn't ask, "Can I take a shower?" He's comfortable enough with what's happened to assume his right to my shower.

If I lean forward slightly in bed, I can see into the bathroom. The shower glass is lime-stained, but I can see the shape of him, the roundness of his gut. He leans back, lets the water hit his face, his eyes closed. I take this opportunity to get out of bed and go to my closet, my arms wrapped across my naked body. I'm not even wearing underwear. This is so unlike me.

After the service, we drove back to Boise for lunch. Gary had found a number of lunch options in Caldwell, but I didn't want to have lunch in Caldwell. Now that I have the urn, now that Jed is with me, I'd be happy to never visit Caldwell again.

We went to a little café on Eighth Street. We sat outside. It's been a warmer-than-usual April. Normally, it's too cold to sit outside at cafés until May, sometimes June. I couldn't help but think of Jed's rants about global warming.

We ordered our food at the counter inside, then took our number to a table out front. A server brought out our glasses of wine.

"Thank you for organizing everything," I said to Gary.

He took a sip of his wine. "I was happy to help."

"I'm sorry about the other day," I told him.

"No need to apologize," he said, though I could tell by the way he sat back in his chair that he was satisfied by this apology, that he needed it.

"It's just been so emotional for me," I said.

"Of course."

The server came with our food. Gary had ordered a pasta dish. I don't know how he could stomach something so heavy. Men are strange that way—never really losing their appetites. I ordered a spinach salad. It came with a baguette. I started with that, nibbling at it like a rabbit with a carrot.

"Anything else I can get you?" the girl asked. She was so young and so chipper. She irritated me. It's not her fault; she didn't know where we'd come from. She thought we were two old people lucky enough to be retired and enjoying a weekday lunch in the sun.

"We're fine, thank you," Gary told her.

After she left, we each took bites of our food. Then I said what I'd been wanting to say, that "clearing the air" thing.

"I know you never liked Jed."

Gary wiped his mouth with the napkin from his lap, took time doing so, as if thinking about what to say.

"I didn't know Jed like you did," he said.

"But you can admit you didn't like him."

He took in a breath so big that his nostrils flared to accommodate it.

"I didn't like the hold he had on you."

"The *hold*?" I asked. "He was my son."

He nodded. "I know. I'm not trying to upset you. I just wished he was more independent, less depressed. I wished the same things as you."

I set my fork on the edge of my plate. "You thought he was depressed?"

He looked at me with pity that made me feel ashamed.

"He was depressed," he said. There was so much certainty to

the statement. I felt my cheeks get red.

"I guess I didn't know it was that bad."

I stared at my mostly untouched salad, picked up my fork, pushed around spinach leaves.

"None of this is your fault," he said,

He's wrong though. Some of this *is* my fault. What I didn't notice, what I refused to realize, *is* my fault. I'm no longer interested in perpetuating lies to myself.

I decided to change the subject. "What do you think Lindsey is going to tell me?"

I asked this knowing full well that Gary would have no idea. It reminded me of being a teenager, asking my girlfriends when they thought my crush would call me. I just liked hearing their guesses. I liked entertaining the notion that one of them had psychic abilities.

"I have no idea," Gary said, not playing along.

"It's just weird—her talking to him the day it happened."

I was trying to incite a conversation, trying to get Gary to guess, to participate in corralling the thoughts in my head.

"You'll find out tomorrow," he said.

That's Gary—straightforward, logical. That's most men, I've learned.

The too-bubbly server asked us if we wanted a second glass of wine when our firsts were three-quarters empty. Gary said yes before I could even consider. I don't know if it's because he was stressed by the day's events or if he just assumed I was.

After our second glass, I felt light, airy. I hadn't been drunk in a good while, and that's what I was—drunk. There was no hiding it. Gary wasn't drunk—he has at least eighty pounds on me—but he was as close to drunk as I'd ever seen him. He laughed more easily. He touched me in small ways—his hand on my back when crossing the street, that kind of thing. We walked around downtown like a couple of bored teenagers in the middle of summer, sampling caramels at the chocolate shop, browsing the trinkets and greeting cards at The Record Exchange. I felt young and silly and smitten. I wondered why I hadn't been drinking too much wine every day since Jed died, or every day of my life, for that matter.

It was just before three o'clock when Gary said, "How about I drive you home?"

When you're old, a couple glasses of wine is exhilarating for about an hour, then you are overcome by the need—the absolute requirement—for a nap.

"We can have a nightcap there," I said.

"It's the middle of the afternoon."

"A daycap then."

WHEN WE GOT to my house, I pulled out a step stool from the bottom of the coat closet and used it to reach the cabinet above the fridge. That's where I've always kept the liquor. Some of the bottles must be twenty years old. I've never been much of a liquor drinker; wine is just fine by me, or a light beer on a summer day. Ed liked a glass of scotch a few times a week. There are a few bottles of that, along with bottles of other things—vodka, tequila, white rum, triple sec, sweet vermouth—remnants of attempts to be the type of person who throws sophisticated parties. I've never hosted a party at this house—not an adult one, at least. When Jed was young, we had a few of his birthday parties here. His birthday was right before Halloween, usually too cold for any outdoor venues.

"How about vodka?" I suggested.

Gary shrugged a "why the hell not?" type of shrug.

I grabbed the bottle by the neck and stepped down.

"I don't have fancy cocktail glasses," I said.

"And I don't have fancy taste."

The late afternoon was turning to evening. It was chilly outside, but we decided to sit out there anyway, at my rusted bistro table and chairs. I bought them at Walmart, couldn't expect them to last.

We drank the vodka out of ridiculously small juice glasses with oranges painted on them. I'd used them when Jed was a kid, when I wanted to limit the amount of juice he drank because I was cautious about sugar. I was that type of parent—cautious. Or I thought I was. Maybe I was focused on the wrong things. Maybe while I was worried about sugar, my son was becoming a monster.

I scooted my chair close to Gary's. After just a few sips of vodka, I reached over, put my hand on his thigh. He raised one eyebrow at me—a curious eyebrow, not a scolding one.

"I've missed you," I said.

I don't know if that's true or not. I think it's more true that I've missed having someone around, another body in the house, another heart beating.

"I've always said you're something special," he said.

He placed his hand over mine, like playing paper to my rock.

"Do you think we could try again?" I felt silly asking this, even with the confidence lent to me by the alcohol.

"Is that what you want?"

I let my hand wander to his belt. I fiddled with the buckle.

"You look nice in a suit," I said, completely ignoring his question.

"I can't wait to get it off, actually."

I raised an eyebrow at him.

WE DIDN'T FINISH the bottle, but we came close; it had been only a quarter full to start. When I stood, I felt like I was

187

standing on a Tilt-A-Whirl at the county fair. I laughed at the absurdity of my inability to walk a straight line.

We went directly to the bedroom, didn't even bother pretending we had another destination in mind. Jed would have thought this was gross, two old people wanting each other with sloppy urgency. It was sloppy—the way I yanked on his belt and nearly fell on my rear end, the way he stumbled while unzipping my black dress. When we were naked, I closed my eyes, but then quickly opened them because my head was spinning. We didn't have sex. Well, we did, technically. But neither of us finished, so it hardly counts. We'd had too much to drink to do anything properly but sleep. I didn't care. I liked just being with him, our warm bodies pressed against each other. I liked the feel of his stubble—already there, even though he was fresh-shaven in the morning. I liked the salty taste of his sweat when I kissed his chest. I liked the reminder of being alive. Jed is dead, and I am alive.

I PUT ON a pair of flannel pajama pants and a T-shirt. When Gary comes out of the shower, he says, "I feel like a new man."

"The shower helped?"

He is naked, just standing there, unashamed. Men have the luxury of this.

"I still need about five Advil, but I feel better."

He grabs a towel off the hook, dries himself off.

"I have Advil," I tell him, "in the medicine cabinet."

I go to it, hand him the bottle.

"You first," he says.

I shake two from the bottle, tilt my head under the sink faucet, fill my mouth with water, swallow. Then he does the same.

"So . . . " I say. I want to ask all the usual female questions:

Does he feel strange about last night? Does he regret it? What does it mean?

He goes to the bed, the towel now wrapped around his lower half. He doesn't have any clothes here, besides the suit he wore yesterday. There's no way Jed's clothes would fit him.

He picks up his suit pants and shirt, sitting in a pile on the floor next to the bed. He puts them on, grumbling as he does so.

"Two days in a row wearing a suit—this is unprecedented."

"I'm sure you want to get home, but do you want some breakfast?"

I tell myself if he says no, that means he regrets what happened and just wants to forget about it. If he says yes, that means there may be something between us still. It would make me happy to be with him, I think. I don't know if I'm saying that because it's dreadful being alone at a time like this or if I genuinely love Gary. Does anyone really know their intentions? It seems like we recognize them only in hindsight.

I make us plates of eggs and toast and bacon. I'm hungry for the first time since Jed died. I feel angry at my body, in a way, angry that it's returning to its usual priorities so soon.

I eat slowly, though I could finish my food in under a minute if I really wanted to; I'm that famished. It's the alcohol probably. That much liquor requires food, proper sustenance. Gary has no problem eating quickly—another luxury for men.

"So . . . " I say, attempting to resurrect a discussion of us, our relationship, where we stand.

Gary tops his last piece of toast with his last bit of eggs, shoves the mini sandwich into his mouth.

"So?" he says.

"About last night."

"Oh," he says. "Right."

"We both drank too much."

"This is a fact," he says.

He wipes his mouth with a square of paper towel.

"I don't know if you're happy about what happened or . . ."

"I'm not *un*happy about it," he says, straight-faced, betraying nothing.

I nod. "Okay, then."

"I wouldn't mind if it happened again," he says. "Minus the vodka. I think that did me in."

I smile. "We should stick to wine."

Right then, my phone buzzes with a text message. It's Lindsey Benton.

Hi, Ms. Ketcher. Still okay if I come by today? Maybe around 11? I'll have the baby with me. Hope that's alright.

I write back:

Sure, of course. You still know the house?

She writes:

Of course. See you soon.

I set the phone down.

"Lindsey," I say to Gary.

"You nervous?"

"I am. Not sure if I should be."

"You want me to stay?" he asks.

This question is how I know we are back together, even if we are not saying it that way quite yet.

"No, you go home. Change clothes. Take a nap. I'll call you later."

"You sure?"

"I'm sure."

He stands, takes his plate to the sink, rinses it. He dries his hands, then folds the dish towel, places it back on the counter. I've always told him his wife, Sandy, trained him well.

"Until later," he says.

Then he kisses me—quickly and softly, as if it's nothing special, as if it's something we do all the time. And that, strangely, makes me feel more loved than any passionate, cinematic kiss ever could.

DAN VELASQUEZ

VICTIM #5

IF YOU WOULD HAVE asked me five years ago if I'd ever be a bartender, I would have said, "No freaking way." I had bigger dreams than that. I still do. I'm in grad school for civil engineering. This bartending thing is just a little detour. I need the extra money. I have scholarship money for school, and my internship pays enough for me to rent a room near campus, but that's not going to cut it for long.

When Kenzie told me she was pregnant, I was like, "Holy shit." We've been together since undergrad and we love each other, but still. This wasn't planned, obviously. I don't know how it happened. She's been on the pill for years. My guy friends say, "Are you sure about that?" But Kenz isn't like that. She's in grad school too, getting her master's in social work. It's not like she wants a baby. Not right now, at least.

We talked about going to Planned Parenthood, making an appointment to discuss our "options." But the more we thought about it, it just didn't seem right to get rid of the baby. We'll be done with school in a year. We'll both be ready to get jobs—*real* jobs. I've always said I want to marry Kenzie. Things are just happening faster than we thought.

First order of business: get an apartment together. She's renting a room in a house with some girls in her social work program; I'm renting a room in a house with some guys. That's not going to work with a baby in the picture. Kenz's family has been supporting her financially while she goes to school, but they've made it clear they won't support her if we move in together. They're super conservative, religious. They hate that my last name is Velasquez. She hasn't even told them about the pregnancy. We both know that won't be a good conversation.

I told Kenz not to worry. I'll save up money for us to get an apartment. I'll just have to bust my ass for a while. I saw that Ray's was hiring a part-time bartender and figured the tips would be good. Plus, the shifts work with my school schedule. Kenz doesn't love the idea of me bartending, but we both know it's temporary.

"HEY, DAN," TESSA says, tossing her purse on the shelf underneath the cash register.

Tessa is the bartender who's training me. She's nice enough. She looks like a teenager, but she must be older if she's serving alcohol.

"Getting busy already, huh?" she says, surveying the bar.

I've been working here only a week, so I don't know what "busy" is. There's a table of girls celebrating someone's twenty-first birthday, and their volume level is making it feel busy. Other than them, there are some old guys in the back. Tessa says they're regulars. I need to make a point of getting to know the regulars, greeting them by name. That's the way to get good tips.

Kenz said she might come by tonight. I hope she doesn't get weird when she meets Tessa. Kenz has a little bit of a jealous streak, and Tessa isn't exactly *un*attractive.

My phone buzzes in my pocket. Tessa doesn't seem to care if I'm on my phone at work. "As long as everyone's drinks get served," she said on my first day.

It's a text from Kenz.

Hey babe, don't think I can come by tonight. Sorry!!! I feel like 😷 **.**

I get this emoji from her a lot. She's been having bad morning sickness. The doctor said it's normal. Supposedly, it'll get better in a few weeks or so.

I text back to her:

No worries, babe. Be home late. Don't wait up. U need ur sleep.

I start to get tired around eleven o'clock. That's when I'm usually in bed.

"You awake over there?" Tessa asks from her end of the bar. I'm mid-yawn. Just as I'm about to explain that I was up late studying the night before, a guy comes in and sits in front of her at the bar. I've seen him before. One of the regulars. I make a mental note to get his name.

Tessa gets the guy a beer. He seems stressed out, like he had a hell of a day.

My phone buzzes. It's Kenz again.

Going to bed. Love u 😚

I'm about to text her back when a guy comes into the bar and I get goose bumps on my arms. Something is not right with this guy.

I look back at my phone screen, at the kissy-face emoji. Somehow, I feel like I need to respond.

Kenz, I love u so much.

Out of the corner of my eye, I see Tessa run past me.
I press send.

ANGIE

I'M SITTING AT MY desk at work, just sitting, staring at the computer screen. I don't have any files or web pages open. I'm just staring at the desktop, the Madison & Brightly logo. I'm always somewhat catatonic after visiting Cale at the hospital. It's a weird transition—like going from purgatory back to heaven. Or maybe this is hell.

There's a knock at my door.

"Come in," I say.

It's one of the account guys, Brandon. Last year, Madison & Brightly was hired by a local brewery who had a very limited budget, and Brandon, Julia (a twenty-something art director), and I were the bare-bones team put on the account. We created a few ads for them to run in local media, and then they cut us loose, said they couldn't afford our services long-term. It was fun while it lasted.

Brandon became a parent around the same time I did; his son, Logan, is just a couple weeks older than Evie. We went through the same things at the same times, all those milestones that seem mysterious even though thousands have done them before—night weaning, sleep training, teething, transitioning to solids. That creates a bond. Many of my coworkers are parents, but I've found that if you aren't going through the same phases at the same time, the connection doesn't happen. Kids change so quickly. What was important a month ago is no longer important. A coworker with a five-year-old doesn't remember the infant stage—protective amnesia, I say. A few weeks ago, a coworker with a five-month-old asked me how often Evie napped at that age, and I couldn't remember to save my life.

One night, a particularly late one at the office, I asked Brandon, "Has it been hard for you—the adjustment to fatherhood?"

This was after I'd started noticing Cale's moods.

Brandon seemed to consider the question. He set down his plate; we were eating pizza, the agency's contribution to the late night.

"I guess it's hard being tired all the time," he said. "And it's hard not to be able to go out and do the same things I used to. I have to think of someone else now. I guess that happened when getting married too, but my wife is an adult who can take care of herself. Logan is a baby."

I nodded, thinking this all made sense to me, thinking maybe Cale wasn't that strange after all.

His face lit up with a smile and he continued.

"But, I don't know. I fucking love Logan. I want to be around him all the time. I just think he's the coolest human."

This did not sound like Cale.

Brandon is young, early thirties. I would imagine fatherhood would be an even bigger jolt to the system at a younger age. Then again, maybe it's harder when you're older and set in your ways.

"HEY," BRANDON SAYS. He closes the door behind him, sits in the chair on the other side of my desk. "I've been meaning to stop by. Figured you were being bombarded."

"Yeah, a bit. It's good to see you though."

"How's Cale doing?"

I've never told Brandon that Cale was having a hard time with fatherhood. Maybe he assumed because of the questions I asked, but he never pressed me on it. Men don't care about gossip in the way women do.

"He's stable," I say. I've said these words so many times that they start to feel funny in my mouth. *Sta-ble*. What does it even mean?

He looks at me, wanting more. Everyone wants more.

"It's a waiting game right now," I say. I don't want to explain the sedation medications, the waking up process, all the things they don't know. It's too much.

He nods solemnly. "I just can't believe you're dealing with this."

"I can't either."

"I have some beer in my mini fridge, leftover from the Blacks Creek account," he says.

That was the name of the brewery—Blacks Creek.

"I might take you up on that."

He palms a stress ball on my desk. There are so many tchotchkes in the advertising world.

"How's Evie?" he asks.

Brandon, Jen (his wife), and Logan came to Evie's first birthday party. We just did a small shindig at the house, had balloons and a smash cake and all the usual things.

"She's fine. She doesn't know anything. I mean, they don't understand much at this age, do they?"

They. Logan and Evie. We'd joked about them dating one day. He probably wouldn't want Logan to date Evie now. Evie may be forever "troubled" because of this traumatic experience.

Brandon shrugs. "Jen had the flu a couple months ago. Logan seemed to understand when I told him mom was too sick to play with him."

He is comparing his wife's flu to my husband's coma.

"Sorry," he says, as if realizing the absurdity of such a comparison. "I know it's not the same."

"No, it's okay. It's probably best if I minimize it for Evie anyway. I guess I was waiting to see what would happen—if he'd wake up or . . ."

"Right, yeah, of course," he says. He shakes his head. "Tough situation."

"To put it lightly."

He sets the stress ball on my desk and presses his palms into the armrests of the chair, helping himself stand. Brandon is more evolved than most men (no other male coworkers have come by to express their condolences or best wishes or whatever you do for the spouse of a comatose person). But, still, this is too much for him. It's too much for me, frankly.

"I've gotta hop on a client call," he says, glancing at his phone, checking the time. "But let me know if you need anything, okay?"

"Thanks, Brandon."

People keep saying that—*Let me know if you need anything*. They must know that this just puts the burden on me. What am I going to do—say, "Actually, I'm really backed up on laundry"? Raquel did set up a meal train. It seems like whenever I go to a meeting, I come back to something on my desk—a casserole, a pan of corn bread, a plate of brownies. I suspect they are checking my work calendar, seeing when I won't be in my office, and leaving their offerings then. They don't want to talk to me. I'm not angry about it; I understand. I wouldn't want to talk to me either.

WHEN WE BROUGHT newborn Evie home from the hospital, I stuck to my plan of sleeping in a separate room with her while Cale slept in our room alone. That first night, when she started crying hysterically, he stumbled into what we started calling "my room" with this look on his face like *What did you do wrong?* He seemed startled and irritated and exhausted. I bounced Evie in my arms, trying to understand why her bright-red face was scrunched up in such agony.

"Did you feed her?" Cale asked me. He glanced at my breasts, these things now known to him as feeding devices.

"Of course I fed her," I snapped.

He couldn't handle the crying. He took her from my arms—a bit too brusquely—and started bouncing her, his eyes big and wild, as if we were in the middle of a crisis. Maybe we were. Maybe all those early days qualify as a crisis.

When she stopped crying after a couple minutes of his frantic bouncing, he looked at me, said, "See? No need to freak out."

"I wasn't freaking out," I said. *You were*, I didn't say.

He handed her back to me, and I placed her in the bassinet attached to the side of the bed, "my bed."

"Go get your beauty sleep," I said, not kindly.

He didn't even bother to respond.

IN THE BEGINNING, I rationalized doing everything for Evie because I was on maternity leave. Cale had to go back to work after two weeks. In those two weeks he was home, he spent most of his time tending to the house—doing laundry, cleaning, organizing. Any time I set down an empty mug of the strange-tasting tea that was supposed to increase my milk supply, he was right there to take it to the sink. When I told Sahana about this, she said I was lucky. But there was something unsettling about his manic efforts. It was like he was going out of his way to do everything ancillary to Evie's care because he didn't want to participate in that care. He seemed uncomfortable with her. "Maybe he doesn't feel confident," Sahana hypothesized. "Maybe he sees you have it handled."

And I did have it handled. Even while I sat in a sitz bath of warm water with Epsom salt, trying to heal wounds that no woman had warned me about, I had Evie resting on a pillow at my feet. She was always with me. When I was pregnant, fantasizing about the early days of parenthood, I had visions of Cale saying, "Why don't you nap while I watch the baby?" I'd heard other mom-friends gush about their husbands doing this. They praised them on social media, claimed things like "Husband of the year" and "Best father ever." Cale never offered me a reprieve though. Maybe I should have asked. Maybe I should have just given Evie to him more, without even asking. Maybe that would have helped his confidence. Maybe my taking control made him feel like I didn't trust him with her. Maybe I didn't.

I went alone to the first pediatrician appointment, carrying Evie in her car seat, the weight of it making me walk lopsided while I struggled up the stairs. My hair was greasy. I had a huge pad between my legs. I was wearing the same stretchy skirt I'd worn home from the hospital. I'm sure I smelled. The doctor's office gave me a form to fill out. It asked questions like "Have you had thoughts of harming yourself?" I wondered if everyone got these forms or if I was selected because of my appearance. Fathers do not get these forms. There is no attention paid to fathers in the beginning. They are considered irrelevant. "She just wants you," Cale said more than once, holding out a screaming Evie to me. "You have the boobs," he said. He stated it as a fact, but maybe there was resentment.

When Cale went back to work, it was almost a relief. His presence in the house had felt strange, like he was in the way, lurking. With him gone, Evie and I settled into a routine with each other. I loved the routine so much that I didn't care when Cale said he had to work late. Sahana kept checking in with me, making sure I didn't succumb to any depression. She thought I would, especially when the initial euphoria of birthing a human faded. I was happier than I'd ever been though, infused with a purpose like I'd never been before. Aria got me a mug that said Goal for today: Keep the tiny human alive. That was exactly right—that was my goal. It was all so crystal clear.

As I felt happier than ever, Cale seemed more withdrawn. Maybe I never felt any baby blues because I could sense Cale was feeling them for the both of us. There is a certain equilibrium to relationships—only one person can be depressed at a time.

Aria offered to babysit one night so Cale and I could have a date night. I'd always rolled my eyes at couples posting their "date nights" on Instagram, pitied their need to schedule specific times for togetherness. Now I understood.

"You guys have fun, okay?" she said, holding Evie over her shoulder, smiling and assuring us that all would be fine. Evie was just six weeks old. It was my first time spending more than five minutes apart from her.

"We will," I said, though I wasn't looking forward to the outing. It was just something I knew needed to be done, for Cale, for our marriage.

We went to dinner at the Bardenay, one of our favorite restaurants. Cale was mostly silent. It wasn't a peaceful kind of silence; it was what I'd come to call an aggressive silence, a silence of anger, frustration, exhaustion, something.

"What's wrong?" I asked.

I had yet to learn that this question just made everything worse. I meant for it to communicate concern, affection, but he seemed to consider it an attack.

"Nothing," he snapped.

We were sitting outside. It was ninety-something degrees.

"Do you want to move inside?"

I thought he might be hot.

"No," he said. "It's fine."

"You seem off," I said, pushing.

"Babe," he said, "I'm just tired."

This was his usual refrain. I resented it because I knew it wasn't the whole truth—something else was clearly bothering him—and because even if he was tired, he couldn't have been more tired than me. I should have been the one who was allowed to claim fatigue. I was getting up with Evie every two to three hours at night, a sacrifice for which he seemed to show zero appreciation.

I took a picture of our beer glasses, posted it to Instagram with the caption, "Parents' first night out." I tried to let myself be comforted by other people thinking Cale and I were happy. In reality, though, by the time our check came, I hated him. I'd spent the entirety of our silent outing resenting the money spent, resenting the time away from Evie, resenting his inconsideration of my needs. I believed it then and still believe it now—men should bow at the feet of the women who bear them children. They should worship them.

When we got home, Cale went straight to bed. Aria gave me a look that asked if everything was okay. I motioned for her to follow me outside, to the front yard. I didn't want to talk inside, in case Cale could hear us.

It was after nine o'clock, but the sun was still up. During Boise summers, it doesn't set until nine thirty or so.

"Does Cale seem off to you?" I asked Aria.

She looked up at the sky, then back at me. "Yeah," she said.

"Kinda."

"Like, how?"

She shrugged. "Just . . . distant. Or something."

"Right?"

I was so grateful for the validation.

"I figured it was just a funk."

"Maybe it is that. I don't know."

"Have you tried talking to him?"

I couldn't help but smile at her. "Yes, dear Aria, I've tried talking to him."

"Well, I don't know. Some couples don't talk."

"I didn't say we talked. I said I've *tried* talking to him."

She nodded once to convey her understanding.

"It'll pass," she said.

"You think?"

"Yeah, give it until the new year. This beginning time is hard."

She spoke as if she'd had a baby herself, as if she'd had a relationship with a man that lasted longer than a few months.

"Okay," I said, deciding to make this suggestion a rule. "Until the new year."

So much can change in so little time. That's what I remember thinking. And it's true—so much *can* change in so little time. The problem is, nothing did.

TESSA

THE SECOND TIME CALE Matthews came to Ray's, it was earlier than the first time—before midnight—and he sat in the same exact seat at the bar. I recognized him. I'm not usually good with faces, but I remembered his. I remembered him looking at me in the parking lot after closing.

"I'm back," he said.

I gave him a small smile. The parking lot incident hadn't really freaked me out or anything. I hadn't thought to analyze it at all until Angie Matthews said Cale had a "thing" for me.

"You're back," I said to him. "What can I get you?"

I set a cocktail napkin in front of him and waited for his order.

"That IPA you got me last time was good," he said.

"The White Dog Hazy?"

"That's the one."

I got him a pint.

It wasn't busy that night. I can't remember what day of the week it was—a Tuesday, probably. Tuesdays and Wednesdays were our slow nights, and I didn't work on Wednesdays. Of all the times he came in—a total of six or seven—this was the quietest night, the night that allowed for the most conversation. I wasn't opposed to conversation. On the slow nights, it helped the time pass.

"So, how's your week going?" he asked me.

"Oh, fine," I told him.

"You work here every night?"

"No. I have two days off—Mondays and Wednesdays," I told him.

"Long days for you—going to classes, then working until two in the morning."

I was surprised he remembered I was in school. "It's not so bad. I'm taking only a few classes right now. It'll take me twenty years to get my degree, probably."

He laughed. "Hopefully not that long. I took my time though, and I turned out okay."

"How long did you take?"

"I had a few starts and stops. I got my bachelor's degree when I was"—he paused, rolled his eyes up, as if searching for the answer in his brain—"twenty-five, I think," he said.

"Well, I'm twenty-three and I'm just starting, so I'll be, like, forty when I'm done."

"Forty. That's old," he said with a smirk that informed me he was in his forties.

My favorite Bob Dylan song came on—"Don't Think Twice, It's All Right."

"I love this song," I said.

I reached under the bar for the little remote control, turned up the volume, sang shamelessly. He just watched me with a bemused expression.

I said, over the music, "I got that line tattooed on my side."

"What line?"

"*You could have done better but I don't mind.*"

I got it when I was eighteen, on a whim. It hurt, the tattooing needle vibrating against my ribs. It was worth it though. I've always loved that line.

"Sounds depressing," he said.

"I don't see it that way. I see it as a peaceful acceptance of someone else's limits," I said.

"Whose limits are you accepting?" he asked.

"Aren't we always accepting a bunch of people's limits?"

He shrugged. "Maybe."

"I guess it makes me think of my mom," I dared to admit. It was something I hadn't really told anyone before. "She did her best, given circumstances."

"Circumstances?"

"It was just the two of us. She was always working a couple jobs, that kind of thing," I said.

"You two close now?"

"Not as close as we were. I moved here. She's back in Bend. We've never lived far apart before."

"How long have you been in Boise?"

"About a year."

"It's a good place to live," he said.

"I like it so far."

A couple guys came into the bar, putting my conversation with Cale on hold. By the time I served them, Cale was done with his pint and said he was going to head home. He left a twenty on the bar—again, way too much.

I DECIDE TO drive by Ray's, compelled by curiosity or masochism, or both.

There is still police tape, but it's hanging limply from the building, no longer pulled taut around the perimeter. There is a makeshift memorial—so many bouquets of flowers, cards, a cardboard sign that says Rest in Peace in black marker.

I just drive by. I don't stop. I can't stop. I'm gripping the steering wheel so tightly my hands are white. A couple streets past Ray's, I pull up to the curb, put the car in park. I'm hyperventilating again. I need to catch my breath.

I think about what I told Cale, about my mom. I look at my phone, sitting in my cup holder. It's time.

The phone rings three times before she answers.

"Tessie girl," she says. This is what she calls me when she's being especially affectionate.

"Hi, Mom."

"It's been too long again."

"I know."

I don't even bother trying to sound normal, and I know she'll notice.

"What's wrong?" she asks, right on cue.

"I have to tell you something," I say.

The tears are already coming.

I know when I say it out loud, it will be real.

I know when I say it out loud, the jig, as they say, will be up. There will be no more pretending to be okay. I am on the verge of a breakdown. I am on the verge of relief.

"What is it? Tess? You're scaring me."

"I know. Mom, just sit down, okay? And I'll tell you."

JOYCE

WHEN I OPEN THE front door, Lindsey Benton is standing on the welcome mat, a screaming, red-faced baby in one arm, a diaper bag slung over the opposite shoulder.

"Here, give me something," I say to her, in lieu of any usual greeting.

She turns to the side and leans so the diaper bag slides off her shoulder. I grab it, hold it against my chest as if it's a briefcase containing a million dollars.

"Thank you," she says, moving the baby to her shoulder, patting her back.

"I think she needs to burp," she says. "I just fed her in the car."

There is a wet spot on her shirt—milk leakage. I remember those days, but they feel like another lifetime.

"Come sit," I say, motioning for her to follow me to the living room, to the couch. She falls onto it, the baby jostling in the process. The crying comes to a sudden stop.

"She burped," Lindsey says.

She sets the baby on the couch cushion next to her, lying on her back. The baby is so small. I forgot babies could be this small. You don't often see the newest of the newborns in public, after all.

I set the diaper bag at Lindsey's feet and join her in staring at the baby. Her skin is so light and pale that I can see the network of veins and arteries all over her body. She is wearing a pink onesie, swimming in it; it is way too big. Her eyes appear dark blue, like the deepest part of the ocean, but I guess all babies have those eyes in the beginning. Jed did. I expected them to fade into a hazel, like mine, but they stayed that color blue.

"She's beautiful," I say.

That's what you're supposed to say. In reality, the baby looks a bit alien. She is completely bald, not a strand of hair. Lindsey has affixed a pink headband to her head, something to clarify gender, something to assist strangers who feel the need to marvel at the infant: *Oh, what a cute little girl*. She has splotches of acne on her forehead and cheeks. I remember this too, the baby acne. It has something to do with the mother's pregnancy hormones still circulating in the baby's bloodstream.

"I think so too, but I'm horribly biased," Lindsey says.

I sit in the chair next to the couch.

"Your first?" I ask.

She nods. "Possibly only. I can't imagine having another one."

"Well, you say that now."

Lindsey takes an orange conical object out of the diaper bag. When she twists it, it starts making a shushing sound.

"It helps her sleep," Lindsey says. "They call it the Shusher. White noise is important—that's what they say. Mimics the sounds of the womb or something."

I shake my head. "They have all kinds of things these days."

There were no Shushers when Jed was a baby. There was no Amazon to deliver diapers. There was no Google.

"It's a total industry," she says. "All these gadgets they say you need. And you're so sleep-deprived and such a nervous wreck that you're like, 'Yes, I need that!' It's crazy. My husband says he needs to take away my credit card."

I bristle at the mention of her husband. I know it's not fair to bristle. It was ridiculous of me to fantasize about Lindsey and Jed ending up together. They were just kids when they dated—and it was never even clear that they dated, officially.

"How long have you been married?" I ask.

"Three years. We met at Boise State," she says.

That was the big thing that happened between them—she stayed in Boise, and Jed couldn't get out of Boise fast enough. He was set on California, Santa Cruz, even though he'd never been there before. Lindsey came over to help him pack up his car—the Mustang. He insisted on driving to Santa Cruz, a ten- or eleven-hour trip. When they were done packing, cramming as much as they could into the trunk and back seat, Lindsey stood with me on the driveway and we waved as he drove off. It was like a scene out of a movie. I told him to call me every four hours until he got there, and he did—three phone calls in total. I assume he and Lindsey kept in touch at first, but then she must have met the man who would become her husband and that was that. No man is okay with a woman keeping in touch with a guy she used to have feelings for.

"And you're still living in Boise, I gather?" I ask.

"Yep. We just bought a place in the North End."

The North End, the trendy part of town. Lindsey Benton has done well for herself.

"Are you working?" I ask. I'm prying, really. I want to know if her husband is rich, if he supports them. I want to know how easy her life is, though I know in my heart that no life is truly easy.

"Well, not now," she says, nodding toward the baby, who has fallen asleep, just as the packaging for the Shusher promised, I'm sure. "I'm a third-grade teacher at Washington Elementary. It worked out well, actually. I'm on maternity leave, and by the time that's up, it will be summer break. But I'll go back in fall."

"That's great, Lindsey, really," I say, giving her a smile that I hope disguises the envy I can't help but harbor.

She leans back against the couch, as if relaxing for the first time since she arrived. She takes a deep breath.

"It's hard, this baby thing," she says, in a soft voice, like she's afraid the baby will hear and be scarred for life.

"It is," I say.

"Why doesn't anyone tell you?" she asks. It's not a hypothetical question. There's an earnestness to her tone, a desperation.

"The people in the thick of it don't tell you because they don't want to scare you. They know ignorance is bliss. The people no longer in the thick of it don't remember that well. The brain has only so much room. You learn to discard the bad stuff and remember only the good times. That's what I did at least."

That's what I'm still doing, I should say.

"Was Jed an easy baby?" she asks.

"I don't believe in easy babies. There are hard ones and harder ones."

She looked at me, expecting more.

"Jed was a harder one," I say. "He was colicky."

I'm still not sure what "colicky" means. Is it related to stomach issues? Gas? Or does it just mean your child is cranky for no discernible reason?

Lindsey groans, says, "My mom thinks Charlotte might be colicky."

Charlotte. So that's the baby's name. I feel stupid for not asking.

"I hated her for telling me that. Like I need a Google diagnosis on top of everything else."

Lindsey Benton's mother's name was a flower—Violet or Rose or Lily, I can't remember which. I never liked her, mostly because she never liked Jed. She was the type of mother who started angling in middle school for her daughter to marry a doctor. I'm too afraid to ask Lindsey if that's what her husband is, a doctor.

"Everything is a phase," I say. "Whether she's colicky or not, she won't be that way forever."

Lindsey looks down at her shirt, notices the expanding circle of wetness around her breast, the leaking milk.

"Oh, Jesus," she says.

She stands quickly. I worry it'll wake the baby, but the baby stays sleeping.

"Can I use your bathroom?" she asks.

"Sure, of course."

She takes the diaper bag with her. A few minutes later, she comes back, wearing a new shirt.

"They say to always have a change of clothes for the baby," she says, "but I've realized I need one for myself too."

"You're better prepared than I ever was as a new mom."

"I feel like a mess all the time."

"Every mother feels that way."

She sits, leans back into the cushion again. The way she exhales—so hard that her bangs flutter—tells me we are about to put an end to the charade of being two old friends, catching up. The real reason for her being here is about to be revealed.

"So," she says, looking at me.

"So."

"I'm sorry I just showed up like that yesterday. And just dumping that stuff on you. I'm not totally myself. The hormones and everything . . . " she says.

She's stalling.

"It's okay," I tell her. "Really."

She exhales again.

"So," she says again. "Jed and I, we hadn't really been in touch for a long time, since high school basically, but we would exchange texts on birthdays, that kind of thing. He congratulated me when I had Charlotte. He must have seen the photo I posted on Facebook or something."

"Jed didn't use Facebook," I interrupt.

I feel the need to say this because Jed was so adamant about his dislike of social media. I want people to understand who he was, to get their facts straight.

Lindsey just shrugs. "Well, I'm not on Instagram or anything else. I posted the birth announcement on Facebook. I don't know how else he would have found out."

I slump a little in my chair, imagining Jed secretly perusing Facebook, spying on the present of his past girlfriend. It makes me ache.

"Anyway," Lindsey says. "He congratulated me, and we exchanged a few texts—we hadn't changed numbers after all these years. He told me he was back in Boise, he was working at Home Depot. He said you were doing well. That was it."

I nod, knowing there is more, knowing that was not it.

"Then, that night. The night of the shooting. He texted me. I can show you."

She digs around in the diaper bag, retrieves her phone, which has a smear of diaper cream on the cover. She wipes it on her shirt, unlocks the phone, finds what she's looking for, and hands the phone to me.

I stare at the text message chain, the name Jed at the top of the screen.

Jed:

Linds, I just wanted to say I've always valued you in my life. You are such a good person. I should have stayed in Boise with you all

those years ago. I'm so glad you are happy. I wish you nothing but the very best. Love, Jed

The message has a timestamp below it:

Thu, April 11, 10:08 pm

Lindsey:

Are you ok?

Jed:

I will be.

Lindsey:

Jed, come on, what's going on?

"I always knew Jed had some depression, even when we were in high school. He would talk about these dark days he'd have, how he couldn't see the point in a lot of things," Lindsey says.

"I didn't know. He didn't tell me." I say this with too much emotion, as if I'm in a courtroom, on trial. Lindsey gives me that dreaded look of pity, a look that says, *Oh, Ms. Ketcher, you don't have to prove anything to me.*

"I don't think he was proud of it. I don't think it's something he wanted to discuss with anyone, really. He said I was the only person who knew certain things about him," she says, lending evidence to the argument that this wasn't all my fault.

"I guess I feel like I should have known."

She gives me that pitying look again, and I have to avert my eyes from hers.

"Teenagers hide all kinds of things. And lots of them are angsty."

But they don't all go on to shoot up bars. That's the part she's not saying but we're both thinking.

I look back at the phone, at the texts.

"So anyway, yeah, I was worried when I got that first text," Lindsey says before going quiet so I can read.

Jed:

I can't do it anymore. I'm sorry. I know you think I'm weak and pathetic. I'm just tired of so much. Just let me say goodbye. Don't mess this up for me.

Lindsey:

I'm calling you.

"This was, like, two weeks after I'd given birth. I was already emotional, you know? My husband thinks the whole thing is weird. Like, why did Jed text me, of all people? Maybe it's because we'd texted right after I had Charlotte and I was on his mind or something. I don't know. Anyway, I had to call him. I just had a bad feeling."

"Did he answer? When you called?"

"Yeah. He sounded like he was in the car so I asked if he was driving. He said yes. I asked him where he was going, and he said he was going to hike into the foothills. Of course I said, '*Now*? It's ten o'clock at night,' and he said, 'I need to do it at night, when nobody is around.' And that's when I understood."

"What?" I ask.

"He was going to kill himself. In the foothills. He'd talked about it when we were teenagers. We had this morbid discussion about how we'd kill ourselves, if worst came to worst. He said he'd hike into the foothills, find a desolate spot, and shoot himself in the head. He was so specific about it. It freaked me out at the time," she says.

"So he was going to kill himself that night?"

"I think so, yeah. I think that was his plan."

"But he somehow ended up at a bar and shot people?"

It doesn't make any sense.

The baby stirs. Lindsey puts her palm on Charlotte's belly, pats it a few times.

"When I was on the phone with him, I told him to wait, that I'd come meet him somewhere," she says. "I didn't know how that would be possible with a baby literally on me, but I figured I had to try."

"And?"

She shakes her head. "I don't know. All of a sudden, he started cursing. Said some guy cut him off. He was furious. I heard him yelling, like maybe he rolled down his window and was yelling at this guy. Then he said he had to go and hung up."

"Did you try to call him back?"

"Of course. Yeah, I mean, I tried a dozen times, at least. Then I texted."

She nods toward the phone. I look at the screen again, scroll through texts she sent to him an hour after the last set, then an hour after that, then again, and again.

Lindsey:

Jed? Call me.

Lindsey:

You're freaking me out. Just text me, ok?

Lindsey:

JED! Come on, are you there?

"That night, or really early in the morning, I was on the

couch with Charlotte. I was flipping through channels, and I saw the shooting on the news. I just knew, before they even shared his name, that it was him."

I hand her phone back to her.

"I'm sorry," she says. "I know this doesn't explain much of anything. I just thought you should know."

"Thank you," I say, though I'm not sure if I'm grateful. From what she's told me, Jed didn't have a plan to kill people. He was going to the foothills. Unless he was lying. But why would he lie to her if he knew she would find out the truth anyway? It's like he got distracted from his original plan—by road rage of all things. Is that what I'm left with—road rage? Why didn't he call me? Or, at the very least, leave me a note. Didn't he think I deserved a note?

"Have the police talked to you?" I ask her, wondering if I should call them myself.

She nods. "I guess they knew that we'd talked that night— phone records or whatever. And they saw our texts. I told them everything. Is that okay?"

She looks scared, as if she's guilty of something.

"The truth is always okay," I say, though I'm not sure I believe this.

I wonder how much Detective Kinsky knows at this point, how much he has yet to tell me.

The baby is adamantly awake now, squirming and emitting little sounds of displeasure that will escalate into crying soon. Lindsey picks her up, unbuttons the first few buttons of her flannel shirt, and unclips her nursing bra.

"Do you mind?" she asks, the baby already latched on, suckling.

"Not at all," I say.

I'd tried to breastfeed Jed, but he had no patience for it.

He would get frustrated—maybe I wasn't producing enough milk, maybe it wasn't coming out fast enough for his liking. He would start to tug on my nipples with his gums, biting that was excruciatingly painful even though he had no teeth. When the milk came out pink, tinged with my blood, I decided we'd had enough. I switched to formula. For a while, I resented how much happier he seemed with that. Did he feel my resentment? I have to wonder these things now.

"We'll probably leave when she's done," Lindsey says, nodding her head toward Charlotte.

"Okay," I say. "I'm glad you came by."

"Are you?" she says with a little wince.

"I am. I don't really know what to think . . . about that night. But I'm assuming the pieces of the puzzle will come together at some point."

Or they won't.

That's the kind of thing that sends people to padded rooms—having a bunch of puzzle pieces that don't fit together at all.

ANGIE

THINGS BETWEEN CALE AND I got worse when I went back to work. I think he would have preferred I become a stay-at-home mom. His salary would cover our expenses; I didn't absolutely *need* to work. But I wanted to. I wanted a career. I wanted my own income. A part of me would never be okay with relying on a man for my lifestyle. I shudder at the idea of having to ask permission to buy a pair of shoes.

When I went back to work, it became obvious that Cale and I would have to split responsibilities with Evie more than we had before. I couldn't work full-time and continue to do everything I was doing for her. She had to go to day care. Someone needed to drop her off and pick her up. There were meals to prepare, baths to give, clothes to wash, diapers to change, appointments to make—all the boring, usual things that go into caring for a small human being.

I cried my first day back at work, and Cale was quick to say, "You can quit, you know." I didn't want to quit though. My body just wasn't used to being apart from Evie's. I liked having time to myself—that's how I came to see work. The ability to sit at a desk and eat my lunch with two hands was a luxury.

I made the mistake every modern woman does and tried to do it all at first. I woke up early to get myself ready for work, then got Evie ready for day care. I dropped her off, then went to the office. I pumped breastmilk every three hours—a logistical nightmare. I ran out of the office by four forty-five to get Evie from day care by five o'clock. Then I came home to give her a bath, put her to bed, and make dinner for Cale and me. I was, in a word, exhausted.

After a few weeks of this, I had it out with Cale. We were in the kitchen. I was doing the dishes after putting Evie to bed.

"You need to do more," I told him. "I know you hate fatherhood, but you need to do more."

I wasn't normally this direct with him, but I simply didn't have the energy to craft my words in a way that considered his feelings.

"I don't *hate* fatherhood," he said.

"It sure seems like you do."

He sighed, hung his head. "Ang, I'm just tired, okay?"

"You always say that. Tired, tired, tired. Don't you think *I'm* tired?"

"I know you—"

"You're depressed. You've been depressed since Evie was born. You need to do something about it. Go on medication. Talk to a therapist. Something. It's affecting our lives."

"I'm not depressed," he said.

I waved the white dish towel over my head, signaling my surrender.

"You are impossible to talk to."

I walked past him, went downstairs to our bedroom. Surprisingly, he followed. As I changed out of my work clothes, he sat on the bed, his arms crossed over his chest.

"I know I've been off," he admitted.

It was the only time he would admit it to me. He'd had a few beers with dinner. It seemed he risked honesty only when he was slightly drunk.

"I'm just working through some stuff," he said.

His offering of this tiny morsel of insight made me hungrier for more. Ravenous, really.

"What stuff?" I asked.

I was standing there, naked except for a pair of threadbare underwear that he often referred to as my granny panties. I'd sworn to myself that I wouldn't become one of those women who loses all interest in sex and romance after having a baby, but that's exactly who I'd become.

"Just some stuff," he said. "I'm working through it, okay?"

I let my arms fall by my side in defeat.

"Why won't you talk to me?" I asked.

"Why won't you trust me to work through what I need to?"

We were always at this stalemate.

ARIA HAD SAID to give it to the new year. The new year came and went. Then, before I knew it, it was Evie's first birthday. Cale hadn't changed. He had some good days, weeks even, when he seemed happier, more engaged, less distracted by whatever "stuff" was bothering him. Those days, I was quick to think, "Okay, we're better. Things are better." But then I'd lose him again. That's what it felt like—like he was by my side, and then he'd disappear into some dark forest, lost.

A few months ago, right before Christmas, I decided Evie was old enough for us to actually enjoy a little family trip. Up until that point, it had seemed like more trouble than it was worth to travel. But she was sleeping through the night, eating regular food. She was fun to be around—smiley and playful. It wasn't overwhelming to go places with her anymore. She just required a few diapers, a sippy cup, some snacks.

When I was a kid, my parents took Aria and me to Seattle around Christmastime. I had fond memories of it—the tree and lights at the Public Market, everyone bundled up and holding cups of hot cocoa, a light dusting of snow on the ground. It was pure Americana, and I was nostalgic for that. I knew Evie wouldn't remember it. It wasn't for her, really. It was for Cale. I was hell-bent on showing him a good time. I persisted in thinking his mood was within my control.

The moment we arrived at our gate at the airport, I knew I'd made a mistake. I'd fallen into the social media trap, lured by images of what seemed like idyllic trips that other families were taking. Yes, they joked about the challenges of traveling with a young child, posted photos of themselves looking bug-eyed and exhausted on a plane with a maniacal toddler in their laps, using hashtags like #prayforme. I thought it was cute, though. I thought Cale and I would look at each other and laugh. I thought it would bond us.

So stupid. Truly.

There was something wrong with our plane. They needed to replace a part, so we were told we'd be in the terminal, waiting, for two hours. I had already presented Evie with every snack I had in my backpack, whipping out a new package of crackers or cookies like a juggling clown. She wasn't having it. I tried my phone. YouTube videos were a last resort in these situations, and I was already there.

At first, she quieted. Then, when "Old MacDonald Had a Farm" came on, she threw my phone and said, "No!" Something about the song had deeply offended her, apparently.

Cale went to her, grabbed her by both wrists, lifted her out of the chair I'd attempted to confine her to.

"What are you doing?" I asked him.

"She wants to walk around," he snapped. Even though I continued to do the majority of the childcare, he had this way of making me feel like I was doing it all wrong.

"Walk 'round," Evie said, completely oblivious to any tension.

He stomped off with Evie in his arms. She loved when he held her, because he didn't do it that often. I told Sahana he was setting her up for a future of chasing after unavailable men.

The plane flight was even worse than the waiting for the plane flight. We didn't get Evie her own seat because babies under the age of two can sit on your lap for free. I guess I was an idiot for thinking she would do that—sit on my lap.

I had her occupied on my lap for a little while, every muscle tight with my attempts to keep her behaving well—not for the sake of the other passengers, but for Cale. She was— still is—obsessed with the Fisher-Price little plastic people, so I put those on the tray for her. When she played with them, I thought, *I'm brilliant. I've got this.* But parenting is the ultimate humbler. It is impossible to feel confident for longer than three seconds.

Without warning, Evie threw her plastic people in all directions. Out of the corner of my eye, I saw one hit the woman across the aisle from us. And one hit Cale right in the face. I thought he was going to scream at me in front of this plane full of people. I thought his outburst would necessitate an emergency landing. Airlines don't take any chances with possibly unstable people anymore.

Cale unbuckled his seat belt, even though the seat belt sign was on. He stood up and climbed over me to get to the aisle. Then he went to the bathroom at the back of the plane. When he was still gone after a half hour, I started to worry that he was causing a line to form. I let Evie walk ahead of me to check on him. Someone else came out of the bathroom, so it was obvious he wasn't in there. I looked up the aisle. He wasn't there. It was like he'd made himself disappear with sheer willpower alone. But no, he hadn't disappeared. As I approached the bathroom, I saw there was a little standing-room area for the flight attendants. That's where he was, just leaning against the wall, his eyes closed. It was the best escape he could manage.

It was afternoon when we got to Seattle, and Evie still hadn't napped. I thought she would nap on the plane, thought the white noise of the engines would lull her to sleep, but that didn't happen. By the time we got our rental car, which took an inordinately long time because they had forgotten to include the car seat, Evie was a manic mess, laughing hysterically one minute and then bursting into tears the next.

"She needs a nap," I told Cale.

"You think?" he said with his unique brand of biting sarcasm.

We decided to drive around for an hour or so. Evie will sleep on car rides. That's one of the few things we've been able to count on with her. So we drove. It could have been a good opportunity for us to talk. But he was silent. Aggressively silent.

"You're tired?" I asked.

"I'm fine," he said.

That was all I got.

We drove up the I-5 freeway to Everett, then turned around and drove back. I'd booked a room at a waterfront hotel, near Pier 66. Evie woke up right as we pulled into the parking lot, and I thought we could reset, start anew. Cale did not share this sentiment.

For the entirety of the trip—just two days—he was quiet. His jaw was visibly clenched; I could see the muscles pulsing. In a way, I understood. It wasn't fun. We had Evie in a Pack 'n Play at night, something we hadn't tried before, and she kept standing up and saying, "Hi, Mama. Hi, Dada," like she was so excited at this idea of all of us sleeping in the same room. I kept going to her, placing her on her stomach, patting her back. But she kept popping up. It felt like a game of Whac-A-Mole. At one point, I attempted to get in the Pack 'n Play with her, but it required way too much contorting on my part and seemed to make Evie more excited. Eventually, I lay on the floor next to the Pack 'n Play, so I could be there if she decided to pop up. She did pop up, so many times. When she finally stayed down, it must have been after two in the morning.

The next day, I tried to make jokes about needing an IV drip of coffee, but Cale was in no mood for jokes. It wasn't just Cale and I who were tired; Evie was too. She was whiny and cranky when we went to breakfast. We ended up asking for takeout. A huge storm moved in that afternoon. There was no dusting of snow in Seattle this year, just sloppy, wet rain. I'd forgotten the umbrella, so the three of us ran back to the hotel, Evie against my chest, Cale holding her stroller over his head. There was nothing to do but hang out in the room. I suggested going to a brewery or something, but Cale said, "You think we should drink beer and then drive in this rain?" He'd become so adept at making me feel like an idiot.

Evie was better on the flight home than she was on the flight there. But it didn't matter at that point. Cale was spent; I was spent. The trip had failed to achieve what I'd wanted; if anything, it'd made things worse.

I probably shouldn't have tried to talk to him the night we got back. We were both so, so tired. I couldn't help it though.

"Are we going to be okay?" I asked him.

We were both in bed, lying flat on our backs, staring at the ceiling, listening to the white noise in Evie's room over the monitor. Or that's what I was doing. Maybe he was already falling asleep because he responded with, "Huh?"

"Are we going to be okay?" I repeated.

He let out a long sigh, a sigh that said I was exhausting him.

"We're not good," I said. My heart was beating fast with this finally released truth.

"Ang, it's just a phase," he said.

"Is it, though?"

"You're making too much of this."

"What is 'this'? Your depression?"

"Ang, come on."

"You're depressed. Sahana says—"

"Don't bring Sahana into this," he interrupted.

It was a fair request.

"I'm just worried," I said, though that wasn't all of it. I was angry, frustrated, fed up.

"You don't need to worry. I'm fine."

I couldn't just let it end there, where it always did. This time, I did what the toddler books advised—I set a consequence.

"If things aren't better by summer, we need to see a counselor," I said.

He didn't respond.

"Did you hear me?"

"I heard you," he said.

I rolled over, comforted by the fact that I'd created a deadline for us. I just had to make it until June, then we could get help. Sahana already had a marriage counselor in mind for us, someone she said was "the best of the best." She'd told me to be patient, that many men are resistant to confronting their depression.

After that talk, he had more good days. On the bad ones, I just thought of summer and the "best of the best" marriage counselor. That kept me going. Now summer seems like this far-off, exotic place. The future, in general, seems like this far-off, exotic place—a place where I don't know the language, a place where I get lost.

By summer, Cale may be back with us—or as "with us" as he'll ever be able to be. There's no telling how his mind or body will function. By summer, I may be a widow. On the bad days with Cale, I daydreamed of single parenthood, of being on my own with Evie. In my fantasies, I breezed through the world, light and airy without the weighty burden of Cale's mood. There was no more tiptoeing around the house, no more energy spent trying to understand or solve his angst. I was free, liberated. Is that how I'll feel if he dies? Free? I don't know. Maybe by summer, I'll know.

TESSA

I DECIDE TO PACK my suitcase while Ryan is at the gym. He's already back to his usual routine, including the Saturday morning two-hour gym session. I told him I'm going to see my mom, so it's not a secret I'm leaving. But I'm packing much more than necessary because I think I may not be coming back.

When I told my mom about the shooting, she reacted in just the way I'd predicted—hysterically.

"What do you mean you were *there*?" she said.

There was panic in her voice.

"I worked at that bar, Mom. Ray's. I didn't tell you because I knew you wouldn't approve and—"

"And you were *there*?"

"Yes. I've been wanting to tell you, but I was just so—"

"Oh my god," she said. "Are you hurt?"

"Mom, it was a week ago. I'm fine. I've been fine."

"How could you be *fine*?"

She was shouting.

"Physically, I'm fine. Nothing happened to me."

"Nothing happened to you?"

The pitch of her voice was higher than I'd ever heard.

"Mom, can you calm down?"

"I'm driving up there."

I hear her calling to someone—probably her boyfriend, Rob—in the background: "It's Tessa. I've gotta get to Boise."

"Mom, wait," I said. "I'll come to you. I'll drive there."

"How can you be okay to drive?"

"It was a week ago," I repeated.

"I don't know. I don't think you should drive."

"Do you hear yourself? I don't think *you* should drive."

That quieted her. I heard her breathing—rapidly, then slower.

"I want to come there," I told her. "I want to get out of Boise for a few days."

"Okay," she said, relenting finally. "I'll have your room all set. Will you be here by dinnertime? I'll make some pasta."

"Yeah, I just have one thing to do before I leave. I'll be there for dinner."

"And maybe some garlic bread?"

This was just like my mom, transferring her anxieties to food preparation.

"Sure, Mom. Sure."

I DON'T REALLY want to see Ryan before I go. I told him last night I'd be leaving while he was at the gym. I told him it would be just for a few days. There's no need to make it dramatic. Besides, maybe I will come back—to him, to Boise, I don't know.

The one thing I want to do before I head out of town is see Joyce.

It's just before ten o'clock, and downtown is bustling with people going to the farmers market. Still, I manage to find a parking spot on the street. A bell dings when I walk through the door of the coffee shop, and Joyce looks up from a table in the back and gives me a little wave. It was nice of her to remember to get a table in the back.

I don't order anything. I just sit across from her, in the chair she's left for me, the chair facing the door.

"It's good to see you," she says.

"You too."

It feels like the service for Jed was a year ago, like the shooting was a century ago. But then, if I close my eyes, it feels like I'm still in the storage closet.

"How are you?" she asks.

"Good," I say.

I reach to the middle of the table, grab a sugar packet from the little plastic container. I turn it over in my palm.

"I told my mom," I say. "I'm driving to Bend after this."

Her eyes widen. "Oh, good. Wait, that *is* good, right?"

"Yeah, I think so. It will be good to get out of town for a few days. And I haven't seen her in so long."

"She'll want to comfort you, I'm sure."

Joyce looks down at the table, just for a second, but enough for me to feel her sadness at the fact that she will never get to comfort her child again.

"I don't really know when I'll be back. Maybe a few days, but maybe longer," I tell her.

"Longer?" she asks, curious.

I shrug. "I guess I'll just see."

I put the sugar packet back in its container.

"How are you?" I ask.

"Oh, well, I don't know," she says. "It depends on the moment you ask me. There are times I feel just fine, like I can tolerate this new life. And, just minutes later, I'll start sobbing."

"I assume that's normal," I say. I meet her eyes. "Do you miss him?"

"Jed?" she says.

Her eyes flicker down, then up again. "I do. He lived with me, so it's just strange that he's not there. And there's so much I want to know . . . about what happened."

230

"There's so much I want to know too," I say.

It's risky, possibly rude, to declare this, but I figure Joyce deserves my honesty.

"Of course," she says. "Everyone wants to know why. The police are interviewing all of Jed's coworkers, his friends, whoever knew him. I asked them what the point was. I mean, he's dead. What does it matter? But I guess they are as determined as anyone to understand the motive."

"Do you have any idea?" I ask.

She shakes her head. "I told the police I'm as shocked as anyone. I'm his mom, you know? People think mothers know their children best, but I don't know if that's true. We have these blind spots, as mothers. There are some things we just can't see."

I nod and sit back in my chair, resigned to coming to terms with leaving Boise without any answers.

"An old friend of his came by yesterday. The girl who showed up at the service," she says.

I remember the woman, hardly a girl—in her mid- to late twenties, I'd guess. I hadn't wanted to pry and ask who she was.

"She said Jed called her the night of the shooting. Said he was going to kill himself. Didn't say anything about a bar or shooting other people."

"So he was suicidal?" I ask.

She shakes her head. "Not that I knew of. Like I said . . . blind spots."

"Maybe you weren't blind. Maybe he was just good at hiding."

"Maybe."

I can't help but wonder if Jed just didn't want to tell his friend his real intentions, his plans to shoot up Ray's. It must have been a plan, something he'd thought about doing for months, years even. Nobody just shoots up a bar on a whim, do they?

"Do you think he just didn't want to tell his friend the truth? Like, maybe he was hiding from her too?" I ask.

I wince a bit, preparing for Joyce to defend her son, his morality, the fabric of his being. But she just sighs.

"It's possible," she says. "But maybe it was impulsive. Maybe something set him off. His friend, Lindsey, she said they were on the phone and it sounded like someone cut him off while he was driving. She heard him cursing and going on. Then he hung up."

Those words—*cut him off*—bring immediate goose bumps to my arms.

"You okay?" Joyce asks.

I must look as shaken as I feel.

"Um, yeah, I think so," I say.

I'm not though.

Those words—*cut him off*.

I feel slightly dizzy, unsteady, like I might pass out.

"Tessa?" Joyce says.

She's staring at me, her brows knitted together with concern.

"Sorry," I say. "I don't know what happened."

I close my eyes. The darkness helps.

I feel Joyce's hand on mine.

"It's okay," she says. "You're safe."

My body feels warm, radiating heat. The nape of my neck is sweaty.

Cut him off.

It means something. From that night. But I can't put it together.

"I had a flashback or something," I say, shaking my head, as if to rearrange its contents, hoping they will make more sense in their new positions.

"About that night?" she says, her brows still colliding into each other.

"Yes. Maybe. I don't know."

She looks at me expectantly, as if waiting for a bit of information about her son. I don't have information though. Or I don't know if I do.

Cut him off.

"It's nothing," I tell her.

Because it might be nothing. I don't know what it is.

My phone buzzes with a text. It's Ryan.

Hey babe. Just wanted to say I love you. Call me when you get there.

"You have to go?" Joyce asks.

She still looks concerned.

I don't really have to go, but I don't want to stay. I don't want to be here, with her, if I remember something else.

"Yeah, I should get going," I say. "I told my mom I'd be on the road soon."

I tap my phone, as if to indicate the text is from my mom.

"Right, of course," she says.

We stand from the table at the same time and then walk toward the door together. She holds it open for me, then we stand on the sidewalk, facing each other.

"You're sure you're okay? Maybe you should wait a bit to drive."

"I'm okay," I tell her.

"Well, then take care of yourself," she says.

She says it like we won't see each other again, like she knows this may be my last day in Boise even though I'm not sure I know that yet.

233

"You too," I say.

"I'm sorry we had to meet the way we did. I'm sorry for what Jed did."

"I know you are."

"Would you mind keeping in touch? Just a text every now and then?"

I nod. "Of course."

I can picture it now—sending her texts when all the happy events of my life happen, texts that assure her that her son's actions did not define my life.

I assume I'll have those happy events, the standard ones—a love, a marriage, a family. This assumption is what keeps people going, isn't it?

"Can I give you a hug?" she asks.

Her arms are already outstretched. As awkward as I feel about this, I cannot reject her.

I hold my arms out, as a show of agreeance, then let her embrace me. It is not a loose hug, a half-assed hug. It is a tight, long, meaningful hug. I don't know the last time someone gave me one of these hugs.

"Thank you," she says, though I feel like I should be the one thanking her.

As she pulls away, she lets her hands run down my arms. When they get to my hands, she squeezes.

"Thank you for letting me mourn him," she says.

Her eyes are glassy. I know when she gets to her car, she will let her head fall to the steering wheel and she will cry.

I return her hand squeeze. "I'm sorry you lost him."

I am still left to wonder when she lost him. It was before that night. Long before, most likely. She might not even know when, exactly.

We part ways, walking in opposite directions toward our

cars. I turn around to see where she is parked, and she is turning around at just the same time.

"Drive safe," she says. "Please."

"I will," I tell her.

When I get to my car, I take a Post-it from my center console and scribble "Text Joyce" on it. As a reminder, for when I get to Bend. Because I'm sure she'll want to know I made it.

JOYCE

LATE SATURDAY NIGHT, WHILE Gary and I were sleeping in his bed, a nineteen-year-old sophomore at the University of Vermont shot thirty people, killing fifteen, during a rampage at a restaurant near campus. It's all over the news this morning.

Just the sound of the reporter's voice makes me nauseated. They all have the same tone when reporting tragedies.

Details are still coming in.

The shooter appeared to act alone.

No names have been released.

It's all too familiar. Every shooting from now on is going to be all too familiar.

"I think I'm going to be sick," I say, bending at the waist.

I heave, but nothing comes up.

"Goddamn it," Gary says, turning off the TV.

For a second, I think he's angry at me for putting his quilt at risk of vomit. But then I realize he's angry at the shooting, maybe angry at himself for turning on the TV, expecting a leisurely start to our day, only to find a horror show.

"You okay?" he asks.

"I don't know."

My palms are clammy, which always happens when I throw up.

Gary grabs a water bottle from his nightstand, hands it to me. I take a tentative sip, not sure my stomach will appreciate having anything in it.

"Thanks," I say.

Gary pushes himself off the mattress, stretches his arms overhead with a sigh. Then he turns around to look at me, hands on his hips, boxer shorts wrinkled and bunched up between his thighs like they always are in the morning.

"In a way, it takes the spotlight off Jed," he says.

I can tell he's not sure this is the right thing to say. I'm not sure either, but it is true, regardless. Jed is no longer "The Latest Shooter." In a sick way, this is relieving; in another way, it is horrifying, horrifying that Jed will just be a name on a list of atrocities, surrounded by so many other names.

"Do you think this guy was copying Jed?" I ask.

I can't help but think this. This nineteen-year-old, this kid, shot up a restaurant. That's similar to a bar. It's less than two weeks after the Ray's shooting. Was this kid inspired by Jed? Or, if not inspired, encouraged? Did Jed's actions validate this kid's own dark thoughts? I will probably wonder these things about every shooter on the news for the rest of my life.

"No, I don't think he was copying Jed," Gary says, with a definitiveness I appreciate.

I want to ask how he knows this, but I resist. He won't have an answer. And, really, I'd rather just take his word for it. "You up for any breakfast?" Gary asks. "I can make a Sunday feast."

There it is again, that resilient appetite of his.

"No breakfast for me, but I'll meet you in the kitchen in a few minutes," I say.

When he leaves, I reach for my phone, curious what people are saying on the message board about this latest shooting, about Jed. I'm hoping what Gary said is right—they will stop talking about Jed, move on. I imagine this message board used to be some other mother's nightmare; now it is mine. Soon, it will be someone else's.

JR2018:

This dude used a Remington 870 pump-action. Crazy mother fucker.

JimJam19:

Prolly saw the Boise dude and was like, 'gotta do better than that guy.'

JR2018:

For sure.

Boyseeeee:

U guys heard the police in Boise are releasing info soon?

JR2018:

Snore.

LvAll21:

I'm sure the families want the info, @JR2018.

JR2018:

You guys are boring as hell. I dunno why I still check this board.

LvAll21:

JR2018:

I don't know anything about the police releasing information. I set my phone on the nightstand and reach for my purse. I have Detective Kinsky's card in the zipper pocket of my wallet. I've been meaning to call him. Well, no, that's a lie. I've been wondering what he knows, but I've been too scared to call him. Now, though, I need to know—before the public, at least. I need to know what people are going to be saying about Jed.

I expect his voice mail because it's Sunday, but he answers after two rings.

"Detective Kinsky," he says.

I sit up in bed, my back ramrod straight against the head-board.

"Uh, hello, this is Joyce Ketcher," I say.

"Hello, Ms. Ketcher," he says, not missing a beat, as if he's been expecting my call.

"I didn't mean to bother you on a Sunday. I was just going to leave a message."

"Well, no need. I'm here."

He's not friendly, but he's not unfriendly. He is businesslike, to the point.

"I guess I was just wondering if you had any information," I say. He doesn't respond immediately so I add, "I heard there might be information coming."

"Word spreads, I guess," he says with a sigh. "Yes, we are planning a press conference for next week."

My face starts to get hot. It seems like if they were planning a press conference about my son, they should notify me.

I hear Jed: *It's not about me, Mom. It's about what I did. They don't give a fuck about me.*

I clear my throat. "When is this press conference?"

"I believe our media relations director said it would take place on Tuesday."

"And can you tell me what I can expect to hear about my son?"

I spit the question at the phone. I've given up on trying to hide my agitation.

"How about you come down to the station tomorrow? I can give you a summary of our findings at this time."

Findings.

There are findings.

"Tomorrow," I say. "Okay."

"Any time is fine," he says. "You have yourself a good Sunday, Ms. Ketcher."

He hangs up before I can say anything else.

I feel like I'm going to vomit again.

Right on cue, Gary calls from the kitchen: "Food's on."

ANGIE

DR. HARRIS CALLED THIS morning, said he wanted me to come in to discuss "next steps." After ten days of waiting and wondering and what-if-ing, it's time for next steps.

When he comes in, he doesn't see me at first. I'm sitting in one of the cold, uncomfortable chairs against the wall. When I say, "Hi, Dr. Harris," he flinches and turns around. I've startled him, clearly. And seeing his reaction makes me like him just a little bit. He is human, after all.

"Good morning," he says, his voice even.

I rise from my chair, as if I'm greeting the president. His ego seems to demand this.

"Thank you for meeting with me," I say.

He called just after eight o'clock, said he wanted me to come to the hospital before he went into surgery at nine. But I had to arrange for Aria to watch Evie; there's no day care on Sunday, obviously, and Aria doesn't wake up until nine. I told him I'd be there at ten, and he seemed irritated. That might be his baseline mood though—irritated.

"I'd like to discuss next steps with your husband's care," he says.

"Right," I say.

He stands on one side of Cale's bed and I move to the other, across from him. It's strange to have this conversation with Cale right there, but not listening. Or maybe he is listening. Last night, when I couldn't sleep, I read this one man's account of his coma, and he said he could hear voices. When he woke up, he knew things that had been discussed in his room, things he couldn't have known any other way. I would guess that Dr. Harris would scoff at this. He seems to be a man committed to what the science proves. Most doctors would have to be, I suppose.

"We are at a point when we are ready to turn off Cale's sedation medications and see how he responds," he says.

I nod slowly. "Okay, so what does that mean?"

"When the medications are out of his system, we can see how his body reacts. We'll monitor his breathing, start removing some of the life support devices," he says.

"What's the prognosis?" I ask. Then, unsure if I want to know that, I clarify: "I mean, what's the best-case scenario?"

He crosses his arms over his middle. "Best-case scenario, he breathes well on his own, we start to see voluntary movements, that kind of thing. Frankly, his MRI yesterday looked more promising than I'd thought it would. The brain is an amazing organ. Think of the waking-up period as his brain rebooting itself. We just have to see what kind of neurological deficits he faces if he wakes up."

"If," I say.

"There are very few 'whens' in this line of work."

He smiles, and I feel oddly proud of my ability to elicit it.

"Okay, so this is the best thing to do, right?"

He must know I am trusting him completely. He must know that loved ones want someone to tell them what to do. In a way, I can't really blame him for his God complex. I want him to be God.

"I don't see any reason to keep him sedated," he says. "He has reached a point when it makes sense to encourage him to wake up."

I nod.

He looks at his pager, which I've realized he always does when the conversation seems to be coming to a natural conclusion. It's possible he's not being summoned; he just wants an excuse to exit quickly. Which is exactly what he does, without a goodbye.

I look at Cale, take his hand like I always do, confirming the warmth.

"Can you wake up?" I ask him. I don't whisper; I use my regular voice. I can't help but think of the man who said he could hear voices while in his coma. I want Cale to hear me.

"Evie misses you," I tell him. "Wake up for her, okay? I miss you too," I add.

Because I do. Even though I'm angry and confused, even though there is still so much I don't understand, I miss him in the most basic way. I miss his presence in the house, his smell, his voice. He has the best voice—deep and strong, a voice made for radio, a voice that gives women chills.

WHEN I GET home, Aria and Evie are playing on the kilim rug in the kitchen. This is Evie's main play area, mostly because we spend most of our time in the kitchen and it's just easiest for her toys to be there. She likes to be near us, isn't old enough to go play independently in another room. It drove Cale nuts to have to navigate around her things. One morning, he stepped directly on one her plastic Little People. He started hobbling around on one foot, as if someone had taken a sledgehammer to the other. He looked ridiculous. I couldn't help but laugh. He didn't find it funny.

"What's my favorite girl doing?" I say, kneeling down next to Evie.

She pats the ground. "All the way," she says.

243

These days, kneeling next to her is not enough. She demands that we sit on the floor next to her and give our full attention as she pretends to assemble meals with her plastic food and plates.

"How did it go?" Aria asks me, while accepting a plastic red apple from Evie.

"They're taking him off his sedation medications," I say. "So he might start to wake up in a few days."

Her eyes go big with hope. "That's great . . . right?" she says.

I shrug. "I don't even know anymore. They still don't know if he'll wake up for sure. He said the latest MRI looked promising, but apparently it's hard to know the damage. Lots of waiting."

"I had no idea so much patience was involved."

"Yeah, me neither."

When Evie's pretend meal is complete according to her strange toddler logic, she says, "All done" and proceeds to tend to one of her baby dolls, leaving Aria and me sitting cross-legged on the rug across from each other. I still haven't told Aria about Tessa, about the note in Cale's phone. I don't want to get into it, specifically. She'll have too many questions, questions that Sahana and I have already mulled over incessantly.

"Can I ask you something?" I say.

"You just did," she says with a smile.

I make the "ba dum tss" sound to acknowledge her dumb joke.

"Do you think Cale would ever cheat on me?"

She looks truly appalled. "What? No. Why?"

I think I asked her because I knew this would be the response.

"I just can't stop wondering why he was at that bar in the middle of the night."

"I assume he wanted a beer."

"Which he could have had at home."

She twists her mouth to the side, considering. "You and I both know he was in a funk or something. He probably just couldn't sleep and wanted to get out."

"Yeah, maybe," I say.

"You don't seem so sure."

"I'm not so sure."

"I really think Cale loves you. Like, a lot."

Sahana is the cynic in my life; Aria is the romantic.

"What if he doesn't even know who I am when he wakes up?" I ask.

Tears start to come. They surprise me. After all, I've had this thought so often recently. I should be numb to it.

What if he doesn't know who I am?

What if he has no memories at all?

What if he can't speak?

What if he requires 24-7 care?

What if I can't do that?

What if I don't love him enough to do that?

While Cale's brain is completely quiet, mine is spinning with these questions. There is no rest.

"You said they don't know what the reality will be when he wakes up," Aria says. "There's no use tormenting yourself with what-ifs."

There may be no use, but pondering all the possibilities makes me feel like I'm doing something, which is necessary for sanity in a situation in which nothing can be done.

"Before he wakes up, you need to forgive him for whatever you think he did," Aria says.

Aria is a believer in things like energy and vibes. I've told her that being named "Aria" probably set her up for this proclivity.

"I don't know what he did," I say.

"Right. And you may never know that."

Aria is also a believer in "surrender" and "letting things go." It's easy for the younger sibling to be this way; the older one usually does enough worrying and planning for everyone.

Just then, Evie turns around and says, "Where Dada?"

She has a look on her face, as if she's just realized she has not seen him in a long time. It's the look I get when I'm halfway to work and wonder if I've left the curling iron on.

Aria and I look at her, then at each other. There is too much purpose and conviction in her question for us to ignore it. But, even if we wanted to, she repeats it:

"Where Dada?"

I open my arms and she runs into them, burying her head in my shoulder. She is in a cuddly, huggy phase. It's one of my favorite phases so far.

"Dada is taking a long nap," I tell her.

It just comes out. It's ridiculous. I'd contemplated a slightly more sophisticated explanation—*your daddy is sick, and doctors are taking care of him*—but I thought that would worry her too much. There is no sense worrying an almost-two-year-old.

"Dada nap?" she says, pushing away from my shoulder, her eyes scanning mine with this intense need to understand.

"Yes, Dada nap," I say.

I see Aria staring at me out of the corner of my eye. I can tell she's suppressing a laugh. The situation isn't funny, obviously, but it's impossible not to laugh at Evie's inquisitiveness.

She doesn't have the language to say much more. She can't ask when he'll wake up, or where he is, exactly. I'm sure her little mind wonders these things, but she seems content enough for now with the lame explanation I've given her.

She gets up and puts her baby doll on a dish towel that she uses as a blanket.

"Baby nap," she says.

Aria and I nod effusively, which is the only way to nod with a toddler. We repeat after her: "Baby nap, baby nap."

She starts to sing "Rock-a-Bye Baby" while draping the dish towel over the doll's face. I don't know why she does this. It makes me wonder if they put Evie's blanket over her face during nap time at day care.

"Baby night-night," Evie says, satisfied with herself.

We compliment her caretaking skills, and then I ask if she wants a snack.

She gives the biggest smile, a smile that shows no recollection of her concern about her father, and says, "Yogurt!"

TESSA

MY MOM HAS KEPT my room exactly the same since I left last year. I thought she would turn it into a home gym or something. She'd been talking for a while about buying a used treadmill on Craigslist, training for a 5K. Since she'd met Rob, she'd been on a self-improvement kick. It didn't seem like she was motivated by a desire to impress him; it seemed like he made her want to be her best self. That, I think, is the definition of true love.

I managed a few consecutive hours of sleep, which is not bad. Since the shooting, I seem to wake up every hour. It's like my brain is afraid to sleep long enough to dream, afraid of what images my subconscious might conjure.

I lie in bed, staring at the ceiling, my bedspread pulled to my chin. Mom bought me the bedspread for my sixteenth birthday—a pretty, romantic, pale-pink quilt from Anthropologie that probably cost a week's worth of groceries. It smells like home. My refusal to take it with me when I moved to Boise shows how utterly stubborn I was about starting anew.

The ceiling is still dotted with the glow-in-the-dark stars I begged for in elementary school. They're probably impossible to peel off at this point. Everything of mine is still here— the twinkly lights strung across the wall behind my bed, my books in their cheap IKEA bookcase, framed photos featuring friends I'm barely in touch with these days. It's sweet, in a way. But it also makes me think Mom expected I'd return. She didn't believe my resolve.

I hear someone moving around in the kitchen, doing dishes, putting them away in cupboards. We had a feast last night, as Mom promised we would. I got into town around four o'clock and helped her make the marinara sauce. She kept saying, "You just sit," but I wanted to help. I missed being her sous-chef.

She made penne pasta, macaroni and cheese, two trays of garlic bread, and fresh-baked chocolate chip cookies with ice cream for dessert. Rob opened a bottle of merlot he said he'd been saving for a special occasion. My coming home was this occasion, apparently. My survival was this occasion.

We talked until one in the morning. Mom wanted to know everything about the shooting, of course. I told her about the man who had told me to run, about the storage closet, about the SWAT team. She and Rob were slack-jawed.

"I just can't believe it," Mom said when I was done.

"I can't either," I said.

It still feels like a dream, or something that happened to someone else.

"You just never think it will happen to you," Mom said.

It's what people always say after things like this. It's one of those overused phrases that is so true.

They had all kinds of questions about Jed Ketcher, and I told them what I knew. I didn't tell them about meeting Joyce. I knew Mom would say, "Honey, do you think that's a good idea?" I didn't tell them about talking to Angie Matthews either, for the same reason.

"It looks like they're doing a press conference on Tuesday," Rob said.

He'd been googling while we talked, his glasses perched on the very tip of his nose.

"Oh, really?" I said.

I hadn't heard anything about a press conference. I wondered if they had more information. I wondered if it mattered if they did. I thought about Joyce, how anxious she must be to hear what the police had to say. I didn't want to text and ask if she knew about the press conference. I assume she knows. If she doesn't, I'm not sure I want to be the one to tell her.

"And looks like there was another shooting," he said, scrolling on his phone.

I thought he meant another shooting in Boise. Adrenaline shot through my body, startling and tingly.

"God, Rob, I don't think we need to hear about that," Mom said, probably noticing my discomfort.

He looked up, guilt on his face, and put his phone down.

"Where was it?" I asked.

I was expecting him to name somewhere in Boise—the Greenbelt, the capitol building, the farmers market.

"Vermont," he said.

"Can we change the subject?" Mom asked.

And then we did. We talked about normal, usual things, and for a brief time, I forgot that life had become anything but normal and usual. We talked about Rob's job at Avion, the local water company. We talked about Mom's job at Berger Construction. She's been their office manager for as long as I can remember. They seem happy—Rob and Mom. Mostly, that makes me happy too, but a small part of me is heavy with sadness. Their life together feels complete. I, on the other hand, have no idea what I'm doing. Floundering, that's what I am. Floundering.

I get out of bed and go to the kitchen, thinking I'll find Mom cleaning up after last night's dinner. It's not her though; it's Rob. Like I said, he's a good guy. He has no qualms about chores.

"Hey, good morning," he says.

He has the coffeepot in one hand. He raises it to me, an offering.

"Please," I say.

He pours me a cup, and I sit at the kitchen table.

"The yard looks nice," I say, staring out the sliding glass door.

When it was just Mom and me, the yard was a mess. We promised ourselves we would turn it into something HGTV-worthy at some point. That didn't happen until Rob moved in.

"Thanks, thanks," he says.

He sits at the table with me.

"There's something I've been wanting to ask ya."

He looks around, as if making sure Mom isn't nearby. That's how I know what he's going to ask me. My heart sinks a little, though I know it shouldn't.

"You want to marry her?" I ask.

He raises a finger to his lips, shushes me. "Quiet, you," he says playfully. Then: "How'd you know?"

"It's pretty obvious you two are crazy about each other."

"I'm crazy about her. She's just crazy. But I love crazy."

I smile. I feel old, like I am their parent, giving permission to the young kids to follow their eager hearts. Will I ever feel young again? Will I ever feel carefree and irrationally optimistic and hopeful? Or did that all die when I survived?

"Do you have the ring?" I ask him.

The way his eyes light up, I know the answer is yes.

He gets up, goes to the pantry. "I'm hiding it at the bottom of a box of bran flakes," he whispers.

We both know Mom wouldn't go near a box of bran flakes. She's more of a frosted flakes kind of girl. Rob is something of a health nut—not in an annoying way, but in an admirable way.

He used to be a smoker, had a heart attack when he was forty-something, and changed his lifestyle. Now he wears one of those fitness trackers on his wrist and, apparently, eats bran flakes.

He takes out the cereal box and brings it to the table. Below the plastic bag containing the bran flakes is a black jewelry box.

"Go ahead," he says. "Open it."

The ring is beautiful—an oval-cut diamond, with two smaller diamonds beside it.

"It's gorgeous. Did she help you pick it out?"

"No way. This was all me," he says.

"Nice job," I say, truly impressed. "When are you asking her?"

"Well, now that I've got your blessing, any time," he says. "Wait, I do have your blessing, right?"

I smile. "Yes, you do."

"And just so you know, you don't have to call me Dad or anything like that," he says.

I hadn't even considered calling him "Dad." I've never given anyone that title before, so I don't know why I would start now. Maybe he thinks I've been missing that in my life. Maybe Mom told him something to that effect. I can picture that: *She's never had a father before.* But the thing is, when you haven't had something for twenty-three years, sometimes you don't even know to miss it. It would be like saying, "Do you miss rock climbing?" to someone who has never been outdoors.

"You'll be my first call if I need someone to walk me down the aisle," I say.

"I'd be so honored," he says, nodding his head reverentially. "Is that in the cards any time soon?"

"Negative," I say.

During our marathon talk last night, they'd asked me how

things were going with Ryan. I was vague because that's yet another thing I didn't feel like getting into. Ryan and I texted a bit last night. He asked again, "Are we okay?" I was honest. I told him I didn't know. I told him I didn't know much of anything anymore. He said we'd talk when I get back. *When.* I didn't have the heart to tell him I wasn't sure I could call Boise home again.

I hear my mom's slippers shuffling down the hardwood floors of the hallway. Rob puts the ring back in its hiding spot and returns the cereal box to the pantry.

"Teresa Rose, what the heck are you doing awake?" Mom calls out.

When she enters the kitchen, her hands are on her hips. She's wearing a maroon robe, her frizzy hair gathered in a bird's nest of a bun on top of her head, glasses on her face. Rob hugs her, lifts her off the ground, spins her around, as if she's dressed in an evening gown for a fancy night out.

When he puts her down, she looks at me and says, "Seriously, Tess, what are you doing awake?"

"Sleeping hasn't been one of my strong suits lately."

"I thought we gave you enough wine last night to solve that problem," Rob says.

"We can try again tonight," I say.

"So you're staying?" Mom says. She makes no apparent effort to hide her excitement.

"If I can."

She waves me off. "That's a ridiculous thing to say. Of course you can. You can stay however long you need to. Or if you're staying for good, we have a job opening at Berger. And do you remember Shelley? Her daughter is looking for a roommate," she says, a runaway train of possibilities.

"Slow down, Mom," I say.

"She gets carried away," Rob says, with a good-natured roll of his eyes.

Mom comes to me, puts her hands on my shoulders, squeezes my tense muscles. We used to trade massages on a nightly basis when it was just the two of us.

"I'm trying to take it one day at a time," I tell them.

Mom knows a thing or two about this. When I was a teenager, she confessed that when I was a few months old, we had to live in her Ford Explorer for a week. It was after her landlord had refused to grant her another chance, and before her first paycheck from Berger.

"Honey, sometimes one day at a time is the very best you can do."

JOYCE

ON MONDAY MORNING, GARY and I make the twenty-minute drive to City Hall West, where the Boise Police Department is located. Gary asked if he could come, probably figuring I would need some kind of emotional support. We sit in the lobby, which is friendlier, less sterile than I imagined a police department lobby to be. There are upholstered benches, even a kids' area with child-size chairs and a toy fire hydrant. The only reminder that this is a police department is the bulletproof glass at the front counter.

A female officer comes out to greet us. She's young, twenty-something. She introduces herself as Officer Evans. Her handshake is loose, the kind of handshake that makes you feel insecure, the kind of handshake that makes you wonder if the person wants nothing to do with touching you. I wonder if this is how she shakes hands with everyone or if this is how she shakes hands with the mothers of murderers.

"Detective Kinsky will be right out," she says.

She offers us cups of water from a cooler, but we tell her we're fine.

A few minutes later, Detective Kinsky comes to greet us. He seems even larger than the first time I met him. He towers over Gary.

"Ms. Ketcher, nice to see you," he says.

His handshake is firm.

"This is Gary, my friend," I say. I don't know what else to

call Gary. I'm too old for "boyfriend" and it's too premature for "partner."

Detective Kinsky shakes Gary's hand too, and then we follow him back to his office.

His office is clean and organized, as if he spends hardly any time in it. He sits in the chair behind his desk, and we sit in the chairs on the opposite side of the desk. I stare at the bookshelf behind him. There are a few framed photos of him with what must be his family. I glance at his hands, confirm a wide gold band on his wedding ring finger. There are two children in the photos—a girl and a boy, around the ages of eight and ten when the photos were taken. His wife is beautiful, with long, thick brown hair that most women in their forties can no longer maintain.

"So," Kinsky says.

He leans forward, rests his elbows on his desk.

"As I've mentioned to you already, we found a journal on your son's computer. It wasn't something he made public, wasn't a blog or anything like that. It seemed to be just for himself," he says.

Gary and I nod simultaneously.

Kinsky pushes a stack of paper about three inches high to our side of his desk.

"That's it," he says. "His journal. Every page of it."

Jed was never much of a writer, always struggled in English class. The fact that he has written hundreds of pages both impresses and frightens me. How did I not know he had so much to say? How did I not see how much he was hiding?

"Wow," Gary says.

Because I'm just sitting there, frozen, Gary reaches for the stack. He turns the first page, starts scanning. It annoys me. I reach over, press my palm flat against the stack.

"I want to read it first," I say, aware I sound like a tantrum-ing toddler. It doesn't make sense, I know that. At this point, many people in the police department have read this. I am not the first. But I don't want Gary to know my son before I can.

Gary does not fight me. He pushes the stack gently, closer to me. I clasp my hands, rest them atop the stack.

"What we've determined in reading the journal is that he was fixated on ending his own life. It was something he had been thinking about for a couple years."

I take this in.

A couple years.

"But there are no mentions of a plan to hurt others," he says. "Which is highly unusual in cases like this."

"What does that mean?" Gary asks.

"Well, we think he would have written about it if he'd been planning it. This journal was hidden on his computer. It was clearly private, as you will see when you read it yourself."

I swallow hard, not sure I want to know what the pages contain.

"He was a very angry young man. Very resentful. He felt vic-timized by the world. These are common things with shooters," he says.

With shooters.

My son is a type now. He is in a category.

"But most shooters have a specific plan, right?" Gary says.

I'm glad he's here. I don't think I'd be able to manage ques-tions on my own.

Kinsky nods once. "They do," he says. "We have reason to believe this was more of an impulsive act. He was acting alone. There wasn't a larger plan. Something that night set him off."

It's just like Lindsey said.

"We pulled surveillance downtown and saw a traffic

incident that we believe may have been the thing that triggered him."

"A traffic incident," I say.

Kinsky turns his computer screen to face us. He clicks play on a video. It's black and white, grainy. The vantage point is a traffic light, looking down on the street below.

"This car, here, runs the red light," Kinsky says, pointing at a nice-looking sedan, a BMW or Mercedes, maybe. "And that happens right as Jed's car is coming down the street."

Jed's Mustang comes into view and tingles go down my arms and legs, as if every nerve in my body has been pinched.

The BMW or Mercedes comes so close to hitting Jed. I wish he'd hit him. I wish Jed had been injured. What if this fateful night had ended with him in an ambulance, not dead, not a murderer?

I cringe as I watch. Jed gets out of his car. There is no audio, but I can tell he is screaming. The other car drives off, and Jed gets back in his Mustang and speeds in the same direction, presumably to follow him.

"So you're saying road rage prompted him to kill five people?" Gary says, his tone skeptical.

Kinsky turns the computer back to face him.

"In talking to people who were in the bar that night, it seems it was a very crazed scene. He was approached by people who saw he had the gun, people trying to stop him, and he shot. More than one person said that a few of his shots appeared to be accidental, like he was flustered."

Accidental.

Flustered.

You would think this would make me feel better in some way, but it doesn't. It makes me angry, at Jed, at his stupidity, at his recklessness.

"We think the man in the BMW was his target," Kinsky says.

"Who was it? Which of the victims was it?" I ask.

"Well, actually, he didn't die."

Gary and I both lean forward at the same angle.

"What?" I say.

"You've got to be kidding me," Gary says.

It's not that I want that man to be dead. It's just that it appears that was Jed's misguided goal.

"He's one of the injured at Saint Al's. We don't plan to release his name or medical information at this time," he says.

"What will you be saying?" Gary asks. "In the press conference, I mean."

"Everything I told you here today, though we don't plan to show the footage of the road incident. We will not be releasing his journal, but we will be referring to it," he says.

"Why? Why share any of it?" Gary asks. He seems mad now. I'm mad too, but I know better than to take it out on Detective Kinsky.

"Mister . . ."

"McKee," Gary says.

"Mr. McKee, we think it's important for the public to know this information. They should be aware of mental health issues, of how something like road rage can escalate. They should know that not every shooter has a specific plan. And that the availability of firearms in our society can allow for these types of impulsive incidents to happen."

I'm surprised by this brief insight into Detective Kinsky's political leanings. Gary sits back in his chair, defeated, deflated. There is no arguing with Detective Kinsky. He is right. The public should know these things.

Detective Kinsky stands from his chair, and we do the same.

"When is the press conference?" Gary asks.

"Tomorrow morning, ten o'clock," Kinsky says.

He leads us through the department, past rows of beige filing cabinets. There's a cliché pink box of doughnuts on one of the conference tables.

Gary thanks him. I can't manage any words. I just offer as much of a smile as I can muster. Then Gary leads me out of the police station, his hand on my lower back.

Outside, the sun is blinding. Gary stands in front of me, blocking my face from the abusive beams.

"I guess it clarifies some things, at least," he says.

I shrug. It does, I suppose. But clarity does not mean peace.

JED

I can't believe I'm back home, living in my fucking mother's house. Fucking Jay. Mom said I couldn't stay at home unless I got a stupid job. So I'm working the front desk at a fucking gym. My god, the people I see—the stay-at-home moms who shove their kids into the Playcare room so they can sweat off their gross breakfasts, the guys who think they're one workout away from professional football. Pathetic. But not as pathetic as me. I can't believe I'm fucking back home.

APRIL 20, 2017 *(entry crossed out, but writing still visible)*

Dear Jay,

It's 4:20 on 4/20. I bet you're getting fucking high on all the product I grew for you. Remember when you said, "We're partners, man"? We shook hands. Lol. What a joke. Can't believe how much time and money and brainpower I gave you and you just peaced out with that stupid bitch. I got Yoko Ono'ed. Whatever, man. I don't need you. I'll get back on my feet and come back and show you up. Fuck you.

JUNE 15, 2017

Got fired from the gym. LOL. That didn't take long. Apparently, some bitch complained that I was rude to her. Lady, I'm rude to

261

everyone. Whatever. They wanted me out of there, I could tell. It's not like I fit in. I haven't lifted a weight . . . ever? I'm going to Home Fucking Depot this afternoon for an interview. If I get this job, I'm gonna have to wear that stupid orange apron and everything. I'll be a real tool . . . selling tools. LOL. It's not like I can find a better job. What am I going to put on my résumé? That I got fired from Boise Bodyworks? That I'm a failed marijuana entrepreneur? That I got fucked over by the guy who was supposed to be my partner? Shit, I have to start all over now. In an orange apron. Like I'm baking fucking cookies.

JULY 1, 2017

I just realized I haven't had sex in two years. TWO YEARS. And even then, it was that chick who just wanted to get high. There are no single girls in Boise. Correction: there are no DECENT single girls in Boise. I kinda want to call Lindsey. Pretty sure she's dating someone. According to fucking Facebook. But dating ain't married.

AUGUST 4, 2017

Fact: Idaho is consistently among the states with the highest suicide rates. Just read that online. Can see why. It's either 1000 degrees in summer (global warming doesn't help) or -1000 degrees in winter. I hate it here.

APRIL 5, 2018

Lindsey got fucking married. She didn't tell me. Saw it on Facebook. Guy looks like a douche. His name is DOUG, which shares lots of letters with "douche." Probably has a corporate desk job, a 401(k), all that shit. That's what girls want. No respect for the path less traveled. I could have been that douche. Being a douche is the easy way. I chose the other way. And it would have worked if Jay hadn't fucking screwed me over. Whatever.

JULY 23, 2018

I hate Home Depot. Same as all the corporations—politics, stupid rules, ass-kissing galore. This guy Adam got a promotion that should've been mine. Total bullshit. There's no justice in the world, not even at fucking Home Depot. I asked Tim why they gave it to Adam and he said Adam is great with customer service. Which I guess means I'm fucking not. Nobody ever appreciates what I bring to the table. Customer service is BS. Who is the person organizing the stock, making sure everything is fucking running smoothly? Me. Whatever. I'm not gonna be here long anyway.

SEPTEMBER 2, 2018

What the fuck is up with all the fancy cars in Boise now? Forbes magazine says Boise is the fastest growing metro area in the US. This is fucking not good. All these rich assholes from Seattle and San Francisco are coming here and ruining the vibe. There didn't used to be traffic here. Is now. Houses are getting too fucking expensive. Mom's lucky she bought her house before all this crap. I can't wait to leave this place. Talking about Boise and the world in general. It's all going to shit. I don't know how anyone could find the point of it all. Global warming, stupid politicians . . . hell in a fucking handbasket.

OCTOBER 15, 2018

Decided I should probably just shoot myself. Used to tell Lindsey in high school that's the way I'd go. Hike into the foothills, far back in there, shoot myself. Point would be nobody would find me. I'd just decompose, be nobody's problem. But with all the fucking people coming to Boise, there are about a billion bikers in the foothills now, so some fucking biker will probably find me. Whatever. Good riddance.

FEBRUARY 5, 2019

I bought it. So now I have it. I'm keeping it in my closet right now, in a shoebox for fancy shoes that I threw away because I don't fucking need fancy shoes. It's not like I'm going to be someone's date to a fucking wedding. Maybe Mom will want me to wear them for my funeral. She's gonna be pissed when she goes to look for them and finds the empty box. Oh well. Keep wondering if I should leave her a note. Seems too cliché. What words could possibly be comforting? It'll suck for her, but this isn't about her. This is about the stupid world and me fucking leaving it.

MARCH 4, 2019

Snow on the ground. FUCK MY LIFE.

APRIL 1, 2019

I'm going to do it soon. Bye, life. You've been a bitch.

ANGIE

WHEN I GO TO the hospital at lunchtime on Monday, I'm more anxious than I usually am. There have been no calls from Dr. Harris, so I'm assuming there haven't been any developments since yesterday. Still, I know how fast these things can change.

I make the now-familiar turns through the maze of hallways and come to Cale's room. When I step inside though, he's not there. The place where his bed used to be is empty. I check the room number, wondering if I've officially gone crazy. But no, it's the right room. He's just not here.

Is he . . . gone?

He can't be gone. Someone would have called me, wouldn't they? What if it *just* happened? What if my cell phone is about to ring?

I stand there, waiting for the ring, staring at the space where he used to be, unsure what to do.

"Ms. Matthews?"

I turn around to see Nurse Nicole in the doorway. I can't tell from her face if she has good news or bad news.

"Where is he?" I ask. I can hear my heart thumping, can picture the adrenaline circulating through my body, my brain preparing for whatever Nurse Nicole is going to tell me.

"Oh, he's in a new room," she says.

Her smile tells me the adrenaline was not necessary.

"Oh," I say, putting a hand to my chest, willing my heart to slow before I go into full cardiac arrest.

"I can show you," she says.

I follow behind her down the hallway, my legs shaky, my heart still pounding. I really thought he was dead. In a matter of just seconds, my mind began preparing for my life as a griever, a widow, a single mother. I saw the text messages to Sahana and Aria in my mind: He's gone.

We make a few turns and then stop in front of a partially closed door.

"Here he is," she says, holding her arm out to one side, as if she's one of the models displaying a car on *The Price Is Right*.

I push open the door lightly. Before I see him, I see the light coming in from the window. The blinds are up. This room is already more hopeful than the old one.

His head is no longer wrapped in gauze. I can see his partially shaved head, his eyebrows. A lot of the tubes that were covering his face are gone. He looks more like a person than a patient.

I go to him, reach for his hand, squeeze it. As I do, I swear I see his eyelids twitch.

"Did you see that?" I say to Nicole, who is standing behind me.

She laughs. "Did he move?" she asks, as if it wouldn't be completely astounding if he had.

"His eyes moved. I saw it," I say.

I squeeze his hand a second time, hoping that will make his eyes twitch again. They don't though.

"He's been having lots of what we call reflexive movements," she says. "Eye twitching, limb movements, that kind of thing."

Right then he coughs. I jump, startled, and look at Nurse Nicole, waiting for her to react in a surprised or stunned way.

She is unfazed though.

"Coughing is common too," she says.

Common? It seems miraculous.

"This all seems good," I say. When she doesn't nod emphatically, I ask, "Is it good?"

"He is doing well. We had to adjust his ventilator because he's breathing so strong," she says. "The two drains in his head are out. We've removed his lines, stopped monitoring his ICP. These are all good things."

I nod, waiting for a "but."

"We're just waiting for some swelling in his throat to decrease, and then we'll remove the breathing tube."

This shocks me. "Are you sure he'll be able to breathe?"

"We think so," she says.

Just then, Dr. Harris walks in.

"Look at that—our patient's two favorite ladies," he says.

It's the first time I've heard him make something resembling a joke. I take this as a good sign.

Nurse Nicole excuses herself, and I resume staring at Cale, watching for more movements. I don't care if they're reflexive or voluntary; they are movements. They tell me he is here.

"We did an MRI this morning, and things are going in a positive direction," Dr. Harris says.

He's in a good mood, better than I've seen. I don't pretend to think it's related to Cale's status; I assume he got laid last night, probably by a nurse twenty years younger than him.

"He is having some neurostorming," he says. "But that's to be expected."

When he doesn't seem like he's going to bother explaining what neurostorming is, I say, "What does that mean?"

My eyes are still on Cale. His lips move just slightly.

"Neurostorming happens when the nervous systems have

difficulty regulating after a brain injury," he says. "Increased heart rate, increased blood pressure, tremors—those are some of the things we've seen in this case."

This case. I don't think he knows Cale's name. He probably never cares to know names.

"It's like overstimulation as the brain tries to reboot," he says. "We've been giving him medication to manage the symptoms."

"Okay," I say.

"I tell a lot of loved ones that the neurostorms are an indication that he's fighting."

That's what he *tells* them; I wonder if that's really the case. The neurostorms might mean nothing, just like the reflexive movements. Loved ones want everything to mean something. Neurosurgeons must bear witness to the extremes of desperation.

I want to ask Dr. Harris if I should be spending more time at Cale's bedside, given recent developments, but I know he won't give me a definitive answer. I doubt he's the type who believes in patients benefiting from the healing vibes of their loved ones. I decide I'll leave work early so I can stop by again before picking up Evie. There is something to watch for now. There are movements now. There is hope now.

Dr. Harris does his usual thing of looking at his pager and then leaving the room. I go to Cale, hold his hand again.

"You're there," I tell him. "I know you're there."

I stare at his face, awaiting anything—a twitch of an eye, his nose, his lips. There is nothing.

"I forgive you, for anything, for everything," I say.

I don't know if this is true. Do I forgive him? It is hard to be angry at him now in the state he's in, this position of ultimate vulnerability. So what if he was pursuing a younger woman? So what if he was using her as a distraction from a life he didn't really want? None of it matters now. Everything has changed now. If he wakes up, he might just be grateful to have any life at all. He may have no memory of his angst. He may have no memory of Tessa.

"You can wake up. We will figure things out," I say.

He may need to hear this. He may need my forgiveness, my permission to come back. Unlike Dr. Harris, I believe in this type of thing. I've read stories online, stories of coma patients who talk about being between life and death. Some say they saw the quintessential white light, encountered deceased loved ones, felt the presence of immense peace that could be described only as God. Then they came back, with a firm understanding that it wasn't their time.

"It's not your time," I tell Cale. "We need you here."

And then, I swear, he squeezes my hand.

There is no corresponding movement on his face, no furrow of his brows, no slight pucker of his lips, nothing like that. Just the faint squeeze. Nurse Nicole would probably call it a reflexive movement, but I don't know how it could be a coincidence that his hand would flex against mine in this exact moment.

I squeeze back, hoping he will respond again, to confirm I wasn't just imagining things. There is no second squeeze though. Of course there isn't. I am too greedy. I am meant to take solace in the small movement I got. I am meant to consider it a gift.

"I'll see you tonight," I tell him.

I wait, holding his hand—one, two, three, four, five minutes. Nothing.

As I walk out of his room, I can't help but turn back at the door, half expecting him to be propped up on his elbows in his bed, a mischievous smile on his face saying, "I got you good."

"I'll see you tonight," I say again.

And, finally, reluctantly, I go.

TESSA

IT'S ALL CATCHING UP with me, the fatigue. I knew I hadn't been sleeping well since the shooting, but I didn't realize how exhausted I was until I got to Mom's house.

It's the middle of Monday afternoon. Mom took the day off work to spend time with me, and all I feel like doing is sleeping. I've never felt this before—the complete inability to engage in any kind of activity, the absolute need to rest.

"I'm sorry I'm so boring," I tell her.

We are on the couch in the living room, watching episodes of *The Bachelor* that Mom had saved in her DVR. We used to watch that show together all the time. It was our thing. It started as a joke—"Let's just see what the hype is about"—and then became a weekly must. We weren't truly interested in the relationships formed; we saw it more as comedy.

"This isn't boring. I've been dying to watch these episodes for months," she says, reaching into a mixing bowl full of microwave popcorn.

"I can't believe you've been saving them," I say.

"For just this moment."

I let my head fall onto her shoulder. When my eyes get heavy, ten minutes into episode two, I let my body lie horizontal on the couch, my head on her thigh. I am safe here. It is something so simple, I almost want to cry.

In the episode, the bachelor and one of the women are at a bar. My eyes are closed, but I imagine this bar to be Ray's.

I am towel-drying glasses behind the bar. Cale is there, standing in his usual spot at the bar. He's just arrived. He seems rattled. He's looking behind him, over his shoulder, like he's worried someone is on his heels.

"You running from the police?" I ask him.

He doesn't laugh, doesn't even smile. "Running from a psycho on the road."

"That bad?"

"I just . . . I ran a red light. I cut him off. He was pissed. I cut him off."

"You need a beer," I say, trying to keep it light. He seems so unnerved, it's starting to scare me.

"Sure, yeah, a beer," he says.

He sits. I bring him a pint of the White Dog Hazy IPA.

"He got out of his car, was swearing at me, saying he was going to kill me," he says.

When he picks up the pint glass, I see his hand is trembling.

"I mean, I cut him off. I get it. I ran the red light as he was coming through. I could have killed him. I was distracted. I—"

"Okay, you need to calm down," I say with a nervous laugh. He is really scaring me now. He keeps looking over his shoulder.

"Yeah, I know. Okay. Yeah."

He takes a big sip, more like a gulp. His eyes look slightly less buggy when he sets the glass down.

"Maybe I should just go ahead and pour you another one now," I say.

Finally, he laughs and I relax a little.

Then there is a bang, what sounds like a firework going off.

"TESSA, TESSA," I hear.

It is not Cale's voice. It is a woman's voice, familiar.

"Tessa!"

My eyes flash open.

I am not in Ray's. I am in my mother's house.

"Tessa," she says, looking at me with concern.

I am sweaty. I can feel my hair sticking to my forehead, the sides of my face. I am breathing fast.

"Honey, you're here, you're okay," she says.

I am sitting bolt upright. Her palms are on my shoulders.

"You had a nightmare," she says. "It's okay."

I look around, ensuring I am where I think I am. Mom pulls me against her chest, rocks me back and forth like I am a baby.

It was Cale.

Jed Ketcher walked into Ray's with a gun because of Cale.

I wonder if I should text Joyce, tell her what I remember. Then again, how do I know if this is an actual memory, not just something imagined, something conjured by my subconscious?

"Honey?" Mom says, pulling away, her hands still on my shoulders. Her eyes scan mine. She looks so worried. I want to tell her I'm okay, but that feels like a blatant lie. I'm shaking, visibly. It's obvious I'm not okay.

"I think I remembered something about that night," I tell her.

She moves her hands to my hands. She holds them steady so they stop shaking.

"Do you want to tell me?" she asks.

"I think I know what made the shooter do what he did. There's this guy who had been coming to the bar pretty regularly for a while. He came in that night and was really frantic, saying he cut off someone on the road and the guy was really angry," I say. "I think it was Jed Ketcher he cut off. And he followed him to the bar. And, I don't know . . . he lost it, I guess?"

She's still scanning my eyes. I wonder if she's looking for

evidence that *I've* lost it.

"Honey, you don't know for sure this is how it happened," she says.

"I do. I talked to Jed Ketcher's mother, and she talked to a friend who was on the phone with him that night, and . . . it's a lot to explain."

Her eyes go wide with astonishment.

"You talked to Jed Ketcher's mother?"

I sigh. "Yes. Look, it doesn't matter. I mean, it does, but it's too much to explain."

Mom nods, slowly, taking everything in.

"But, this guy, the one Jed Ketcher was so angry with, I think he may have saved my life. He told me to run when I was just frozen behind the bar. He saw him coming. He knew what was going to happen."

"Okay," Mom says. I can tell she still doesn't know what to think.

"Like, maybe I should tell his wife about this. It will help it make sense."

"Whose wife?"

"The guy, Cale."

"Who?"

"The guy who told me to run. The guy who cut off the shooter on the road," I say, impatient for her to catch up.

"Cale?" she says, seemingly stuck on the oddity of the name.

"Yes, Cale."

"Cale what?"

"Cale Matthews," I say, unsure why she cares.

"Cale Matthews?"

Mom goes white. I've never actually seen someone go white right before my eyes. I've heard the phrase, of course, assumed it was an exaggeration of a real phenomenon. But it's not; she really does go white.

"What is it?" I ask.

Her eyes look pained.

"Oh, honey, there's something I need to tell you."

JOYCE

GARY SAID IT WOULD be best if I didn't watch the press conference. "What's the point?" he said. "You know everything
they're going to say. It will only upset you."

And he was right. But I felt the need to know, firsthand,
what was being said about my son. For the rest of my life, I will
be the only one advocating for him, speaking for him. It is my
responsibility, as his mother.

I decide I will attend the press conference in person. Gary
doesn't agree with this decision, but says he will go with me
anyway. I don't want to risk staying home because I don't know
if the stations will cut to the live press conference or if they'll
just save clips of it for their evening news programs. I want to
see the whole thing, in its entirety.

When we went to the police department yesterday, the
parking lot was three-quarters empty, just a few people milling
about. Today, the parking lot is full. There are news vans sporting logos for all the local stations. A crowd of people is congre-
gated in front of the station, everyone facing toward what must
be a podium. I can't see over the tops of everyone's heads.

I'm wearing sunglasses and a large sun hat to shield my face,
a hat I used to wear when gardening. I can't imagine life being
calm enough again for me to have interest in gardening. Gary
says I look like someone in disguise. He says I will draw attention to myself by attempting to not draw attention to myself.
Maybe he's right; we will see. I know there are reporters here

hoping to catch a glimpse of me or loved ones of the victims. Not much happens in Boise; these reporters are hungry. They know a human-interest angle for the Ray's Bar shooting could get them jobs in bigger markets.

We stand at the back of the crowd, though Gary says that's exactly where a hungry reporter will look for me. I tell him we'll take our chances. He grumbles to himself.

At exactly 10:00 a.m., there's a commotion and the crowd surges forward. I assume the police chief has come outside. With everyone's attention focused ahead, I stand on the edge of a concrete planter so I can see.

"Jesus Christ, Joyce, what are you doing?" Gary says, tugging on my arm. "You are literally putting yourself on a pedestal."

I slap his hand away. "Nobody is looking at me. They're looking up there."

Up there, Police Chief James Barnard is at the podium. There are the clicks of photos being taken with professional cameras, a sea of cell phones held overhead, attempting to get the best shot possible.

"Hello, everyone. Today I'm going to give you some updates on the Ray's Bar shooting, as we feel we've come far enough along in our investigation to share critical details that may affect the lives of our citizens going forward."

The camera-clicking slowly dies down, and the crowd goes silent. The sea of cell phones remain, videoing.

"At this time, we have found it safe to conclude that Jed Ketcher acted alone during this event. We have pored over his personal writings and have determined that he suffered from depression and had plans to commit suicide. His firearm was purchased legally in February, and he had no prior record of violence. Nowhere in his writings was there a plan for harming others, though he did express profound anger with the world at large. In looking at surveillance footage from the night of the shooting, we observed that Mr. Ketcher was involved in a verbal altercation with a man traveling south on Ninth Street after that man went through a red light and nearly collided with Mr. Ketcher's vehicle. We believe this altercation motivated Mr. Ketcher to follow this man to Ray's Bar. When he arrived, patrons attempted to confront him, which escalated his rage, resulting in the shooting deaths of five people and injuries to two others. At this time, we will take questions."

I expect the crowd to erupt with inquiries, but there is just a low rumble of discussion, people turning to those around them and commenting. I don't know what they're saying. I probably don't want to know.

"Can we go now?" Gary says, tugging on the sleeve of my sweater.

The first question Barnard addresses is about the identity of the man who had the altercation with Jed. He does not share it, as Detective Kinsky said they wouldn't.

"Joyce, come on," Gary says.

He wants to slip away now, before the crowd starts to break apart and people turn back toward their cars.

I accept the offering of his hand and step down from the planter. When we get inside our car, unscathed, he breathes an audible sigh of relief.

"I wonder who he is," I say.

"Who?"

"The man who almost hit Jed's car on Ninth Street. I mean, how do you think he feels, knowing he may be the reason for all this?"

Gary takes his eyes off the road to look at me.

"Joyce, nobody but Jed is the reason for this."

He says this carefully, as if it's news to me.

"I know that," I snap. I refuse to be cast as the delusional mother defending her angelic son. I know what Jed did. "I'm just saying, it could be assumed that this wouldn't have happened if that man hadn't run the red light."

"It wouldn't have happened if Jed didn't own a gun either," he says.

I roll my eyes, look out the window.

"You don't have to make me feel worse than I already do," I say.

He reaches over, puts his hand on my thigh. I ignore every instinct and let it sit there.

"I'm sorry," he says.

He doesn't clarify if he's sorry for what he said or sorry that the truth of my son will always cause me pain.

"Me too."

I'm glad they didn't say much about Jed's journal. I want to burn the thing, the entirety of it. I want to never see it again. The person it reveals is not the person I knew. He is so angry and bitter and entitled and mean and pathetic and sad—all the things a parent never wants to see in their child. Gary wanted to read it, but I refused. He never had any fondness for Jed; the journal would only confirm his suspicions that my son had no redeeming qualities. Jed was kind to me, though. He cared for me, or I thought he did. I still cannot understand why he didn't leave me a note, something to explain, something to console me. I'm left to assume that he hated himself so much that he thought I would be relieved if he died. He didn't presume I would need any consolation. How did I raise someone with so little value for himself, for life?

GARY AND I have decided to make his place "home" for now. Yesterday, someone left an anonymous note on the welcome mat of my house, telling me I would burn in hell, among other things. It doesn't feel safe there. I would sell it, except I'm not confident I could afford to buy a new house right now. As Jed said in his journal, the housing market in Boise is crazy. I never would have guessed Jed paid attention to things like the housing market. There were so many things in his brain—annoyances, grievances—that I had no idea about.

Gary goes to his garage to tinker when we get home. I know that means he wants time to himself, to think. I'm sure he wants to fast-forward a year or two, to put distance between us and this horrible thing that happened. I don't know if I'll ever feel sufficiently distant from it though. It will always be *right here*.

While he tinkers in the garage, I turn on my laptop, go to the message board. I can't help myself. I know the message boarders will have watched the press conference. I know they'll have opinions, opinions I should probably avoid hearing, but, like I said, I can't help myself.

LvAll21 says:

5 people dead over road rage. What a waste.

JR2018 says:

TBH, I was kinda disappointed. Thought there was gonna be more to the story. Turns out just a loser with a temper. Snore.

LvAll21 says:

Imagine how the victims' families feel. Like, this could have been so easily prevented.

Boyseeeee says:

I dunno. Clearly the guy was gonna snap somehow.

JR2018 says:

Coulda snapped and just killed himself. That woulda been the right move.

I read these words without much reaction. I understand their feelings, in an objective way. I hate them for talking about Jed so flippantly, like his life meant nothing, but I understand. They didn't know him. They are just people with too much time on their hands on a stupid message board called "Shooting the Shit."

I dare to type a question, my first contribution to the thread.

MamaBear208:

Does anyone have any idea who the man was? The man in the altercation on Ninth Street?

It takes only a few minutes for a response. The fact that these people respond so quickly makes me think they get alerts on their phone when the thread is active. They live for this. Their hearts skip beats over this.

Boyseeeee says:

Prolly one of the dead guys. Jason Maguire, Robert Lang, or Rick Reed. My money's on Jason Maguire cuz he was kinda young, seems like the type to run a light.

I know something these people don't know. Detective Kinsky told me the man who incited Jed wasn't killed.

MamaBear208:

But they didn't release his identity, which makes me think he was one of the injured people.

JR2018 says:

@MamaBear208, where u been all this time? Got ourselves a
regular armchair detective now.

LvAll21 says:

Lol.

Boyseeeee says:

Ha. Well, could just be the dead guy's family doesn't want his name
out there as the person who caused this thing.

There it is, another person saying that this event was
"caused" by someone other than Jed. I know it wasn't. I know
Jed is to blame. But still.

MamaBear208:

Does anyone know the names of the injured people?

Boyseeeee says:

Ya. Someone posted that a while back. Kat Reynolds and Cale
Matthews. I'm guessing Cale is a guy. WTF is that name? If ur
theory is right, maybe it's him.

Cale Matthews.
It must have been him.

Boyseeeee says:

How ridic if the guy he was targeting lived and these other people
died.

LvAll21 says:

"Ridic" is one word for it. Tragic is another.

JR2018 says:

@LvAll21, the resident poet.

I hit the power button on my phone; it goes dark.

I want to meet Cale Matthews. I'm not angry with him; truly, I'm not. I just want to talk to him about what happened. I want to see Jed through his eyes. I want to understand this rageful version of my son.

He's one of the injured at Saint Al's.

That's what Detective Kinsky said.

Saint Al's is just ten minutes away.

"Gary?" I call out toward the garage.

"Yep?" he calls back.

"I'm going out to get some lunch."

If he's smart, he'll know this is strange. I don't often go out to get some lunch. And if I was going to, I would invite him.

There's a long pause. I think he might be getting off his stool, coming to investigate my true intentions.

"Okay," he says finally.

There's a tentativeness to the "okay," as if he knows I'm up to something but he's going to let me be. It's not apathy; it's trust. It's love.

KAT REYNOLDS

VICTIM #6, INJURED

I'VE NEVER BEEN TO a therapist before. So far, it's just like it is on TV. I'm sitting on a couch, across from this woman named Tracy who's sitting in an armchair you'd see in someone's grandma's living room. She seems nice enough, but I'm having a hard time keeping eye contact with her. I feel like she's staring into my soul or something. It's creepy.

"So, how does this work?" I ask her, fidgeting with a loose thread in my jeans. They're the "distressed" jeans that are in right now. I paid fifty bucks for them—on sale—and they came with holes in the knees.

"It works however you want it to work," she says.

"I don't know how I want it to work."

"Well, let's start with what motivated you to call me," she says.

The truth of it is that I made the appointment at the insistence of my parents and my girlfriends—Carrie, Michaela, and Britt. They were the three with me that night, at Ray's. Carrie is the one who recommended Tracy. "She's helped me so much already," she said. "Please call her."

Carrie has been in therapy for years—ever since her parents divorced when she was eleven. So when the shooting happened, she already had someone to call to help her "process" it (her words). Carrie has tried to convince Michaela and Britt to call Tracy too, but I can tell Carrie's most worried about me. I was the one who got shot, after all.

I was trying to find the bathroom when the guy with the gun came in. Even now, I refer to him as "the guy with the gun." I know his name, but it's weird to think of him as an actual person. I prefer he remains a shadow in my mind.

I was drunk—so drunk, too drunk. I guess I was supposed to be—it was my twenty-first birthday—but I didn't like the feeling. I hardly ever drink, can't rationalize the calories. In preparation for my birthday dinner, I hadn't eaten all day. I live in fear of someone presenting a pizza and cake to me, forcing me to eat it. That didn't happen, of course. I got a salad, dressing on the side, like always. My friends didn't question it—either because they completely understand how I am or because they completely don't. The waiter brought a slice of cake when they told him it was my birthday. We passed it around the table, sharing. I took a few tiny bites—less than a hundred calories, I'm guessing.

I didn't know where the bathroom was in Ray's because I'd never been there before. And I was so unsteady on my feet, my head fuzzy with the few shots of tequila I'd had. I chose tequila because I knew it was only about seventy calories per shot, as opposed to vodka, which has about a hundred. I don't know what I would do without Google. Well, I guess maybe I wouldn't be anorexic.

I was heading to the bar to ask the girl working there where the bathroom was. That's when everything happened. It was all so fast. I don't think the guy with the gun *wanted* to shoot me. He was crazed and I was just sort of . . . there. When I saw him shoot the others, I moved toward him. I don't know why— instinct? Maybe I wouldn't have moved toward him if I hadn't been so drunk, so inhibitionless. Maybe if I'd eaten more that day, I wouldn't have been so drunk. Somehow, it comes back to this being my fault.

I don't know what I thought I was going to do—tackle him with all ninety of my pounds? I must have scared him because he fumbled with the gun and it went off. There was this immediate pain in my shoulder, but I didn't know what had happened at first. Everything around me slowed down. It was like when you're underwater and you can't hear anything and you're just in this other universe. Then I saw him shoot himself. He held the gun right to his temple and pulled the trigger. He collapsed so quickly, hit the ground with a thud. I stared at the blood spatter on the wall next to him. That's what I see every time I close my eyes now—the blood. That's why Carrie says I need to see Tracy.

"I was at the Ray's Bar shooting," I begin. I've already told her this, on the phone, but she nods intently, paying close attention. I can't handle that attention, so I stare out the window.

"You were shot," she says. Again, we've already covered this on the phone. Even if we hadn't, my injury is pretty obvious. He shot me in the shoulder. I'm still in a sling. According to the doctors, I was incredibly lucky; the bullet missed the subclavian artery by just a few millimeters. I needed surgery to repair some blood vessel damage, and they don't know if I'll get full motion back, but I'm alive.

"Yes, I was the last person shot," I say. "I mean, before he shot himself."

"That must have been so traumatic," she says.

Her eyes get teary, and I'm taken aback. She barely knows me, and she's crying.

"Maybe I'm still in shock," I say. "I don't know."

"You probably are," she says, composing herself. "It wouldn't be uncommon."

"I kind of wonder why I lived," I say, running my finger up and down the seam of the couch cushion.

"Why?" she asks.

I shrug. "Those other five people died. I just wonder why I lived."

"Do you feel guilty that you lived?"

I shrug again. "I don't know. Not guilty. Just, like, I wonder if it means something. Am I supposed to do something different with my life now?"

"I don't know. Is there something you want to do different with your life now?"

I stuff my hands under my thighs, dare to look up at her.

"I want to stop thinking about food all the time," I say.

I look for judgment on her face, or surprise at the very least. There is nothing. She just nods. Maybe she knew, just by looking at me, what my secret was. Maybe I'm not as clever as I think.

"Tell me more about that," she says.

"Okay," I say.

I start from the beginning, figuring she may as well know the whole story. I haven't told it to anyone except the therapist in the treatment center I went to when I was seventeen. Mom and Dad still think that three-month stint cured me. I've lost twenty-five of the thirty pounds I gained there, but they insist on believing I'm okay. They never ask me if I'm not; they don't want to know.

I tell her about my autistic little brother, Aidan, how he got all the focus and attention, for obvious reasons. I tell her how my parents didn't have time for me, how they still don't have time for me. When they showed up at the hospital the day after the shooting, the look of concern on their faces made me giddy.

I'd never seen them concerned for me before, just for him.

"I'm aware this all makes me a selfish brat," I say to Tracy. "Just to get that out there."

She shakes her head. "Because you have needs? As their child?"

"Aidan has more needs. That's just a fact."

"His neediness has nothing to do with yours. You are still allowed to have needs."

The therapist at the treatment center tried to tell me the same thing. I left there with the understanding that my anorexia was about making myself smaller, taking up less and less space. It was like I was saying to my parents, "You want me to have no needs? Look, I don't even need food!" It was a subtle fuck-you to them, and they didn't even seem to notice, not even when I dropped to eighty-five pounds. My high school friend Michelle's mom had to intervene and tell them, "I think Kat might have an eating disorder." That's when they put me in that treatment center, so they would look like good parents.

After I got out of treatment, I started at Boise State. It wasn't my top pick—I would have preferred to stay in Oregon—but I got a scholarship, and I knew that was important to my parents. They both had good-paying jobs, but care for my brother is really expensive—and they need care for him in order to keep their good-paying jobs.

"Is that when things got hard again, with the eating disorder?" Tracy asks.

I nod. "Yeah, I mean, I guess the treatment center helped me put weight on because I literally could not escape meals and stuff. But when I was on my own again, I was back to my usual ways."

"And what about now, after the shooting? I'm assuming a traumatic event like that would make you want to cling even tighter to your coping strategies," she says.

The morning after my surgery, they brought me a tray of food and I ate it, thinking, "I almost *died*. I will eat these dry eggs and these terrible pancakes because I'm *alive*." I told myself I'd stop counting calories. I wanted to reserve the brain space for something else, something better. But just a day later, I was fretting about the sugar in the apple juice they gave me with lunch.

"I want to live differently now," I say.

I feel embarrassed saying this, speaking as if I've been transformed or something.

"How so?"

"I just don't want to think so small anymore," I say. "My old therapist, the one at the treatment center, used to say, 'Your eating disorder is your way to make mountains *into* molehills.' Like, I'm too afraid to deal with these big things in life, so I focus on controlling my calories."

"That makes sense."

"Does it?"

She nods. "Of course. Like I said earlier, it's a coping strategy."

"I don't want it to be anymore," I say. "I can't survive this shooting and just go back to being this pathetic girl who knows how many tortilla chips are in a serving."

Twelve. There are twelve in a serving—140 calories.

"You are not pathetic," Tracy says.

I roll my eyes. "Yeah, yeah," I say.

"Look at me," she says. The command startles me. I look at her, obedient.

"You are not pathetic," she repeats.

My face gets tingly, like it does before I cry.

"Okay," I say.

"You did survive this for a reason."

I want to believe she has psychic powers, that she is going to tell me all these amazing things I'm going to do with my life.

"And you get to decide what that is," she says.

So, the mystery remains.

"How do I not be anorexic?" I ask.

She gives me a smile. "The simple answer—you learn to accept your needs, trust your needs, and feel empowered by your needs."

"What's the complicated answer?"

"We work on it, over time, together," she says.

"That doesn't sound that complicated."

She smiles again and glances at her watch. "Our time's about up for today, so I'll consider those famous last words."

ANGIE

I DIDN'T GO TO work today. I went straight to the hospital this morning because I wanted to be there when they took out the breathing tube. That happened at eight o'clock. There were several people in the room, probably in preparation for the worst. While it was happening, I closed my eyes, feeling like a little kid going through a dark tunnel on a road trip drive. The room went silent. I held my breath while waiting to see if Cale would be able to find his. It was like I wanted all the oxygen in the room available to him, should he need it.

"Alright, he's doing it," Nurse Nicole said.

"It" meaning breathing on his own.

That's when I opened my eyes.

I couldn't believe it really. I watched his chest move up and down on its own, in awe of his body's ability to perform this basic skill.

It's been two hours now and he's still breathing. I, on the other hand, am holding my breath for long intervals.

Nurse Nicole comes in around ten thirty and quickly turns off the TV. I always have it on when I visit. I figure it's good for Cale to hear familiar sounds. The look on Nurse Nicole's face—a mild panic—makes me turn around to look at the now-black screen.

"What was it?" I ask.

Clearly, there was something she didn't want me to see.

"Just the news," she says. "Nothing good."

She's nervous.

"What is it?" I ask again.

I reach for the remote, push the power button. Her shoulders slump in defeat.

It is the news. But it's not "just" the news.

There is a reporter in front of the police department. The ticker at the bottom of the screen says:

Press Conference on Ray's Bar Shooting

I turn up the volume. The reporter is summarizing what apparently just happened.

"Police Chief Barnard says they have determined that the shooter, Jed Ketcher, was triggered by a traffic incident on Ninth Street the night of the shooting."

She goes on to repeat this same thing, with slightly different wording, then adds that Jed Ketcher acted alone and had no apparent premade plans for the attack.

A traffic incident?

This whole thing was caused by a traffic incident?

I turn off the TV.

"Why even have a press conference?" I say. But when I turn, Nurse Nicole is gone. I am talking only to Cale.

Cale is in a coma because of a "traffic incident." The absurdity is infuriating.

I go to him, hold his hand. Just as I do, his entire body starts to tense. I'm excited, at first—*something's happening, something's happening*—but then scared as his breathing becomes heavy and his jaw clenches. Is he seizing? Sweat beads form in seconds, dotting his head. I can see a thin layer of sweat break out on his arms. Machines start to beep, probably because of how fast he's breathing, and Nurse Nicole rushes in, along with another nurse I met earlier whose name escapes me.

"What's wrong?" I ask.

The nurses ignore me, relay numbers back and forth to each other.

"What's wrong?" I ask again.

"Probably a storm," Nurse Nicole says.

A neurostorm, the first one I've witnessed.

I wonder if he heard the reporter on the TV. Maybe it upset him as much as it did me. Or maybe he could feel the anger in the grip of my hand. Maybe I transferred it to him, emotional osmosis.

"Is he going to be okay?" I ask.

They administer something, a sedative I assume, based on the way his body starts to calm.

"He'll be okay. It's just a small one," Nurse Nicole says.

I watch the red heart on the monitor blink as his heart rate goes down—185 to 155 to 120 to 100 to 85. I let go of a breath held so long that I feel a little dizzy.

"It's scary, I know, but he'll be okay," she says. Then she leaves, says she'll page Dr. Harris.

I sit in the chair at his bedside, watching his chest move. I'm afraid to touch him again. His head starts lolling from side to side a bit. It seems like he's in the midst of a dream. Do people in comas dream?

"Cale?" I whisper.

His lips move just slightly.

"Cale?" I say again.

Then he whispers one word. I swear he does. I swear I'm not just hearing things. At first, I don't understand. But then I do.

The one word he whispers is:

"Tessa."

CALE

I DECIDED I HAD to tell her. It was time. I never intended for things to go on as they had, with me coming to the bar, burdening her with small talk while I tried to work up the courage to tell her the truth. I'm a coward. Always have been.

Here's what I haven't told anyone. Here's what I should have told Angie in that beginning phase of dating, when confessions about pasts are standard.

I was only twenty-four when she was born. I guess that's considered an appropriate age to be a father, but I felt like a child. I met her mother, Janine, at a party. I wasn't even supposed to go to the party. I was working at an outdoor gear store called Wild World and a coworker invited me to come along, promising weed. So I went. When I got there, Janine was sitting in a beanbag chair, taking a hit off someone's joint. When she saw me, she said, "And who are you?" with a flirtatious smile. She was a little drunk. There was a keg of cheap, watery beer and some flasks of bourbon going around. We ended up in an upstairs bedroom, like a couple teens at a post-prom party.

We exchanged numbers, but I didn't call her. I didn't have much interest in a girlfriend at that time. I'd broken up with someone a few months before, was relishing alone time. (Or that's what I told myself. The truth is that I was probably a little depressed and dealing with it by escaping into the mountains on long hikes.) I was planning a solo backpacking trip—the Timberline Trail around Mount Hood. The night before I was set to leave, Janine called me, said she was pregnant. I didn't believe it. I asked how she knew the baby was mine, and she hung up on me.

I went on my backpacking trip, came back a week later to a message on my machine: "It is yours, you asshole. I'm due in March. Would be great if the child had a father."

I didn't call back. I'm a coward, remember?

She came to my door two months later, got the address to my shitty apartment from the coworker who had invited me to the party where I'd apparently conceived a human being.

She was clearly pregnant. I still couldn't believe the baby was mine though. I had spent maybe three hours with this person. I just couldn't see how we would be forever tied together by those three hours.

She was furious, of course.

"So you're keeping the baby?" I said.

She rolled her eyes.

"We're a bit past that discussion. If you had an opinion on the subject, you should have expressed it a while ago," she said. "And, yes, I'm keeping the baby."

I knew I couldn't be outwardly angry about this, but I was pissed. I'd had no part in the decision. None. I guess I assumed she would have had an abortion. I assumed most unmarried, unexpectedly pregnant women in a liberal town like Bend would get an abortion.

"I just want to clarify—you want no part of this?" she asked.

She drew an imaginary circle around her belly.

"I mean, I'm not going to abandon my kid," I said.

I knew that was the right answer. I saw a flash of hope on her face.

We talked for two hours—about logistics, plans. We decided I would move in with her (she had the nicer apartment). We would be parents, not lovers ("I mean, if it goes that way, fine. But that's not my focus," she'd said). It made sense to share expenses, share childcare. She had it all worked out. I nodded along, even though I felt my throat constrict, like I was choking on something.

When the baby came, we named her Teresa. Well, Janine named her. I let Janine take the lead on everything. I felt like a stupid puppy on a leash with her. I tried to play the role of the proud dad, but I was terrified, panicked. I'd never held a baby, first of all. She was so small—not exceptionally small by baby standards, but I had no baby experience. I started working more at Wild World, took a second job at a bike repair shop. I told Janine it was to earn money for us, but I really just wanted out—of the house, of this strange life.

When Teresa was about six weeks old, she had one of the worst nights of her young life. People say babies cry, but she was howling. It was an animalistic, primal expression of dis-content, and neither Janine nor I had any idea what to do. She didn't want either of Janine's breasts, the usual soothers in these situations. Janine collapsed in a heap on the floor, said, "You take her. I can't do this." I thought it was insane of her to presume that I could.

The next morning, while Janine and Teresa slept off the hor-rible night (Teresa had finally fallen asleep around four o'clock in the morning, after hours of rocking her that left my biceps sore), I packed all my things into my car. It took just a couple trips. I left a note for Janine, telling her I was sorry, I wasn't capable of being a father. I left her all the money in my wallet, told her I would take out all the money in my bank account and send her a check in the mail. I did do these things, by the way. I'm not a *total* piece of shit. Well, maybe I am. After all, I left. I just *left*.

I went on a monthlong backpacking trip in the Three Sisters Wilderness, a trip without any destination, just meandering. There was this girl I worked with at Wild World who joked, "Camping is really just living like a homeless person." And that's how I felt—like a vagrant, a vagabond. I grew so much facial hair that I didn't even recognize myself when I finally emerged from the forest and looked in the mirror of my car. On that trip, I thought about what I'd done—abandoning my daughter. It was the thing I'd said I wouldn't do. I decided she was better off without me. Maybe I decided that because it was the easy conclusion. If I'd decided she needed me, I would have had to go back to them, reenter the life I'd left.

While in the wilderness, I'd thought about where to start over. I needed somewhere new. I picked Boise. I'd been there once, as a kid, and I'd liked it. I went to school, got a business degree. Then an MBA. I felt like I had something to prove— to Janine, to Teresa, to myself. When all was said and done, I was a thirty-five-year-old investment banker with a life people seemed to envy. It was strange. I dated, thinking when I met the right person, I'd tell her the secrets I'd kept for so long. But I never did. I thought it would be different with Angie. I felt like she understood me, saw me for who I was. But as more time passed, I knew I'd never tell her either. At a certain point, it was just too much to say, "I have a daughter somewhere." I couldn't do it.

I thought about Janine and Teresa over the years. I googled, kept tabs. But it wasn't until Evie was born that I started to unravel. I hadn't had much emotion about the whole thing over the years, had started to assume something was seriously wrong with me. But the emotion was there; it was just hidden until Evie came.

Evie looked so much like Teresa. It was uncanny. It was like the universe was punishing me on a daily basis—rightly so, I guess. Every time I looked at Evie, I was forced to think about what I'd done. It got to the point when I couldn't stand being around Evie. It's awful, I know. Evie didn't do anything wrong, of course. She didn't deserve a dad who was a detached asshole.

I was getting the strangely familiar itch to leave Angie and Evie. It scared me. I didn't want to leave them. I just couldn't stand myself. I started to think the only solution was making peace with the past.

I knew Teresa had moved to Boise, which I took as a slight shove from the universe. She was going to Boise State, working at a local bar—what were the chances? That's when I started going to the bar. I'd get to know her, I thought. Then I'd tell her. And she'd forgive me. It was a simple plan, stupidly simple.

The night of the shooting, Angie and I went to bed before nine, as usual. We weren't doing well. I was distant. I didn't know how to tell her why. If she knew, she would leave me, I thought. If I were her, I'd leave me.

I couldn't sleep. I knew I was going to the bar that night. I was going to tell Teresa the truth. Or Tessa, rather. She goes by Tessa—one of the many things about her that I should have known, as her father.

Sometime after ten, when I was sure Angie was asleep, I went upstairs, paced the kitchen while rehearsing my speech. I poured myself some scotch, threw it back. When you lack courage, you drink to create the illusion of it.

Tessa, I've been meaning to tell you something for a while. I'm sorry it's taken me this long. I understand if you never want to speak with me again, but I need to tell you the truth. I am your father. I left you and your mother when you were just six weeks old. I'm not asking for forgiveness. I just thought you should know.

I kept rehearsing after I got into the car.

That's what I was doing when I ran the red light—rehearsing. I was distracted. I wasn't paying attention. I was a little buzzed on that scotch.

I realized what I was doing about halfway through the intersection, but it was too late. Out of the corner of my eye, I saw the Ford Mustang coming at me. I heard the screech of his brakes. He came within a foot of hitting me. Adrenaline rushed through me. He got out of his car, yelling.

"What the fuck are you doing, motherfucker. You could have killed me."

He was young—twenties or thirties. There was this fury in his eyes. I'd never seen anything like it—pure rage. I put my hands up in the air, a motion of surrender, apology. He didn't seem at all placated by this. He kept yelling.

"You entitled fucker in your fucking Beemer. Fuck you."

"I'm sorry, man," I tried.

"You're sorry? Is that what you'd say if you'd killed me? Jesus Christ, man. Fuck you."

He was coming toward me, his pace fast and determined. He was still screaming.

The only thing I could think to do was leave. Just drive away. I put the car in drive. He ran toward me, slammed his fists against the back window before I drove away, my tires screeching against the asphalt.

When I pulled into the parking lot of Ray's, I wondered if he could have followed me. I parked, my heart still racing. *Just go inside*, I told myself.

So that's what I did.

I went inside.

I was fixated on sticking to the plan, telling Tessa the truth. I knew I would need a couple beers to do it, but it was going to happen. I would tell her, and she would forgive me. Even though my speech claimed I didn't seek her forgiveness, that's all I really wanted. Then I would tell Angie. And I would be able to look at Evie without hating myself. These were my hopes when I walked into Ray's that night. *This night will change everything*. I had that exact thought. I was right, I guess. I was right.

TESSA

WHEN SHE'S DONE TELLING me the story—of how they met at a party, how she got pregnant, how he left when I was six weeks old, how she knew he'd moved to Boise and still lived there—I'm shocked.

Then angry.

She'd told me my father was dead. And not just dead-in-a-car-accident dead, but dead-from-a-drug-overdose dead. There's a difference. She intentionally made him into someone I would never want to know. She lied.

"He left us, Tess," she says. "That's still the truth."

"But why didn't you just say, 'He left us. He lives in Boise'?"

I understand now why she didn't like the idea of me moving to Boise. She had to wonder if something like this would happen, if our winding paths would cross.

"I was afraid you'd go looking for him. I didn't want you to be disappointed. I was trying to protect your feelings."

There's not much to say in response to this. I know she meant well. It's hard to lash out at good intentions.

"I just wish you would have told me," I say, the anger leaving me. "I'm not a kid anymore. I could have handled the truth."

"I guess I always thought he would come looking for us and I'd tell you then. When he didn't, I thought, 'Well, he really is an asshole.' I didn't think there was any good reason for you to know him."

"You shouldn't have decided for me. Not once I became an adult. I had a right to know."

She nods, looks down at her lap. "I think maybe you're right about that."

Sometimes, that's all a person needs—an admittance of wrongdoing. Too often, egos don't allow for this.

When she looks up again, there are tears in her eyes.

"Mom, stop," I say, reaching toward her, even though I'm still upset.

"I'm just sorry," she says. "They say, 'mother knows best' . . . that's the real lie."

I sit next to her on the couch, our hips touching. She takes a tissue from a box on the end table.

"Okay, now you're being dramatic," I say, trying to lighten the mood.

She dabs at her eyes with the tissue.

"It's just so strange, you two finding each other."

"He must have known who I was, right?" I ask her.

She looks at me like she pities my naïveté. "Yes, honey. I don't think this was coincidence."

I think of what Angie said about how Cale might have had a "thing" for me. She misunderstood. She didn't know he'd had a daughter. I was his secret.

"What do I do now?" I ask her.

She shrugs.

"Should I tell his wife?"

She starts shaking her head before she responds.

"Honey, I don't know if that's your place. She might be angry at you."

"For what?"

"For existing," she says plainly. "You are evidence of his lies. He's in a coma. She's going to need someone to get mad at."

"It just seems strange to not tell her," I say.

"How would you even tell her? It's not like you *know* her."

I'm about to explain that I do kind of know her when my phone buzzes with a text message.

I look down and see the name "Angie Matthews" on the screen.

"What is it?" Mom asks. I must look dumbfounded.

"It's her," I say.

Three more texts populate the screen. I read them.

"Who?" Mom asks.

"She says he's waking up," I say.

"Who?" Mom asks again, still not getting it.

"She wants me to come there," I say. Then, finally answering Mom's question: "Angie. Cale's wife."

"What?" Mom says.

"She says he whispered my name."

JOYCE

WHEN I ASK THE woman at the Saint Al's reception desk for Cale Matthews's room number, she types his name into her computer and gives me the information without hesitation. I thought it would be more difficult. It's possible the press conference did what Detective Kinsky intended it to do—alleviated fears about Boise being under threat of additional violence. Jed acted alone. The threat is gone. That is the message meant to bring relief to our city.

I keep asking myself what my purpose is in being here. I guess it's the same purpose I've had since that night—apologizing on my son's behalf, making things right however I can, trying to understand. I am not angry at Cale Matthews. He made a mistake on the road. He ran a light, the most fateful, impactful mistake of his life. What happened next is Jed's fault. As tempting as it is to add an asterisk to the event—*But he was triggered by someone else*—I have to accept the statement without the footnote: Jed killed people. Jed is responsible for this evil thing.

When I get to his room, I see he is lying in bed, asleep, it seems. A woman is seated in a chair next to his bed, her back to me. Her elbows are propped up on the railing of the bed, her arms collapsed, hands stacked on top of each other, creating a little pillow for her forehead. I don't know whether to say something or just leave. I don't want to intrude. Before I can decide, she turns around, startled.

"Oh, you scared me," she says.

"I'm sorry," I say. "If this is a bad time . . ."

"For what?" she says. "Are you with the volunteer organization?"

"The what?" I ask.

We stare at each other with mutual confusion.

"I'm sorry, I'm here to visit Cale Matthews," I say.

"Oh," she says. "I'm his wife, Angie."

She stands from the chair, extends her hand to me. I use both my hands to take it, as if it is something fragile, precious.

"It's nice to meet you," I say.

Her eyes flick down to glance at my hands holding hers. I release, sensing she's uncomfortable.

"And you are . . . ?" she says.

"Oh, I'm sorry," I say.

Here is where I have to do the thing that scares me most:

"I'm Joyce Ketcher."

I do my best to remove fear from my voice, but I still hear it.

"Joyce Ketcher," she says, her eyes rolling upward, as if she's flipping through a Rolodex in her head, asking herself how she knows the name. It's obvious when she's figured it out. Her eyes roll down and she stares at me.

"His mother," she says, not as a question but as a statement of fact.

I nod.

She sits in her chair again, facing away from me.

"I'm sorry," I say. "I don't want to upset you. I really just wanted to tell Cale how sorry—"

"He's not exactly able to accept your apology," she says, not angrily but curtly.

I don't know if she says this because he's sleeping or because she knows how much he despises me.

Assuming the latter, I say, defensively, "I don't expect forgiveness for my son. I know what he did was awful. I just want to apologize to Cale for my son's actions. I can come back when he's awake or—"

"He's not *sleeping*," she says, a bitter bite to her words. "He's coming out of a coma."

A coma.

My son put this man in a coma.

"Oh," I say. "I didn't know . . ."

She turns to look at me now. Her face softens, as if seeing my probably-haggard-looking face zaps her antagonistic energy. We are just two women, here in this hospital room because of the men we love most.

"I guess the press has done a good job of keeping his medical situation private," she says.

I don't know what to do now. She's already dealing with so much. It seems cruel to tell her what I know about that night. She will think I'm subtly blaming her husband.

"I suppose I can just apologize to you then," I say. "I'm so sorry about Cale's . . . condition."

"You weren't the one who shot him," she says.

She slumps in her chair as she says this, as if this fact is a disappointment, as if she wishes I were the one who shot him, so she could unleash whatever pent-up feelings she has on me.

"Still. He was my son. I feel responsible."

That is the plain, simple truth of it. I decide in this moment that I will contact all of the victims' families, by letter first, then in person if they'll have me. I need to.

"Cale's had damage to his brain," she says. I can tell she doesn't say this to make me feel worse, but I do anyway. She goes on: "So we don't know what he'll remember or not. If you give me your number, I can let you know when he's up for a visit."

She gives me a small smile, a smile that says *I'm trying not to hate you. I'm trying to take the high road.*

"*If* he's up for a visit," I say. "I don't expect him to want anything to do with me."

She nods. "Okay then. *If.*"

We do the modern-day exchange of phone numbers—she tells me hers and I send her a text that says, "This is Joyce Ketcher." So she has my number. I doubt she will use it, but at least I can go home knowing I tried.

Just as I'm about to thank her and say an awkward goodbye, I hear the footsteps of someone else entering the room behind me.

"Tessa," Angie says.

Tessa? I wheel around. There she is, standing in the doorway, her eyes jumping from my face to Angie's.

"Joyce?" she says. "What are you doing here?"

"You two know each other?" Angie says.

The three of us stand very still, unsure how to proceed.

"I was just coming to apologize to Mr. Matthews," I say.

"Oh," Tessa says, understanding, though still seeming dumbfounded by this run-in.

"What are *you* doing here?" I ask her. I have no idea how she knows Angie Matthews.

"I asked her to come," Angie says.

This confuses me more.

Angie moves past me to Tessa. "Look, I don't know why he said your name, but he said your name. Maybe you can help him wake up. I think he was in love with you or—"

"He's my father," Tessa says.

The room goes silent. I must not be the only one whose mind is taking a moment to process this revelation.

Cale is Tessa's father?

"What?" Angie says. She takes a step back, as if this announcement has disturbed her balance.

"That's why he was at the bar," Tessa says. "He was trying to get to know me, or something."

Angie shakes her head. "Cale doesn't have a daughter. I mean, he has Evie. He doesn't have *another* daughter, certainly not a—how old are you?"

"Twenty-three," Tessa says.

Angie crosses her arms over her chest. I can almost see her doing the math in her head.

"He would have told me," she says.

There are tears welling up in her eyes. It's obvious this is what upsets her—his keeping of this apparent secret.

Tessa just shrugs, like, *Well, he didn't.*

Suddenly, the thing I came to say seems so irrelevant.

Suddenly, everything seems so irrelevant.

Cale Matthews went to Ray's Bar to see the daughter nobody knew he had.

On the way, he cut off the wrong person on the road.

That person happened to be my son.

My son shot Cale Matthews and five others.

It's a chain of events that simultaneously makes no sense and all the sense in the world.

Suddenly, life seems so absurd.

"How do you know this?" Angie asks, arms still crossed over her chest.

"My mom told me."

Angie looks perplexed, disbelieving. She stares at Cale, lying still in his bed, then turns back to Tessa.

"His daughter?" she says.

A single tear rolls down her cheek. I watch its slow descent, wondering how she must be feeling. If I'm not mistaken, she seems relieved in some way, like maybe this explains something, like maybe this explains many things.

Tessa nods, slowly.

"His daughter."

ONE YEAR LATER

ANGIE

"AM I READY FOR my close-up?" Cale asks.

We are sitting on our couch, chatting with Charlie, the twenty-something filmmaker who is going to interview us for his documentary about the Ray's shooting. His working title: *Remembering Ray's.*

"You look quite handsome," I say.

"Thanks to you," he says.

He's referring to the fact that I have to shave his face and style his hair every day. Cale's come a long way, but he still lacks some fine motor skills.

"So, before the others get here, I wanted to get some footage of you two reflecting on the road you've traveled since the shooting," Charlie says.

We are his first in a series of interviews. After us, he'll visit with Kat Reynolds (the young woman who was shot in the shoulder), Jenna Maguire (Jason Maguire's sister), Greta Lang Ferber (Bob Lang's daughter), Sherry Reed (Rick Reed's wife) and her two grown children, Mari and José Velasquez (Dan Velasquez's parents), Kenzie Baron and baby Olivia (Dan Velasquez's girlfriend and the daughter he never met), Joyce Ketcher, and Tessa.

"People need to see the lasting impact these events have," Charlie says.

It's just him and his cameraman, Joey, another twenty-something. They both have sleeves of tattoos. They are impassioned liberals, committed to making a film that will motivate lawmakers to ban assault rifles. I suppose I've become a bit of an activist myself. I have to do something with the residual anger; that's what Sahana says.

"Are there any topics off-limits?" Charlie asks.

The question scares me. I can tell it scares Cale too. We look at each other, shrug. What could this man—this boy, really—want to ask us? I flush at the thought of him inquiring about our sex life, which can only be described as incredibly awkward. He wouldn't ask that though. This documentary isn't about Cale and me. It's not even really about Cale. It's about this sensational thing that happened to him.

"I don't think so," I say, trying to sound like a woman with nothing to hide.

He points a finger at Joey, and I see the red light on his camera flash on.

"Tell us a bit about the recovery process, what you guys have gone through over the past year."

Cale looks at me, takes my hand, squeezes. He relies on me to say so much. His memory just isn't there.

"It hasn't been easy," I say, adding a little laugh because that's what I do when I'm uncomfortable.

Charlie makes a "go on" motion with his hand.

"In the movies, they make it seem like people just wake up from comas, and that's just not how it works. For Cale, he was in a state of what they call 'emerging consciousness' for weeks. Soon after waking, he was able to speak, so we knew that part of his brain was functioning. That was a huge relief for me. But he has had cognitive difficulties. He has no memory of the shooting—"

"Which is probably a blessing," Cale interjects.

"Yeah, and he doesn't remember many things from before

311

the shooting. He doesn't remember significant years in his past. Thankfully, he remembers me."

I give another little laugh.

"How could I forget her?" Cale says.

I roll my eyes good-naturedly.

"He was in a rehab center for a few months, then came home. But he's remained in therapies since."

"I've gone through several speech therapy sessions where they focus on teaching me memory strategies. I've had to learn little hacks, like taking my iPad wherever I go and jotting down things as they come to me."

He holds up his iPad, evidence.

"And he's had occupational and physical therapy to help with his fine motor skills and some ongoing fatigue and weakness," I say.

"What's the prognosis, long-term?" Charlie asks.

"They think I can get back to ninety percent of where I was, eventually," Cale says.

"His doctor actually said they've never seen somebody do so well after such a massive injury. Usually, people who survive the type of damage Cale had stay in a chronic vegetative state. It's kind of a miracle, how far he's come."

I never thought I would be this person, a person claiming miracles. But it's true. It's also a minor miracle that the ad agency has let me work from home full-time, so I can be there to help Cale. He's stubborn, tries to do everything on his own, but he's had to learn reliance on me. He's had to accept that he's no longer an island.

"We're very lucky," Cale says.

As if on cue, Evie bolts into the room, Aria chasing after her, muttering, "Sorry, sorry." Aria and her new boyfriend, Brian, are supposed to be confining Evie to the kitchen. They're at the stage in their relationship when they can't keep their hands off each other; it's nauseating, but I'm happy for her. I'm sure Evie snuck off while Aria and Brian were gazing into each other's eyes.

"She's just so fast," Aria says.

Evie laughs maniacally, and we can't help but laugh in return. Even Charlie and Joey are laughing, the camera still rolling.

"She can stay," Charlie says. "Evie, do you want to say hi to the camera?"

She sits on the couch next to Cale. "Hi, camera!"

Somehow, quiet and reserved Cale and I have created this sociable ham of a child. When I first brought Evie to see Cale at the hospital, I was worried he wouldn't remember her, though he said he would. When she came, there wasn't a hint of confusion on his face; he knew her. He doesn't have memories of much of her baby life, but I've started to think that's okay. It wasn't an easy time for him, for reasons I understand more now.

"How old are you?" Charlie asks, encouraging her.

She holds up two fingers. "But almost three!"

"What do you think of your dad?"

She looks at Cale thoughtfully, taking this question seriously.

"He's a superhero," she says.

She's never said this before. And I've never referred to him as that before. Cale and I look at each other, perplexed by this human we've created.

"What's his superpower?" Charlie asks.

She puts one finger to her chin. "Hmm," she says. "He can take very long naps."

We all laugh, and then she jumps off the couch and scurries

off, Aria on the chase again.

After Evie is gone, Charlie waits a beat. His hesitation unnerves me.

Finally, he asks, "What about Tessa?"

I exhale. Talking about Tessa is far less frightening than talking about our sex life.

"Of course, getting to know Tessa has been one of the big blessings of this whole mess," Cale says.

Word has spread about Cale and Tessa's father-daughter relationship. It's a captivating story, after all. Everyone also knows that Cale was the person who apparently triggered Jed Ketcher's rage that night. Puzzle pieces have come together, as they say. It's all fascinating, I guess, to the general public. It's my life, though, and it's complicated.

Cale has no memory of Tessa. At first, I wondered if he was just saying that, because it would be convenient to not remember. But his injuries had taken away his abilities to be that conniving. It was obvious on his face that there was just no recollection of Tessa, of his visits to her at the bar, of leaving her as a baby—none of it. If I'm honest, it relieved me, in a way. His memory loss has meant there is no point in attempting to unravel the past. It cannot be unraveled. We cannot fully understand his intentions, his thoughts, his feelings because he has no memory of them. It's like the person who had those intentions, thoughts, and feelings died at Ray's Bar that night. Now we have this new person. It is the epitome of a clean slate.

I imagine it's harder for Tessa. She has just learned who her father is, and he looks at her as if she is a total stranger. We've explained the facts to him, of course. He understands the truth of the matter. He's apologized to her profusely for his past actions, even though he doesn't remember them. They—we—have a standing weekly breakfast date at Goldy's. I go along to help in any way I can—filling in memories, answering questions for Tessa that Cale may not be able to answer. I know as much as she does, though. His existence had been unknown to her; her existence had been unknown to me. We're both kind of fumbling around in the dark. Sometimes, I wonder if that's what the entirety of my marriage is going to feel like from now on. But, like Cale told Charlie, the doctors are confident Cale will continue to progress. Everyone, including Cale, seems fixated on getting him back to who he was before. Secretly, I've let go of that expectation.

Sahana is the only person who has dared to ask about our sex life. We've just started trying to be intimate again. Cale has the physical ability; it's just . . . strange. The first time we successfully finished—well, he finished—he said, "I guess it's like learning to ride a bike." I laughed when I really wanted to cry. "You've been mothering him for a year," Sahana said. "It's bound to feel weird." She told me about this famous psychotherapist, Esther Perel, who specializes in counseling couples. In one of her TED talks, she says, "Most of us are going to have two or three relationships or marriages, and some of us are going to do it with the same person." My life with this new Cale feels like my second marriage, a marriage from a reality TV show in which the two people saying their vows barely know each other.

There are times I daydream about leaving him. Because it's hard. Because I'm human. I've done all the cliché things—screamed into pillows, downed bottles of wine, perused old boyfriends' Facebook pages, wondering what my life would be like if I'd married them instead. These truths will stay with me. They will not be part of any documentary. People want a fairytale ending, a happily ever after. They want it all to be neat and tidy, even though life is never like that.

"How's it been for you, Angie? You have a new daughter in your life, in a way," Charlie says.

"Well, Tessa has a mother. And she's an amazing woman. I wouldn't pretend to be Tessa's mother. Cale is her father, and I guess I'm a . . . friend."

I look to Cale, to confirm this is accurate. He nods, then says, "Tessa loves Angie."

I don't know if that's true, but it makes me feel good anyway. Tessa likes me. Tessa appreciates me. I am her liaison to knowing her father.

"How do you think the shooting has changed you, individually, as a couple?" Charlie asks.

Cale and I look at each other.

"I've become annoyingly dependent," Cale says, giving his own little laugh.

"He used to be annoyingly independent," I add.

"I mean, I don't really remember much of before, of who I was. So much of that is gone. In a way, the shooting has given me a chance to start over," Cale says.

He's taken this optimist view because we've both learned it's better than dwelling on what was lost. When my parents visited a few months back, meeting both Cale and Evie in person for the first time, they refused to pity me. As distant as we've been over recent years, they know me well enough to know I don't want pity. Their goodbye hugs were tight, but not lingering. "Just keep moving forward," my mom said. "And come visit us in Maui when you're ready," my dad added.

"Obviously, daily life has changed a lot," I say. "Cale's rehab has been intense—physically, emotionally. My entire focus has changed. But all the platitudes are true—about gaining perspective, gratitude, all that stuff."

"Are you angry at Jed Ketcher?" Charlie asks.

I shake my head, immediately. This answer is simple.

"I've talked so much with his mother, Joyce. I can't be angry at her son. I'm sad about it all. He was a troubled person. It's just . . . anger doesn't solve anything."

My throat starts to feel thick, like I'm going to cry. Cale squeezes my hand.

"I'm angry I ran a red light," Cale says, trying for comic relief and failing.

I can feel Joey focusing the camera on me, on my coming tears.

"I'm sorry," I say. "I don't know why I'm crying."

I really don't. I've cried so many tears over the past months—tears of frustration at Cale's rehab, tears of joy at Cale's progress, tears of sadness over the difficulties in our life now, tears of gratitude for Evie having a father, so many tears. I'd thought I was all dried up.

"It's just that . . . this kind of thing, it's life-changing. You see these shootings on the news and there's no follow-up. You don't know what becomes of the victims, their families, the shooter's family. There is a whole network of people, all tied together by this terrible thing. It just makes you realize how strange and fragile and crazy life is. It's overwhelming, I guess, how little control we all have, how unfair things can be, how fate works. That's what it is—overwhelming."

Cale wipes a tear from my cheek with his thumb.

Charlie gives Joey a nod. He has what he needs.

"And . . . cut," he says.

TESSA

I LOOK AROUND MY apartment one more time, in search of a surface to dust, something to keep me busy. I don't know why I'm so nervous. I brought this whole thing on myself, after all. Joyce told me about the documentary, and I emailed Charlie and Joey, telling them I wanted to participate. I guess I just wonder if what I have to say matters. They keep referring to me as a "survivor," and that makes me feel kind of lame. I ran into a storage closet. I'm not some kind of hero. Cale is a survivor. Kat Reynolds is a survivor. I'm someone who escaped.

My apartment is spotless, thanks to my early morning manic cleaning episode. It doesn't take much for it to be spotless; it's just a studio, a few hundred square feet. My bed is about two feet from my fridge. Sometimes in the middle of the night, when I can't sleep (which is still a pretty regular occurrence), I reach over and grab a yogurt. Then I think about how strange it is that I'm sitting in bed, eating yogurt at 3:00 a.m. It's almost always 3:00 a.m.

There's a knock at the door at noon. Right on time. I take a deep breath, open the door. It's my first time meeting Charlie and Joey, but I've done enough Facebook stalking to recognize them immediately.

"Tessa?" Charlie says, confirming.

I nod. "Come in, come in."

They take in their surroundings, likely plotting where to sit. There are only so many options.

"Cozy," Charlie says.

Everyone knows that's just a nice word for "small."

"Yeah, I don't think I've ever had three people in here at one time, actually," I say.

There have been only a couple times when I've had two people in here—study sessions with my new friend, Ashley. Not surprisingly, Ryan and I ended things after I came back to Boise. It wasn't a bitter ending. We're on fine terms, and we text occasionally. There are no hard feelings. The shooting changed me— that's how he explains it. *We grew apart. It's not you, it's me.* Our breakup is a collection of clichés, but our relationship wasn't. We were good for each other, for that time we were together. He's the one who encouraged me to go to nursing school. And I am. That's the main reason I came back to Boise. That, and I want to get to know Cale. My father. I still don't refer to him as that. It's too strange.

Charlie and Joey agree that I should sit on the love seat for the interview (my place isn't big enough for a proper couch). Charlie will sit across from me, on the bed, off-camera. Joey will stand by the fridge, filming. I expected some kind of preinterview, something to help me warm up, but they say they'd rather jump right in. "Sometimes it's better to get your thoughts before you have a chance to polish them, ya know?" Charlie says. My heart starts beating a little faster.

"Just remember, nobody will see me asking you questions. It'll just be you on screen. So when you answer, use full sentences. Okay?"

I swallow and nod.

"Tell me how the shooting has affected your life," Charlie says.

He wasn't kidding. He's jumping right in.

I shift on the couch, finger-comb my hair behind my ear

self-consciously.

"I mean, I think about the shooting every day still. I have nightmares at least a couple times a week. I still have a hard time in public places, like if I can't face a doorway and see what's happening. It's gotten better, but it's still, like, a thing."

"How has it been for you getting to know Joyce Ketcher?"

I shift again, then mentally chastise myself. I'm sure it looks better on camera for me to be still, not moving about nervously like a mental patient.

"It's been good," I say.

"Full sentences," he whispers.

I start again. "It's been good getting to know Joyce Ketcher. I know some people think it's weird, but it's been good for both of us to be in each other's lives. I wanted to understand what happened, why Jed did this, and she wanted to understand the same thing. We've been a comfort to each other in that way. What people don't realize is that lots of people are affected by shootings. There are ripple effects. It's been a year and, sometimes, I still feel like it's *right there*, like it just happened. Joyce says we both have PTSD, and that's probably true."

"What about your father—how has it been getting to know him?"

Crazy. Painful. Confusing. Weird. Fascinating.

These are all the words that come to mind, but not necessarily the words I want the public to hear.

"Getting to know my father has been . . . unbelievable," I say.

He looks at me expectantly, wanting more.

"I didn't even think my father was alive, let alone in Boise, coming to the bar where I worked. Because of his memory loss, we've had to really start over, from the beginning. It's a slow process."

We do weekly breakfasts, a standing date. Angie comes along. I've actually developed more of a relationship with her than I have with Cale. It's just hard to get to know someone who comes with no past, basically. He feels like such a stranger. Angie can tell me more about Cale than he can tell me himself—not just the timeline of his life, but his personality, his traits, things I might have in common with him. When I requested no mushrooms in my omelet, for example, she said, "You must get your mushroom aversion from Cale." Cale didn't even know he had a mushroom aversion.

"Has your mother been in touch with Cale too?" Charlie asks.

The truth is she hasn't, but I feel like if I say this, it will make her out to be a grudge-holding bitch. When, really, he's the asshole of the situation. Nobody will ever call him that now. He has pity on his side. It's so hard to be angry at someone who looks at you blankly, without knowledge of his own mistakes.

"My mother hasn't been in touch with Cale yet. She lives in Bend. But we have talked about them meeting," I say.

Mom says she's not up for it. She knows he will apologize to her—because he has been told what he did all those years ago—but the apology will be inherently inauthentic. He doesn't remember, so his remorse is stiff, awkward.

I visit Mom once a month, call her a few days a week. We talk more now than before because I feel the need to remind her that she is, and always will be, more important to me than Cale. She won't admit she worries about that, but I can tell she does. She gets so quiet when I mention my breakfast dates with him. It's not fair, really. He gets this big, fat, convenient pass. She gets nothing—no award or acknowledgment for busting her ass as a single mother, raising me to be who I am. The media cares only about Cale and me reuniting; that's the exciting story. Cale is portrayed as this victim, this good-hearted man who got shot while pursuing a relationship with his long-lost daughter. The truth is so much more complicated. My mother is the victim in many ways, and I'll never be fully convinced of the goodness of Cale's heart.

"What are you doing for work now? I know you said you could never work in a bar again," Charlie says.

I'm grateful for the change of subject.

"I can't even go to bars now," I say.

I haven't set foot in a bar since the shooting. I get invites sometimes, from school friends who don't know what happened or have forgotten (it's amazing how fast people forget).

"So, safe to say you're no longer a bartender?"

I laugh. "I'm no longer a bartender. I still serve drinks though. At a coffee shop," I say.

It's the coffee shop where Joyce and I met—Bean There, Done That. The pay isn't as great—people don't really tip baristas—but I can pay my rent and have a little left over, so it's fine for now.

"And I'm studying to be a nurse, hoping to work in emergency medicine," I say. It's something I'm proud of, something I want people to know.

Predictably, Charlie asks, "Is that inspired by what you've been through?"

"I've always wanted to be a nurse, but I didn't decide that I wanted to focus on emergency medicine until after the shooting, so I guess it was inspired by that. I want to be on the front lines, comforting people when they're most scared."

Sometimes, I think it's masochistic of me to want to put myself in chaotic crisis situations. But I also hope that enough exposure to those situations will be healing, in a way.

"Have you forgiven Jed Ketcher for what he did? Or where

do you stand with him in your mind?"

"Honestly, I rarely think of Jed Ketcher anymore—not in the sense of Jed Ketcher the shooter. I think of him as Joyce's son who died after doing a terrible thing. He's not a monster in my mind. Maybe he would be if I'd never been in touch with Joyce, if I hadn't come to call her a friend."

These days, Joyce and I don't see each other all that often. We text more than anything. But I know she'll always be in my life.

"I love Joyce," I say.

My own declaration startles me. I haven't even said those words to her before. I imagine her seeing the documentary, tears coming to her eyes. I've seen so many tears in her eyes over the last year.

Charlie looks to me to say more, but I'm still taken aback by myself. After a few seconds, I say what has become my truth:

"To know Joyce Ketcher—as a mother, as a person—is to forgive her son."

"Has *she* forgiven him?" he asks, leaning forward, interested.

I know she hasn't. She hasn't forgiven herself either. She's started seeing a therapist to help with that. But this is not for me to disclose.

"You'll have to ask her," I say.

I know it's not the complete sentence Charlie wants, but I don't care. I don't want him to have me on camera saying anything about Joyce's thoughts or feelings. Those are hers.

Charlie gives Joey a nod, and the red light of the camera goes off.

"How about we get some footage of you talking about the night of the shooting?" Charlie says. "Most people know the details, but we should get it anyway."

"Okay," I say.

I sit up straight, clear my throat. This is the easy part.

The red light goes on.

"It was a typical Thursday night at Ray's," I begin.

And then I tell the story, a story I've told so many times that it's finally starting to become "a thing that happened to me" rather than a thing that continues to happen to me. There is power in voice, in sharing. Maybe that's why I wanted to do this documentary. It is my way of reaching out, saying, "Can you help me hold this? I don't want to carry it on my own." And even though the film won't be released for a while, I already feel lighter.

JOYCE

MY PHONE BUZZES WITH a text from Tessa:

> We just finished. They're on their way to you. It was totally fine. You'll be fine.

I text back:

> If you say so.

She knows I'm nervous. We're both nervous about this whole thing. I'm especially nervous because their documentary started with me. They wanted insight into the mind of the shooter, vis-à-vis his mother. The old cliché lives on: Mother knows best. It was me who told them there was so much more to the story. I didn't want to focus on Jed, glamorize his actions in any way. I wanted to focus on the victims, the lives he affected. I wanted people to see the full picture.

"They'll be here any minute," I tell Gary.

He brings me a glass with a little bourbon in it, sits with me on the couch to wait for Charlie and Joey to arrive. Gary won't be in the documentary, says it's my story to tell. I can't help but wonder if he just doesn't want to be publicly connected to Jed. It's not like it's a secret, at least not in Boise. We don't hide the fact that we're together. But maybe he doesn't want the whole world to know. I'll always wonder if he's a bit ashamed to be with me, the mother of Jed Ketcher. He would never admit as much, but I wonder if it's a truth that's buried beneath his logic, a truth he's not even brave enough to confront.

I officially moved into his place six months ago. It took me that long to agree with him that selling my house was for the best. It was bittersweet; I have so many happy memories of Jed there. But it was more painful than anything to be in that house, to walk by Jed's room and ask myself again and again what I did wrong. I didn't want to believe Gary when he said I would feel better if I sold the house. I thought he was saying, "You'll feel better when you forget Jed." But that's not what he was saying. Gary is a simple man. He means exactly what he says; there are no layers. We sold the house for much less than its value. We had to, given the history it carried. The new owners have completely renovated it—maybe to fit their taste, maybe to erase whatever evils it may have contained. Gary was right—I do feel better now. And I could never, ever forget Jed.

GARY WELCOMES IN Charlie and Joey. They set up in the living room. I sit on the couch, waiting for them to tell me what to do. Gary stands off to the side, hands on his hips, like he's working security at a club. He's protective of me, even though I stubbornly insist I don't require any protection. Secretly, I like his old-fashioned chivalry. Secretly, I like being taken care of. Eventually, maybe I'll admit that, settle into it, instead of denying it because of fear he will disappear. I seem to live in fear of loved ones disappearing. It doesn't take a psychology degree to figure out why.

"Okay, Joyce, you ready?" Charlie asks.

He is sitting in a chair Gary has brought from the kitchen. Joey is standing against the back wall, the camera on his shoulder.

"I'm ready," I say.

They ask me to recount the night of the shooting, how I came to know what Jed had done, what my initial thoughts were. I feel my cheeks flush as I recall my denial, my disbelief. I imagine the families of the victims watching, shaking their heads at me. I don't know if I'll ever shake off the guilt, the feeling that I should have known.

"How does the shooting continue to impact you today?" Charlie asks.

"There's not a day that goes by that I don't think about what Jed did. Some mornings, I wake up feeling like a boulder is on my chest. There's nothing I can do to make right what he did. There just isn't. I'll spend my life trying."

"What are some things you do to try to make it right?" He already knows the answer to this question; I told him when we spoke on the phone. He wants other people to know. He wants them to see that I'm a good person. I don't know if I'm a good person though. I'm a desperate person.

"I've reached out to surviving victims, the families of those who died. I've tried to connect however I can."

I feel like an idiot, saying these things. It's embarrassing to reveal my pitiful efforts. I started with letters to the families of Leigh and Jason Maguire, Bob Lang, Rick Reed, and Dan Velasquez. In the letters, I expressed interest in meeting in person. Bob Lang's daughter, Greta, met with me. She was as understanding as she could be—or she faked it well. Sherry Reed, Rick's wife, talked to me on the phone (meeting in person wasn't feasible; she moved to California after he died). She was short with me, seemed angry, but she restrained herself, which was almost worse than if she'd just yelled at me. The Velasquez family never responded to me. The Maguires sent me a nasty email. They hate me. My therapist says I have to allow them that. "You can only control yourself. You cannot control others' thoughts or feelings or opinions," she said. I wanted to say, "Well, duh," but clearly I've struggled to accept this basic fact.

"I started a support group here in Boise for mothers of children with mental illness," I say. "I've become very involved with Everytown for Gun Safety. We're organizing a march here in Boise this summer."

"It must be hard for you to continue to see shootings on the news. Can you talk a little about that?"

I look to Gary, because he's had to bear the brunt of my emotional breakdown every time there is a shooting. He gives me a small nod, a nod that says, *Go ahead, sweetie. You're okay.*

"It seems like we can't go a week without a shooting. It's just awful," I say, the tears coming. "Every time, I'm brought right back to that night. I think about the shooter, the shooter's family. I think about the victims. It's just so much heartache. There have been times I've gotten physically ill hearing the details. I've thought about never watching TV again, never going online again. But that's just denying the problem. I have to face it. We all do. I'm a mother of a shooter. That's a cross I have to bear for however many years I have left. There are many who haven't been touched personally by a shooting yet, and it's those people we need to join us in solving this problem."

"Do you think it's a problem that can be solved?" Charlie asks.

"That's a tough question," I say. "What I've come to accept is that there is evil in the world. It's not always visible. I had it under my own roof, and I didn't even realize. We cannot solve for the existence of evil. But we can make it more difficult for evil people to arm themselves."

I'm aware I've become obsessed with this topic, because it appears to be the one thing that is a controllable factor in all this. I'm on my computer at all hours of the night sometimes, gathering statistics, writing letters to congressmen, connecting with others affected by gun violence. I'm nearly manic sometimes. Gary doesn't say anything. He lets me be, even when I know my ideas are grandiose. Just the other day, I told him I wanted to organize a Million Mom March 2.0 in Washington, DC, like the one they did back in 2000. He just nodded, said, "Go for it."

"In your heart, have you forgiven Jed for what he did?" Charlie asks.

"That's another tough question," I say.

I look to Gary again. More tears are threatening. He must see them too because he comes to me, obviously not caring that he's on camera. He sits next to me on the couch, puts his arm around me, kisses the top of my head. That just makes the tears come harder, faster.

"This is Gary," I say to the camera, ugly crying and not caring at all.

Charlie gives me a moment to compose myself. Gary remains at my side. I wipe my eyes.

"I'm working on forgiving Jed," I say, "and myself."

Charlie leans forward, elbow on the arm of the chair, chin in his palm.

"We all have things to work on in life, don't we?" I continue. "That is . . . and forever will be . . . mine."

ACKNOWLEDGMENTS

THIS BOOK STARTED WITH a much less interesting title. Thank you to Stephanie Beard for the title brainstorming, and for everything else.

Thank you to Todd Bottorff and everyone at Turner Publishing. I've said it before and I'll say it again—you are a writer's dream.

Carey Nelson Burch, I heart you so much. Thank you for supporting this book (and all my books).

Thank you to Sue Klebold, whose book *A Mother's Reckoning: Living in the Aftermath of Tragedy,* planted the seed that became this book. Her story is heartbreaking and reveals the complexity of who we are as humans. The media likes to capture our attention with tidy stories, but life is rarely tidy.

Thank you to Caitlin and Michael Hocklander for reading this when it was just a Word document. You are my Boise experts. I can't wait to visit again.

Thank you to Randy and Jan Fredrickson for answering my questions about police and hospital protocols, respectively. I am completely to blame for any mistakes made.

I am so grateful to my early-early readers—Wendy Paine Miller, Huong Diep, my husband, and my mom. Thank you for getting me.

Chris and Mya, you are my everything. I don't think it's a coincidence that I've been more inspired (and productive!) with you two in my life. Thank you for loving me in a way that makes me feel safe and secure enough to undertake writing these crazy books.

No Hiding in Boise is Kim Hooper's fifth novel. Her previous works include *People Who Knew Me* (2016), *Cherry Blossoms* (2018), *Tiny* (2019), and *All the Acorns on the Forest Floor* (2020). She is also a co-author of *All the Love: Healing Your Heart and Finding Meaning After Pregnancy Loss.* Kim lives in Southern California with her husband, daughter, and a collection of pets.